LOVE HEALS ALL

Once Broken Series, Book Two

By Alison Mello

LOVE HEALS ALL

Limitless Publishing, LLC
Kailua, HI 96734
www.limitlesspublishing.com

Formatting: Limitless Publishing

ISBN-13: 978-1-64034-161-6
ISBN-10: 1-64034-161-7

Prologue

Brooke

I'm so excited! My big brother is coming home today and it feels like I haven't seen him in forever. He's bringing a friend with him. They're renting a car and driving here for their leave since they can't afford to fly. I run to the bathroom to take a quick shower and throw on my bikini with some clothes. My parents have a pool, and I'm so grateful, because in this weather it's totally necessary. It's summer here in Georgia, and it's been extremely hot. I throw on a tad bit of makeup and run down to see if Rem is here yet. I'm the only one in the family allowed to call my brother Rem. His full name is Remington, but his friends and family call him Remy. I smile to myself. Rem and I have always been close. He's extremely protective of me and we talk over the phone as often as possible. I have two other brothers as well. They're both local but I'm nowhere near as close to them. There's Dawson, who is married with kids, and Keaton, who is single and will probably stay that way forever.

"Mama, I'm home." I hear Rem's voice coming from the front door. Mama and I both go running into the living room. Mama hugs my brother and he kisses her on the cheek.

The second she steps aside, I jump into my brother's arms like I always do. "I've missed you, Rem!" He kisses me on the cheek and puts me down on the floor.

"Rem?" the tall, dark-haired man behind him questions.

"Oh, I'm sorry. Mama, do you remember Vaughn from my boot camp graduation?" Remy steps to the side and points to his friend.

Mama gives him a welcoming smile. "Of course. Welcome."

I can't help but look the guy up and down. He's toned, and his hazel eyes are like a curse; they lure you in and hold you. "I'm not sure we've met. I'm Brooke." I hold my hand out to him.

He looks down into my eyes, holding out his hand. "It's a pleasure to meet you."

Remy slaps his arm. "Come on. You can stay in my brother's old room." The trance is broken and Remy pulls him away from me. I can't help but watch them run up the stairs together carrying their bags.

"I'll be out by the pool. Let me know when you need me to help get lunch together, Mama." I slip off my clothes and lay on one of the loungers we have set up on the patio. I take my time rubbing sunscreen into my skin before I lay back and close my eyes. The second I do, visions of Vaughn pop into my head. His hazel eyes with the golden freckles and his perfect smile. His short, wavy, dark hair that he gels and slicks back to control. His lips look so soft and full, I bet they would feel heavenly on my body. Damn, I have to stop this, my bikini bottom has grown damp from my visions. I smile with my eyes closed, the sun's warm rays tan my skin. It's beautiful out here today. I'll have to take a dip in the pool soon to cool off before I flip to tan my back.

When I can no longer take the heat, I get up from the chair. I peek up to my brother's bedroom window and sigh when I see no one there. I jump into the pool, do a few quick laps, and then climb back out. At this time of year there's no need for a towel since the sun will have me dry in no time. When I get back to my chair I begin putting on more sunscreen, this time making sure I pay extra attention to the back of my legs, shoulders, and neck. I can't reach my lower back, but I won't be lying on my stomach for long, so I should be fine. My mind starts drifting to Vaughn again and his big muscular hands when I hear his voice.

"Want some help with that?" I jump, not realizing he was there. I look up. "Sorry. I didn't mean to scare you. Remy told me to pack a suit, and I'm glad I did. It's so hot here and we've been cooped up in the car. I asked him if I could take a swim. He told me to go for it."

"Of course you can take a swim, and I'd appreciate the help." He picks up my sunscreen and I get settled on my stomach. Suddenly his hands are on my back rubbing the lotion into my skin, but it feels like so much more than an act of help. His touch sets my skin on fire. My body suddenly overheats.

"What are you doing?" I hear my brother's stern voice from behind me.

"Relax, Rem. He's just putting sunscreen on me so I don't burn." This is when I hate my brother's protectiveness. Now Vaughn will probably never touch me again.

"You're good. I'm going to cool off now."

"Thank you." *If your body reacted anything like mine did, I'm sure you do need to cool off.* Shit, I need to cool off, but with my brother here, I certainly can't get up and jump in the pool now. He'll be all over us, and the only person I want all over me is Vaughn. I chose to lay in the sun for a few more minutes. I want to be nice and tan. Once I start college there will be little time for this stuff.

"Brooke, can you help with lunch, please?"

"Yeah, can I cool off quick?" I squint my eyes to see Mama standing in the slider.

She gives me a knowing smile. "Sure."

I jump up from my chair and run toward the pool, doing a cannonball right between Vaughn and Remy. Mama bursts into laughter the guys spluttering from the splash I made.

"Oh, you're going to pay for that." Remy picks me up and throws me across the pool. I can't help but giggle while Vaughn stands awkwardly at the other end. I wink at him and climb the ladder. I need to help Mama with lunch. I can feel his eyes on me, but when I turn back and look over my

4

shoulder, Remy gives him crap. "Dude, watch yourself with my baby sister. I would hate to kick your ass."

"Dude, relax. She's eighteen, right? You're not going to be able to protect her forever. Besides, even if I were to go with her, you know I'd never hurt her."

"Yeah, well. It's a good thing for you we're leaving next week and I don't have to worry about it."

I shake my head and storm off into the house, slamming the door harder than I intend.

"Brooke Leah Bennett, what has gotten into you?"

"Sorry, Mama. It's Rem and his meddling again. The man is never going to let me grow up." I cross my arms and lean on the counter.

She walks over to me putting her hand under my chin forcing me to look at her. "He adores you and worries about you."

"Mama, I'm eighteen and going to college in the fall. He needs to let me live."

"I know that, so do you, but that's his friend out there, and they are similar in age, which means he's probably eight or nine years older than you. You need to find someone your own age."

My brows shoot up. "Mama, you know darn well even if he were my age, Rem would scare him off."

She chuckles. "You're probably right, but he's only here for a week, so enjoy your time with him. You know you love him as much as he loves you." The woman is right, as always. This doesn't mean I won't be having a conversation with my brother the

5

first chance I get.

When we sit down to lunch, Mama tries to make conversation. There's a bit of tension at the table since I stormed off. "Are you three headed to the county fair tonight?"

"I don't know, Mama." Remy takes a bite of his sandwich.

I look at Mama. "I'm going. I'm not sure who I'm going with yet, but I'm going. It's fun and I want to win me another stuffy."

Mama laughs. "Brooke, I don't think you have room for another one."

"Yes, ma'am, I do. I donated some of my old ones." She shakes her head with a grin because she knows I'm forcing my brother to go by saying I'll be there.

Remy growls under his breath. "Dude, you good with going to the fair tonight?"

Vaughn shrugs his shoulders. "Sure, why not?" Vaughn's cell phone rings. He looks and his eyes go wide. "Will y'all excuse me? I have to take this." He answers with, "Yes, sir." Then walks off to the other room, leaving the three of us at the table.

I scowl at my brother. He scowls back. "He's too old for you. Cut the crap, Brooke."

"I'm eighteen now. That's not your decision."

"Yeah, and when he leaves for his next tour, then what?" Remy's brows shoot up, waiting for my response.

"I'll cross that bridge when I get there."

Vaughn comes back to sit at the table with us. "Everything good?" Remy asks nervously.

He sighs. "I ship out as soon as we get back."

"Fuck," Remy mumbles.

Mama huffs. "Remington Scott Bennett, language," she reprimands.

"Sorry, Mama. I forgot my place for a moment." Remy turns to his friend. "I guess we better make the best of this week, huh?" He nods but says nothing more.

When we arrive at the fair, we meet up with Amelia and her older sister, Kathleen, who has the hots for Remy. Of course I arranged that on purpose. We all walk into the fair, stocking up on tickets for rides. Remy enjoys the rides, but I like the games, so we argue for a minute over what to do first, but eventually Remy agrees to let us play some games. Kathleen walks next to Remy and Amelia, Vaughn and I are walking together. The guys always take the outside 'to keep us safe,' or at least that's what Remy says. Vaughn and I have intentionally bumped hands periodically. Our fingers have even locked slightly from time to time and I couldn't be happier.

We walk up to the squirt gun race and Vaughn takes a seat next to me while Remy watches from behind as Amelia and her sister duel it out on the game beside us. I beat Vaughn the first game, but we race again. I'm hoping to get a bigger prize, but he beats me. I look over at him with a full on pout. He gives the guy two more dollars and we race again...this time he lets me win. I turn in my small teddy bear for a much bigger one. I thank the man and we walk away. "Dude, you totally let her win."

He grins. "I have no idea what you're talking about."

He shakes his head and we walk off to check out some rides. "I'm hitting that ride." Remy points to this huge ride that would scare the crap out of me.

I look at him wide-eyed. "You can go on that, but I'm not. As a matter of fact, here—you can have my tickets."

Vaughn laughs, but Kathleen claps her hand. "I'll go on with you. I love rides like that."

I laugh because Remy flinches slightly, but Kathleen is too busy checking out the ride to notice. "There you go, Rem. You have a partner for the ride."

Amelia follows him. "I'm in." I can't help the smile that spreads across my face. Vaughn and I are finally going to be alone.

"Shall we get some cotton candy?" Vaughn smiles at me. I nod, he links his fingers with mine and we wander off to one of the small food trucks. "Can I get a cotton candy, please?" Vaughn says to the woman in the window. She hands it to him and he gives her the money to pay for it.

"Thank you." We walk off with a huge cone of cotton candy. He pulls some from the cone and pushes it into my mouth. "What are you going to school for?"

I bite my lower lip. "I'm going to be a veterinarian."

"That's awesome."

"Thanks. My dad and oldest brother are doctors, and I wanted to do something similar but I love animals, so I decided I would take that road. I'm going to have to bust my tail during my first four years of school to even get accepted, but I'm up to the challenge."

His brows shoot up. "It's hard to get into school for that?"

"Extremely." I pluck some more cotton candy from the cone and plop it into my mouth. "I love cotton candy." Vaughn chuckles. We lean against a tree beside a booth while we wait for the others. He looks down into my eyes, his thumb goes to my lip, wiping away the sugary treat that was stuck to it. I stick out my tongue, licking it, causing his breath to hitch. His eyes are bouncing between my lip and my eyes, waiting for permission to press his lips to mine. Lord, how I want to feel those lips on me. He finally leans in, my eyes are about to close, when once again he ruins it. "What are you two up to?"

"Your sister had something in her eye." He backs away.

I take a deep breath. "I'm ready to blow this place." I'm frustrated and my panties are once again wet.

Remy shakes his head. "I still have tickets left."

"Well, hurry up and use them then."

"Come on, dude. You hitting a ride with me."

"Sure." The guys walk off with Kathleen, who's also ready to hit another ride.

Amelia and I stay by the same tree. "What's up with you and that guy?"

"Nothing, thanks to my damn brother. Every time we get close, he breaks it up." I sigh. "I would happily give that man my v-card."

She laughs. "I don't blame you. I'd give him mine too."

***

It's finally the night before the guys are scheduled to leave and Mama even made a special dinner for them. We've also packed food for them to take in the car. They leave at three a.m. to drive back to the base in Virginia. The remainder of the week has gone on in a fun, flirty fashion. Vaughn and I have rubbed legs under the table. He continued putting sunscreen on my back, and one night we all went out and he came so close to kissing me, our lips were about to touch when Remy appeared. We quickly pulled apart and he gave Remy some crap about removing a piece of hair from my face that was bothering me. I was so mad at Remy for ruining my moment with him. He may have nine years on me, but I couldn't give a shit. This man is hot has hell and we have some serious chemistry together.

"I'm hitting the shower." Remy runs upstairs to clean up before bed, leaving Vaughn and I in the living room with Mama and my dad.

Things get really quiet. "Come help me in the kitchen, dear," Mama says to my dad.

"Yes, dear." He gets up and follows her into the kitchen, leaving Vaughn and I sitting in the living room. Now things feel even more awkward. "Listen." He looks down. "It's been a fun week. Thank you."

"Vaughn. I like you."

He chuckles. "I like you too, but your brother is not too thrilled with the flirting we've done over the past week, and I have to take a road trip with him."

He chuckles. "I want to live long enough to deploy." He looks down for a second and then looks back up at me. "You're only eighteen, Brooke. Live a little, date some guys your own age." I'm getting mad because I'm tired of everyone telling me what to do. "This deployment is dangerous, and I have no idea when I'll be anywhere near here again. That's no way for you to spend your first serious relationship." He gets up from the couch, kisses me on the cheek, and walks up the stairs.

As much as it sucks, he's right. A long distance relationship with a man eight years older than me is no way for me to live. Especially with me starting school in a few short months. I sigh, running up to my room to dream about the best week of my life with a man I can't have.

Chapter 1

Vaughn

"You guys meeting me at Crossroads tonight?" I lean against a broken down Humvee.

Liam pops his head out from under the vehicle. "Fuck, yeah. I've had a shit time with this damn thing." I laugh at him. He's been cursing at the thing all day long.

My team runs the shop for the military police on base. We work hard to make sure their vehicles are always running at peak efficiency and it can be stressful trying to keep up.

We tend to go out a couple of Fridays a month to blow off some steam. I find it not only fun, but it brings us a lot closer as a team. I can push my guys harder when I need to and I think part of it is because of the time we spend together on and off the field.

"I'm in." Callen slaps me on the shoulder.

"Me too, Sarge." Max joins our conversation.

"You joining us, Nolin?"

"Nah, I promised to take my girl out tonight." He wipes his hands on a dirty rag.

"Well, let's clean this place up and get out of here." There are tools everywhere, as well as dirty rags and water bottles. I always make my guys clean the place up before we leave on Friday. Sergeant First Class Blake came in one Monday and the place was left a mess. I got my ass chewed out for an hour, and then I had to chew my guys out. He counts on me to take care of this team, and that means ensuring the place is kept the way it should and my guys are working safely.

When everything is cleaned up, I tell my guys to call it a day, but first I confirm what time we're meeting up. "I'll see you guys at Crossroads at six for dinner and beers."

"See ya there, Sarge," the guys call out as they walk through the door. I lock up and climb into my vehicle.

We all live close by. Max, Liam, and Nolin live in the barracks on base, but Callen and I rent apartments in base housing. We live in the same neighborhood in a town called Hinesville. His apartment is the next street over from mine. It's one of the luxuries of being a staff sergeant. Once you hit sergeant you can rent off post if you want to. Callen got his sergeant rank almost a year ago and got off base as soon as he could. We're pretty close, we work out together and sometimes we drive in together.

When I pull up to my place, I run inside and straight to my room. I pull out a pair of jeans and a polo shirt. I grab my boots from the closet and jump into the shower. There's nothing I hate more than being late. I actually like to beat my guys there. I make quick work of cleaning up and getting dressed. I quickly down a bottle of water before I throw some gel into my hair. It's so thick and wavy that if I don't do something with it, it becomes a mess. One of my personal missions is to always set an example by looking my best around my men. The younger guys sometimes have no idea how to dress or behave, and it's up to us upper enlisted to lead the way. If one of my guys gets into trouble, I can get into trouble for not guiding them, and I'm not having that.

Callen knocks on my door. "Come in." When he opens the door, I shout, "I just called the cab."

"Cool. Did he give you a time?"

"Yeah, he'll be here any minute." Callen and I are always telling the guys to take a cab if they plan on drinking. It's that or someone doesn't drink. I toss my empty water bottle into the trash.

"Our ride is here." Callen opens the door and waits for me.

"Let's have some fun." I shut my door, locking it behind me. I stick my house key into my wallet and put my wallet into my pocket. I don't even bring my car keys with me. The cab lets us off right in front of the pub and tells us to call him when we're ready. He hands me his card. I thank him and stick it in my back pocket. When we get inside, we discover it's already getting busy despite the fact it's still early. I find us a booth and slip in. We luck out and get a table not far from the door so we can watch for Max and Liam. They're pretty good about being on time, so they should be here any minute.

A girl wearing short shorts and a tight tank top walks over. "Good evening, boys. What can I get y'all tonight?"

"We're waiting on two more, but we'll have a draft beer while we wait." Callen smiles at the girl.

She winks at him. "You got it, big fella. I'll be right back."

I burst into laughter. "Big fella?"

"Hey, you know some women can just tell when a man has the goods." He grabs his junk, causing me to laugh even harder.

A yawn escapes me and I shake my head. "You're not too full of yourself, are you?" I love my best friend, but sometimes he seriously needs to be brought back to reality.

"No, actually I'm not. Stop hating. You sleeping all right?"

Fuck, here we go again. He's always on me about my sleep. "I'm sleeping fine."

His brows shoot up and he gives me a look that screams *really* as the girl comes back and places two beers on the table along with some menus for us. "I'll be back to check on you boys in a bit."

"Damn, you went from big fella to a boy in a hot minute." I poke him with my elbow, changing the subject. I'm not a fan of discussing my sleeping or any other issues I may have since I got back home.

"Fuck you, dude. She didn't want to make you jealous." He has laughter in his voice.

"Why is Sarge jealous?" Max and Liam slip into the booth across from us. Thank god they're here. Callen would never carry on in front of the guys.

"He thinks he's the stud of the night because the waitress was flirting with him." I nudge Callen one more time as the waitress approaches us.

We look at the menu really quick and decide on a variety of appetizers and we all order more beers. When she walks away, we all go back to talking. "What are you guys up to this weekend?"

Liam and Max shrug. "It sucks being on base…there's nothing to do. Nolin has a car, but now that he's seeing that chick, he never hangs with us anymore, so we're stuck around here." Nolin, Liam, and Max are all specialists, so they can't live off base yet. They can have a car, but most guys their age don't because it's expensive to move around if their next duty assignment takes them overseas.

"Come on, guys, it's not that bad." Callen tries to sound positive but fails.

"Really? Then why the fuck did you move off base?" Max shoots his mouth off.

Callen starts to feed him a line of shit, but I'm not listening, because I spot someone I know. I can't believe she's here, and damn, she's looking good. I've been admiring this girl for years now. Her long blonde hair sits in gorgeous waves down her back. She turns toward me and scans the room. She has just a touch of makeup on, and her eyes are bold and beautiful.

She's my boy's sister, and I don't want him pissed at me for asking her out, but I've thought about discussing it with him a few times now. She must feel me checking her out because our eyes connect, and a small smile spreads across her soft, pink gloss-lined lips. She taps her friend and nods in my direction. I swear she's exaggerating the sway of her hips as she approaches the table. "Hey, Vaughn, what are you doing here?" Her voice is soft with that thick southern accent I love.

I slip out of the booth, trying to play it cool. I give her a brief hug. "Hey, Brooke. Hanging with my boys for the night." Feeling her small body pressed to mine causes my cock to twitch slightly, but I mentally talk it down.

She smiles at them politely. "How y'all doing?"

"Brooke, this is Callen, Max, and Liam. They work in the shop with me. Guys, this is Major Bennett's beautiful baby sister." I look back, her head drops, and the sweetest blush creeps up her gorgeous face.

"You need to stop that now, ya hear?" She smacks me playfully.

"Who's your friend?" Callen holds his hand out.

"I'm Courtney. Nice to meet you, Callen." He takes her tiny hand and gives it a gentle shake. "I work at the clinic with Brooke." His signature *I want to fuck this one* smile spreads across his face. I want to elbow him and tell him to behave, but I leave it be.

"We just ordered some food. Would you ladies like to join us? We'll make room." I really hope she says yes. This would be the perfect end to a long week.

"Oh, we don't want to intrude on your guys' night." Brooke shakes her head.

"It's fine," the guys all insist.

Courtney squeezes in, sitting next to Callen,

Brooke sits next to Courtney, and I sit on the end. It's a tight fit, but we make it work. The waitress comes over and laughs when she sees our party has grown. "Listen, y'all can move to that big round booth right there. I was just about to clear it off."

"You don't mind?" I ask, not wanting to give her more work.

"Not at all. Come on, y'all, follow me." We all grab our drinks and follow her to a much bigger booth. Now there's plenty of room for us to sit comfortably.

Once we're all settled, the waitress takes the girls' drink order and tells us she's going to grab our food, and then she'll be back with their drinks. "How's your brother?"

"He's good. They're working on the wedding. As you know, they want to have a backyard wedding this summer at Mama's house."

"That's cool. I'm surprised they're not getting married in a church."

The waitress interrupts our conversation to drop onion rings, bacon cheese fries, nachos, buffalo chicken fingers, and barbecue chicken fingers on the table. "Y'all enjoy now, and I'll be back to check on you soon." She walks away, this time without flirting with Callen. She must assume now that Courtney's here that they're together.

"Nah, she's cool with it. The family pastor will come to the house to marry them, but we don't practice nearly as well as we did when we were small." She takes the plate I hand her and she helps herself to some food.

"My mama would forbid me to marry any girl

who didn't want to marry in our family church. She's a stickler for religion," Max says.

I shrug my shoulders. "Not me, my mom was kind of like Brooke's. We went to church as kids and I had to make confirmation, but the older we got, the less we went because sports and other things got in the way." I chuckle. "It's funny though, Mama always goes to support the craft fairs and other events the church puts on. She always tries to show some form of support." I smile thinking about my mom and how sweet she is.

"Your mama sounds sweet," Brooke gushes.

"What about you?" Courtney asks Callen.

Callen has had a bit of a tough life, but I say nothing, waiting to see how much he decides to share. He sighs. "My mom tried hard, but wasn't around much, and my father was pretty much a piece of shit. It's why I joined the Army. I wanted to make something of myself." Callen shrugs it off like it's no big deal.

"Good for you." She gives him a big smile.

"Hear, hear." Max raises his beer glass. "I'm in the same boat, my man. My father got my mom pregnant and then left her high and dry. She busted her ass to raise me by herself, but I never had shit growing up." He downs the remainder of his beer and slams the glass down.

The waitress is back. "Did I hear the telltale sign that someone needs a beer?" We all laugh and ask for another round.

This is turning into a great night. I have Brooke by my side looking damn good in some shorts and a white top that's so see-through she has a skimpy cami under it. The music is playing and the boys are all laughing and having a good time. This is what every Friday night should look like. Brooke starts tapping her feet to the music. I can feel her body swaying as *I'm Only One Call Away* by Charlie Puth plays. I slip out of the booth, holding out my hand. "Want to dance?"

A huge smile spreads across her face and she takes my hand. "I'd love to." I lead her out to the small dance floor. Pulling her small body close to mine, we start swaying to the music. I look down into her gorgeous blue eyes, lost in how clear they are. Suddenly we're the only two on the dance floor, swaying to the music. I'm a bit taller than her but I like the way her head comes to my chest.

"I can't believe it's been eight years. You look amazing." The connection is as strong now as it was eight years ago. I know she must be feeling it too, because she lets out a gentle breath, and suddenly I'm dying for a taste of those gloss lined lips. She stares up into my eyes as I lick my lips and we continue to dance right into the next song. We're so wrapped up in each other that neither of us noticed the song change, until someone bumps us, breaking the trance we're in.

She giggles and looks down, blushing. "We should go back to the table. Our drinks are probably there." I lick my lips again, wanting to argue, but I nod my head. She shows me her bashful smile and grabs my hand, pulling me from the floor.

"I thought we lost you two." Callen busts my balls.

"Shut up, man." Poor Brooke blushes even

harder slipping in next to Courtney.

"If you will excuse me, I see a female on the dance floor that needs a dance partner." Liam slides out next to go in search of a girl.

"Where?" Max asks, squinting to see who he's talking about.

"I haven't found her yet, but I'm sure she's out there. Come on. I'll show you how it's done." Liam smacks Max on the arm. We laugh watching the two of them head out onto the dance floor in search of some ladies.

It gets quiet at the table, but I don't want things to get awkward between us. "How's school?"

Her face lights up at my easy question. "Great. I graduate in May, and I can't wait."

"I'm so proud of her. She'll officially be a veterinarian," Courtney brags putting an arm around her friend.

"Well, I have to pass my exam first." She looks to her friend.

"That's awesome! I've been thinking about getting a dog," I blurt out and instantly regret it. Shit. I don't even know why I said that. I haven't told anyone about wanting a dog. I hope Callen doesn't start asking questions.

"Since when?" Fuck, here he goes.

I shrug my shoulders. "Since we got back from our last deployment." He knows I'm having some issues with sleep and stuff after the last one. It was a rough deployment and it's not something I like talking about. I give him a look that says *leave it be*, and lucky for me, he does. "The only fear I have is if I got called on another mission I would need

21

someone to watch it. It's the only reason I haven't gotten one."

"I'm sure we could find someone to watch him for you. There are foster homes just for that reason," Courtney explains.

"Really?" I had no idea they had foster homes for pets. I just asked if I could have pets in my base home and they said yes. I just have to pay an extra deposit, and as long as the dog hasn't done any damage to the place, I'll get my deposit back.

"Really. As a matter of fact, we have a few foster families, as does the local shelter. I could help you pick a dog that would be good for you. That is, if you want?" Brooke offers with a hopeful look on her face.

A smile spreads across my face. "I'd like that."

"Cool. Let me know when you're ready and we'll chat. Have you ever had a dog?" Brooke leans on her hand continuing our conversation.

"No, my mom was allergic to most animals, but I've always wanted one." I turn my body to face her and lean my arm on the back of the booth. Callen and Courtney are talking to each other, paying us no mind.

"It's a lot of work, but it's very rewarding. I can help if you run into any problems."

"Don't make any promises you can't keep, now. I'll hold you to them." I smile to let her know I'm partially joking.

She crosses her arms over her chest and raises one brow. "Vaughn Anderson, if there is one thing I'm good at, it's keeping a promise, yah hear?" Damn, she's fucking cute when she gets all sassy on me.

I laugh. "Well, I guess only time will tell."

She looks down at her watch. "Speaking of time, Courtney, are you ready? I'm beat."

"Yeah. It's been fun, guys. Thanks for letting us join you."

"Let's do it again some time." Callen stares into Courtney's eyes.

She bites her lip. "You bet."

"Are you ladies good for a ride?" I don't want these girls driving home after the drinks they've had. Not only is it not gentleman-like, but the Major would have my ass.

"Yeah, we'll get a cab." I slip out of the booth to let them out, and she looks up at me like she wants to say something, but doesn't. I pull her in for a hug, and this time it feels a bit awkward compared to the hug I got when she walked in. I want to walk her out and tell her I had a good time. Ask her if I can see her again, but I really need to talk to Remy first. They're halfway to the door when we both watch them burst into giggles. At the same time, they turn around and give us a wave before walking out the door.

Chapter 2

Brooke

It's been a week since I saw Vaughn at the bar. The memory of his tall muscular body still plays in my mind like it was yesterday. I close my eyes and inhale, remembering his delicious woodsy scent as he held me while we swayed to the music. I've had the most delicious dreams of his body pressed against mine, his pink tongue poking out from behind those full lips, wishing he'd lick my body in all the right places. A smile spreads across my face, but I shake off my thoughts. He is one fine man, and I've prayed for quite some time now that he would ask me out, but he hasn't, and I know it has to do with the fact that he and my damn brother are good friends. I even thought about going back to that bar tonight in hopes of running into him again, but I can't. I have so much to do to get ready for my exams. I have always been a straight A student, and I can't let him get in the way of me finishing my degree off strong. Instead, I'm going straight home

24

after work to study. It's less than two months until I graduate, and then I'll officially be a veterinarian.

The clinic I currently work in is small, and we only house one vet. He's the owner of the clinic, but I've been working for him for so long that he's promised to give me the roll of vet here as soon as I have my degree. I probably won't make nearly as much as if I went to a bigger clinic in a nearby city, but I love our town, and I love this place, so I'm okay with that. Dr. Kramer is a sweet man, and I enjoy working for him. He's taught me a lot. We've already discussed what my salary would look like, and since my parents covered my first four years of college, my loans aren't too bad. I'll be able to afford to live on my own and pay what loans I do have without any problems.

I smile staring in the mirror, slipping on the lab coat I wear to work. Remy thinks I like to mooch off my parents, but in reality, I can't wait to get out of here and get a place of my own. I've been saving as much as I possibly can. My goal is to move by the end of the summer or early fall. It depends on how quickly I find a house for rent. I've seen a few around town, but I'm not ready just yet. I shake off my thoughts, running downstairs to grab some breakfast before I have to leave for work. "Good morning, Dad." I find my father sitting at the kitchen table.

"Morning, sweetie." He sips his coffee.

"Are you going into work today?" I place an English muffin in the toaster and then go about making my lunch.

"Yeah, your brother is already there, but since

25

my first appointment isn't until ten, there was no rush for me to go in."

"Good, that means I can have breakfast with you. Did you eat?"

He shows me his gentle smile. "I did, sweetie, but thank you." I shrug and finish making my lunch. As soon as I hear the toaster pop, I gather my coffee, English muffin, and apple, and then take a seat at the table with my dad. We're both silent and while I eat. He reads his paper, but I can see him glancing over the top of it periodically. "What's wrong, sweetie?"

I shrug. "I kind of have a lot on my mind. I graduate in a few months, and I want to start looking for a house. Especially since I know I have a job as soon as I get my diploma." I pause for a moment. "It's bittersweet, ya know?"

"I do. You're our baby, and you're about to move out of our home, but you're an adult now, and we have to let you go and hope we taught you well. That said I also don't want you to rush into buying a house."

I smile at my father. "First, you did, Dad, and don't you worry. I'll always be your little girl. Second, I actually want to rent. I want to have a yard to enjoy and maybe even get a dog."

He gives me a proud smile back. "Damn right you'll always be my little girl." He lifts his paper and begins to read again, but mumbles, "God help your boyfriend."

I giggle and finish my breakfast. My father and brothers have always been very protective of me, but I haven't had a really serious relationship in a long time. I dated a guy for a while when I was studying my undergraduate program, but I broke it off with him because he was too much of a distraction. He didn't understand that I had days I had to focus on my course work and couldn't drop everything to go out dancing. I tried to study around date nights and such, but it was hard. There are times when things pop up or you've studied, but don't quite feel ready for that big exam. I would want to study a bit harder and he would get pissed. He was the first guy I had ever slept with. We had great chemistry, it was just too bad he couldn't be more supportive of my career. I loved him, but I loved my desire to become a veterinarian more. I've dated a few guys since then, but nothing serious. It never made it past the second or third date. We either didn't have the chemistry or it just didn't seem to work out. Now, Vaughn and I have chemistry. I can feel it already. He hugged me and my body lit up, it was like bolts of lightning had struck me, sending shock waves through me. My stomach did flips as we danced.

I bite my lip. I've contemplated asking Remy how he would feel about me dating him, but I figure I should finish my degree first. The question is, can I wait that long? It's been so long since someone other than my vibrator has touched me. "Are you okay, sweetie?" Holy shit, I'm thinking about vibrators with my father sitting across from me.

"I'm fine, Dad."

"You're all flushed." His face shows concern.

"Sorry, I was thinking about an embarrassing mistake I made yesterday. I tripped over a cat carrier, causing the cage to open and the cat escaped. He ran all over the back room. We had the hardest time catching him."

He laughs at my story. Thank god he buys it. I'm not usually clumsy, but I think that makes it all the funnier. "You need to be careful."

"I know. It was really embarrassing. I'm thankful the owner wasn't there to witness it. I finally grabbed some treats and got her to come to me that way."

He shakes his head, folding the paper up and setting it to the side. "I have to go to work. I'll see you for dinner tonight."

I nod. "Yes, you will." He kisses me on the top of the head and walks out of the room.

I let go of the breath I'd been holding. I'm not big on lying, but there was no way I could tell my father what I was really thinking. I'm very lucky in that my parents give me total privacy.

I pull up to the clinic, and of course the lot is empty except for staff. We don't open for another fifteen minutes, but I want to get inside and see what our day looks like. It isn't a huge clinic, but we're big enough to handle all of the local animals and we have a great reputation. We have two small rooms where we can treat the animals in private and one open room with a table in the middle of the room for everyday exams, and a wall full of crates for pets that need to spend the night. Dr. Kramer is already here. Courtney pulls in behind me. We both climb out of our cars and exchange good mornings. "I hope you're ready. We have a busy day today."

"We do?" I question using my key to open the

door. Dr. Kramer always keeps the doors locked right up until it's time to open. He likes to work in the back, and some mornings he's here really early.

Courtney nods. "Yup, and you know we'll end up with emergencies as well." I shut the door, locking it behind us. We find Dr. Kramer at the front desk.

"Good morning, ladies." He greets us with a smile. He's about my father's age, but he looks older. He has a full head of completely white hair. He keeps it cut neatly and always has it styled. He's a pretty fit man. He works out regularly to keep up with the animals. They can be tough. I feel for him though, he has no real family left. His wife and son died in a hit and run car crash years ago, and he's made this clinic his life ever since. My parents have invited him for holidays, but he always refuses, only making appearances at the annual block party and occasionally at the Fourth of July cookouts.

"Good morning," we both return.

"Brooke, I need you to prepare room one. Mrs. Thompson is coming in with Bruno today." His voice is sad. Bruno a beautiful chocolate lab and is very ill. Mrs. Thompson has been bringing him to Dr. Kramer since he was a puppy. The tone of his voice and the look on his face tells me the time has come. We're putting Bruno down today. This is the part of my job I do not like. It's sad not only for the pet owner, but all of us here at the clinic as well. We love these animals as if they were our own…we definitely feel the loss. Some of them we've been treating for years, they're like our friends. Their faces light up with excitement when they see us for a checkup, and we can see the sadness in their eyes when they are not well. Courtney was right—today is going to be a tough day. I let out a deep breath, trying to maintain my composure as I walk off to do as Dr. Kramer asked.

***

Vaughn

"SSG Anderson, front and center!" I hear my commander's voice from across the room.

"Yes, sir." I run over to approach my commander, standing at attention.

"Get you and your men squared away. We have two vehicles that need recovery from the same area. You'll have all the info you need in the next twenty minutes."

"Yes, sir." He nods and walks out of the room.

I turn to my men. "You heard the man, gear up." The men all jump up and rush around grabbing the gear they need, along with their rifles. We don't go anywhere without a rifle. I begin making a mental list. I need to sign out vehicles, to collect the two Humvees and get them back. I grab my helmet and my rifle and head out to the motor-pool.

"Hey, Sarge. I need to sign out some vehicles."

"I heard. I have a HET-Heavy Equipment Transport, a HEMTT -Heavy Expanded Mobility Transport Truck, and three gun trucks all fueled up and ready to go." He gives me a clipboard and has me sign on the appropriate lines for each of the vehicles.

"Thanks, man." I start to walk away. I need to meet with my men quickly before we take off.

"Hey," the sergeant calls out. I turn back around. *"Be careful out there. I hear shit's brutal."*

I nod and keep walking. Damn fucking straight it is, and it's my job to not only recover these vehicles, but get my men back here safe. When I get back to our makeshift office, my boy, Lieutenant James, is there gathering the guys. *"You got my vehicles, Sarge?"*

"Yes, sir. All signed for and ready to go."

"Good. Let's get our team together and get this shit done." He nods to me.

"Listen up, guys! We want to get this mission done quickly and safely. We roll out in a few minutes. Here is your assignment. Freight, you're driving my HET. Lieu, are you good being his A driver?"

"You got it."

I nod. *"Bull, you're driving my HEMTT and I'll be riding with you as your A driver. Jones, you're the third in my vehicle, and Porter, you're riding in the HET."* I look around to see them nodding. *"Burke, Falcon, and Callen. You'll each jump into one of the gunner trucks. Truck one will be the lead, driven by Eagle Eye, truck two will be driven by Hawk, and truck three will be driven by Liam. My gunners—you know who you are and who your drivers are. Any questions?"* Complete silence spreads throughout the room." *Let's do this shit."* The room erupts into one big HOOAH.

As soon as everyone settles into their vehicles, we do a quick radio check, and then take off with

Eagle Eye leading the convoy. The HET is next, followed by Hawk. Bull is next, and we end the convoy with Mercy protecting our asses. It's a bit of a drive with the speed limits we must abide by while in a convoy. Eagle Eye is always our lead, because he spots fucking everything, dude's amazing. We finally approach our vehicles, and an eerie feeling comes over me. They're in the middle of fucking nowhere. One of them is practically blown to shit, and god knows what's wrong with the other one. The gunners take their positions around us to cover our asses while the maintenance team gets busy. "Hey, Vibe. How's that gut of yours?" the LT asks when he jumps out of his truck.

"Not good, sir. Let's get this done and get the fuck out of here." He started calling me Vibe because I have this gut instinct that tells me when shit ain't good, and I can tell you right now my gut is fucking flipping the hell out. He shakes his head and we get to work, while the others are keeping an eye out.

It takes us a little bit, but I manage to get the dead truck up on the HET. The LT works with the other guys to get the other one hooked up to the HEMTT. One is like a flatbed truck, and the other is like a tow truck. We're sweating our asses off in this fucking heat, but after a short time, we've managed to get the trucks loaded. The LT comes over to me and says, "We're good, are you?"

"Yeah, we did it. Let's get out of here." I wipe the sweat from my forehead with the back of my sleeve.

"Hey, Vibe. I guess you're off today. You feeling

all right?" He nudges me with his elbow.

"I have no problem being wrong once in a while, sir." I chuckle.

We're about to mount up when we find out I wasn't off at all. No sooner did he finish his last word, than one single shot rings out from on top the hill, hitting Burke, who was standing right on the side of me. Fucker dropped. I grab him, pulling him behind the truck for protection.

Eagle Eye has already set himself up in a safe position, and is hooking up his scope. "Where are you, motherfucker?" He pants as he scans the area. "One guy on the hill. I only see one," he screams to me. The LT is calling in for a med flight for Burke. Everyone is quiet except for Eagle Eye, who's mumbling something as he squeezes the trigger, taking out the motherfucker who shot our guy. "Got you, you fucking bastard."

"Hey Sarge," Burke grabs onto my shirt panting in pain. "Give this to my wife. Tell her it never left my pocket." He slips the other hand into his pocket, pulling out a picture of him and his family...his two little girls in pretty pink dresses, his wife wearing a formal black dress, and him in his dress uniform.

I shove his hand back. "Fuck you, give it to her yourself. You're not going to die." His eyes start to roll. "Fuck, hold on, man. You got this." I press my hand over the huge hole in his body, trying to stop the bleeding, but it's everywhere.

LT comes over with a medical bag. "They'll be here any minute. You hold on, kid." He presses a bandage to his stomach.

I'm holding him on my lap, rocking him, while

we wait for the flight. "Come on, man, hold on." He chokes, a streak of blood runs from the corner of his mouth and he goes limp. Suddenly there's more gunfire from the hill. My guys take position, lighting that shit up. There are bullets flying, but I can't manage to let go of my guy to do a fucking thing about it. "What the fuck? They told us this hill was clear." LT is pissed.

"I know, LT." A tear runs down my face as I look at Burke's dead body. I don't fucking lose men. My men are always my top priority. Suddenly we hear the chopper overhead, lighting up the hill with my guys, and the gunfire stops. It lands, we load Burke up, and we all stand watching them take off with him.

My guys are all looking as devastated as I am, and I can't blame them. We lost a good guy today.

I shoot up straight in bed, drenched in sweat. "Fuck." I pant. It's been six months since I've been home, and I still can't rid myself of these damn nightmares. I trudge to the shower to wash it away, and as soon as I'm done, I text Callen. It's four a.m. and I need to run this off.

Vaughn: Going for my run now.

I put on shorts, deodorant, and a t-shirt. By the time I'm done, I get a text back.

Callen: Another nightmare?

Vaughn: You could say that.

Callen was there with me that dreaded day. He understands how I feel, and has tried to help me move past it, but it's a struggle. He didn't have the responsibilities that I had. Liam was there as well, but the remainder of my current crew came in after, and some have moved on. I walk out my door and Callen is already there, ready for our run. We take off, quiet at first, and then he finally speaks. "Want to talk about it?"

"Nah, you were there. It's the same thing it always is. If it's not a repeat of that day, it's roadside bombs going off. What's there to talk about? I need to figure out how to get that shit out of my head." My voice full of frustration. He nods his understanding and we continue our run in silence. He too suffered from nightmares, but he seems to have his under control. I guess that's why we make a great team, we understand each other. We have a routine. We run, shower, go for breakfast, and then go to work. I'm told routine is supposed to help. I've also done some research and discovered having a companion such as a dog can help.

Chapter 3

Vaughn

I need to get my ass in gear. Grabbing my keys from the table by the door, I run out to get a start on the day. I'm tired as fuck from my lack of sleep, and the less sleep I get, the more the nightmares affect me. I don't like taking my sleeping pills, but tonight it's going to be a must or I'm going to lose my mind. I pull up to the pump at the little convenience store we call the shoppette to fill up my car. I climb out to pump my gas and a yawn escapes me. Damn, I'm fucking tired. I need to get this shit under control. The last thing I need is for me or one of my guys to get hurt because I can't focus. Another yawn escapes me as the pump stops. I return the nozzle and replace my gas cap before moving my car to a parking spot. We all take turns picking up coffee during the week, and today it's my turn. Pulling the door open, I nearly walk into a female soldier. "Excuse me." I hold the door allowing her to step through.

"No worries, Sergeant." I nod and head straight to the coffee station. I know exactly how to make everyone's coffee just the way they like it. As soon as I'm done, I grab a sandwich from the deli fridge for my lunch, along with a diet soda and a bag of chips. I turn to carry it all to the counter, but I bump into my boy, Remy. "Let me help you with that." The Major smiles at me.

"Hey, sir. How's it going?" Remy and I shake hands. I try hard to slip my mask into place but I fear I'm too late.

"It's going well. How about you?" He looks me up and down.

"I'm doing okay, sir." I give him a tight smile. I can tell from the look in his eyes he's not buying it.

"Are you sure? You're looking a bit tired." He narrows his eyes at me.

"Ah, you know how it is, sir. Overworked and underpaid. How's Kenzie?" I try changing the subject, but again it doesn't work.

"She's great, actually." He takes the sandwich, chips, and soda from my hands and walks them back to their appropriate spots.

"What are you doing, sir?" My one eyebrow raised in confusion.

"Buying you lunch." He narrows his eyes again. "I need to get going, but I have a feeling we need to talk. I'll meet you at the commissary food court for lunch at noon sharp. Don't be late." He says nothing else and gives me no chance to argue, he turns and walks out the door.

"Fuck," I whisper to myself. I have to figure out how to get around this. I know Remy has some demons of his own, and he's worked to fight through it, but I'm not sure I want to talk about it anymore than I have. I've tried talking to Callen about it and it hasn't done shit for me.

"Next," the guy at the counter yells, pulling me from my thoughts.

Shaking it off, I step up to the counter. "My bad." I put the coffees down on the counter and pull out my wallet to pay the man. "Thanks." I nod at the guy after paying him. I grab the coffees and put them on the front passenger's seat. What am I going to do? Remy already sees through me, there's no way I'm going to be able to convince him I'm fine. That the nightmares haunting my nights are not really there. This is why I keep to myself. I start the car and slam it into drive before pulling out of the parking lot. The guys are going to be waiting. It's already zero eight-thirty, and we're usually there by zero eight hundred hours. I'm tired, slow, and bumping into the Major didn't help.

When I pull up, the bay doors are open and my guys are busy working on their assigned vehicles. There are four bays, and each bay has a vehicle in it. Two are on lifts, and two are regular maintenance. I can't help but notice there are a few new ones in the yard that must have broken down sometime over the weekend. Guys are always on training missions, so vehicles show up all the time. I'll have to check them out first thing to see what they need.

I walk through the door and the guys all begin clapping. "It's about fucking time," Max shouts from across the shop.

38

"Fuck you, guys. I ran into Major Bennett at the shoppette. I couldn't exactly tell a major to fuck off—that my guys are waiting for coffee." I put the coffees on the counter and they all come running over to grab them.

Everyone but Callen takes their coffee and walks away, to continue working. "What's up with the Major?"

I look to the ground for a second. "He picked up on my lack of sleep. Asked if I was all right."

"What did you tell him?" Callen leans on the counter sipping his coffee, like we're making casual conversation. He knows damn fucking well this isn't easy.

"I tried to tell him I was fine, but he didn't buy it. Bastard took the food I was buying for lunch from me and told me I needed to meet him at noon."

Callen starts laughing. "I guess we know where you'll be this afternoon." He puts his coffee back down and walks over to the vehicle he's working on.

"We have a lot to do. I may not go," I call out, taking a swig from my coffee. Callen turns back, his brows shoot up, and the face he makes screams *really,* but I ignore it.

"What? Let's get to work," I shout back to stop him from staring at me.

"Fine. I'll get to work, but you know damn well what that look was for." Fuck yeah, I do. He wants me to meet with Remy because he knows Remy won't stop until he feels he's gotten me to agree to help. I don't need help. I need sleep. When I'm not overtired, the nightmares stay at bay, but if I'm stressed and not sleeping, well, fuck me, they're fierce. I shake my thoughts and jump onto my computer. I need to check emails and see what's going on with some parts we need for vehicles we have waiting for repair before my commander kicks my ass.

After a long ass morning of emails, repairs, parts tracking, and a brief meeting, I'm running out the door late. I was supposed to be at the commissary to meet with Remy five minutes ago. No sooner do I pull out of the maintenance parking lot than my phone rings through my in care system. "I'm on my way. Sorry, man."

"I thought you were blowing me off. I was going to come drag your ass out of that bay."

I laugh because he would too. "Nah, I'll be there in a minute." I cut the call. I thought about blowing him off, but he would only use that against me to try and prove a point. I'll have lunch with him, explain I just need a little sleep, and all will be good. I pull into the parking lot a few minutes later, and of course the place is packed. This place is always a zoo at lunch time. It's why if I don't pack my lunch, I grab it from the shoppette in the morning. First, I typically work through lunch, and second, I hate dealing with crowds. When I get inside, Remy is already sitting at a table with a large pizza. "I figured we could share a pizza, and since you were late, I took the liberty of ordering." I laugh and take a seat.

"Thanks, man. Sorry about that. The shop is really busy right now, and I have two guys that are still somewhat new, so they're slow and can't do all the stuff Callen and Max can do." He hands me a bottle of diet cola and I take a slice of pizza.

"No problem. I heard you saw my sister." Easy conversation, this I can handle.

"Yeah, she was at the same bar the guys and I hang out at. They ended up joining us. Your sister's pretty cool." I take a bite of the pepperoni pizza.

He wipes his mouth with a napkin and then places it on his lap. "Listen, I try not to get involved in her life, but I heard her telling her friend that she thinks you're hot, and that she's had a great time with you." Fuck, maybe this isn't going to be easy conversation. He didn't call me here to discuss my sleep issues, he's pissed his sister likes me.

"Listen, I think your sister is gorgeous and yes, we had fun, but say the word and I'll stay away from her. I'd never disrespect you like that. We've been friends for far too long." Remy and are the same age, and we've always gotten along really well. Every time we've been stationed near one another, we've gotten together.

"I appreciate that, but my sister would cut my balls off if I tried to interfere. My point was to let you know that she likes you. All I ask is that you be good to her. Don't lead her on if you're not interested." He has laughter in his voice. He's probably right, Brooke is one sassy woman. She adores her brother, but she doesn't take shit from him, either.

Well, that went better than I expected. "I wouldn't do that to any woman, especially not your sister. You're like family, man."

"Good, now onto more important things." He

takes a swig of his soda. Fuck, here it comes. "What's up with you and this shit about not sleeping? Are you having nightmares again?"

"Only once in a while. It's really no big deal." I shrug my shoulders to try and persuade him it's really not an issue because it's not. I'm a little tired, but this is nothing I can't handle.

His brows shoot up in disbelief. "When is the last time you slept through the night?"

"Night before last. Listen, man. I get it you're concerned, and I appreciate it, trust me I do, but I'm good." Crossing my leg, I lean back in my seat. "I'm relaxed, calm, and I'm not easily agitated." Remy stares at me for a moment, trying to figure out his next move. I can see the cogs spinning in his head. He's been in my shoes, only he had it worse. It was him who took a bullet—twice. That's not something you can easily move on from. I sigh. "I spoke with your sister about getting a dog. I need some focus in my life, that's all. Once I have a dog to take care of, everything will fall back into place. I'm telling you, I'm good."

"You think it's that easy?" He crosses his arms and narrows his eyes at me.

"I don't think it's that easy, but I think it will be helpful."

"Okay, fine. Have you spoken to her since the bar?" I shake my head. "What are you waiting for?"

I shrug. "I never got her number." It's a lame ass excuse, since I could have picked up the phone and easily gotten it from Remy. "Plus, I know she's graduating soon. I don't want to bother her while she's studying." Truthfully, I'd love to take her out.

42

I've had my eyes on her for years, and was stoked when Remy got back and invited me to his parents for their annual cookout. She was looking mighty fine, as always.

Remy bursts into laughter. "Dude, really? Are you a man or a kid in high school? You should have called." He shakes his head and pulls out his phone. My phone pings a minute later. He sent me a text with Brooke's phone number.

"Are you going to tell her you gave out her number?" I have laughter in my voice. "Or is that something you do on a regular basis?"

"First, you know damn well I don't. Second, hurt my baby sister and I'll kill you. Third, call her and get the dog squared away. I don't like seeing you like this." He stands from the table. "If I don't see improvement, you better believe we'll be having another conversation." He puts his hand on my shoulder. "I have to get my ass back to work. Take the rest of the pizza back for your guys. They'll love you for it."

"My guys already love me." I close the lid to the pizza and we walk out together.

He's a few feet away when he turns back. "Do me a favor."

"Anything."

"Promise me if this shit gets out of control, you'll get help."

"Sure." I muster as much conviction into that one word as I can. There's no way I'm going to allow this to get out of control.

"Good. I don't want to have to kick your ass." He chuckles and walks out the door.

43

I pull up to the shop. The guys are all standing around looking at one vehicle in particular. "What's up, guys?" I walk over carrying the pizza and they all turn to face me. "I brought some pizza back."

Callen comes over and tells me that the two newbies made a mistake on the truck they were working on and now it needs added repairs. The repairs aren't major, but they'll put us further behind in our schedule. "Callen, you help them fix their mistake, and I'm going to go check out the last of the vehicles that were dropped off this weekend so we can get out of here at a decent time. We're working late tonight, boys." They all grunt and groan heading back to work, but I don't give a fuck. We're a team, and if one guy stays late, we all stay late.

Chapter 4

Brooke

It's been a long ass week and I'm beat, but looking forward to the family coming over for dinner tonight. Mama has the family over at least every other weekend for dinner, and as tiring as it is, it's nice to see everyone. Tonight after we eat, Mama and I are sitting down with Kenzie and her aunt to finalize wedding plans. They're getting married on the Fourth of July, and it will be here before we know it. Mama is really excited. She keeps planning all these parties and telling everyone her family has a lot to celebrate this year. I'm graduating college in a few weeks, and Remy and Kenzie are getting married.

"Brooke, will you come down here and help me out?" Mama shouts from the bottom of the stairs.

"Coming, Mama." I run down the stairs, knowing she's in a panic over dinner. Kenzie's aunt and uncle are joining us as well. They don't usually, but given that we're talking about the wedding and

45

her aunt wants to be involved, Mama invited them as well. We have seen a lot more of them since Kenzie's nana passed away. Her aunt has children, but they don't live close by. Mama says she includes them because they're part of the family now, and she doesn't want them to feel lonely. I swear Kenzie treats them more like parents than their own children do.

"What do you need, Mama?"

"Can you peel these potatoes, please?" Mama hands me a bag of sweet potatoes, a bag for the peels, and a peeler. I set up at the snack bar and work on my task. My mind drifts back to Vaughn. I realized the other day that I never gave him my number. I wonder if Remy would give me his number, and how would Vaughn feel about me reaching out to him. I bite my lip thinking about it as I work on getting these peeled. I'm about done when my brother Remy comes walking in.

"Hey, Mama," Remy greets Mama and gives her a kiss. "Brooke." He leans in and gives me a hug.

"Where's Kenzie?" I ask him, shocked she's not with him.

"It's nice to see you too." I giggle and he shakes his head. "You know, I remember a time when you were thrilled to see me. Now it's like I don't exist."

"I'm sorry. I am thrilled to see you, but I grew up with three brothers, and now I'm going to have another sister-in-law. You have no idea how exciting that is." A smile spreads across my face.

"I'm here." Kenzie walks in. "Trust me, I'm thrilled to have a sister as well." She gives me a hug.

Don't get me wrong, I love my sister-in-law Kayla, but we're not close, not like Kenzie and I. Kayla's family is quite big, and she's used to having sisters around, where Kenzie is an only child. "Are you excited to finalize your wedding plans tonight?"

A huge smile lights up her face. "I'm so excited." My mom takes the sweet potatoes and starts to prepare them for dinner.

"I saw Vaughn yesterday," Remy interrupts our conversation, changing the topic.

"Oh yeah?" I don't want to give it away that I like him because I don't want Remy to freak out. I'm not sure how he'll feel about my dating one of his friends. Last time he caught Vaughn flirting, he wasn't happy about it. Vaughn is older than me, not that I care. He's really hot with his muscular build. His dark wavy hair makes me want to run my fingers through it, and when we were on the dance floor, his big hazel eyes pulled me in. I couldn't break eye contact with him, we were connected if only for a minute. I bite my lip thinking back. When I left that night, all I could think about was running my hand down the bumps of his chest and his abs.

"Earth to Brooke." Remy shakes me from my thoughts.

I giggle. "Sorry."

"You like him," Remy accuses, his eyes wide.

"I do not." I laugh and try to leave the kitchen, but Remy steps in front of me.

"You do too, and you know what? He likes you too." Remy looks amused.

"What? How do you know that?" My laughter

stops.

"I have my ways." He wiggles his eyebrows at me. He's being childish but I'm not mad. He's my brother, and he's always been like this with me. Plus, who can be mad with news like this?

"Will you excuse me?" He continues to stare at me and says nothing. My mother and Kenzie are standing behind us, amused by the banter taking place between my brother and I. "What do you want?" I can't help the smile that spreads across my face.

"Admit it." He crosses his arms and blocks me from leaving the room. I want to escape to the bathroom, if only for a minute, but he's not having it.

"Why?" He continues to look at me. "Are you going to interfere?"

"No." He's fighting a smile, but failing miserably.

I match his stance. "Fine. I like him. I've liked him for a long time now, but didn't say anything because I thought you would freak out." I'm full of sass.

He bursts into laughter. "Vaughn asked me today if I'd have a problem with him seeing you. He likes you. I told him if he hurt you, I'd kill him."

"Of course you did. I have one question for you, big shot." My brows shoot up. "If he likes me so much, why hasn't he called? He obviously could have gone to you for my number." It's been a little over a week since I've seen him. I even offered to help him find a dog, figuring it would give him excuse to call. I didn't give my number, but he could easily get it from you. He didn't even have to say it was because he liked me…he had the puppy as an excuse."

"He didn't have your number until we spoke. I'm not sure why he hasn't called you yet, but give him a chance. He's trying to sort out some things right now." Remy steps to the side, letting me by. I run up the stairs to wash my hands and wrap my head around my thoughts.

What could he be trying to sort? I'm graduating soon, and the last thing I need is a distraction. Staring in the mirror, I contemplate what I should do. Now that Remy has told me he's okay with me seeing him, I'm pushing him away. I know he won't treat me poorly like my ex did, but if he's having issues, can I handle that and deal with graduation and a new job title? What am I saying? He hasn't even tried to contact me, but damn, I wish he would. I shake my head, I'm a mess.

I hear voices downstairs. Aunt Kenderly and Uncle Jasper are here. I sigh and run back down the stairs to say hello. When I get to the bottom, my brother Dawson and his clan are walking through the door. Becky is getting so big, and Kayla is carrying Beau in a car seat. He's only a few months old, but he must eat like a beast, because he's huge. No sooner does Kayla put the carrier down than Remy scoops up his godson and starts to play with him. He looks so sweet holding the baby. I hope they have kids someday. They will make great parents.

"Brooke, can you help me with beverages, please?" Mama calls from the kitchen.

I ask everyone what they'd like to drink and then Kenzie and I head into the kitchen to grab beers, wine, and water. Mama's busy finishing off dinner, which is almost done. She, as usual, has made a feast, and now that the family is growing, we no longer all fit around the dining room table. I'll sit in the kitchen with Becky and Keaton while everyone else sits in the dining room. Mama made a joke of telling my dad that they needed a new house with a bigger dining room. Dad didn't find the joke very funny. Kenzie and I hand out the drinks and I go back to the kitchen to make sure Mama's all set.

"Brooke, will you mash these for me?" Mama hands me a pot of potatoes. It's always my job to mash them. She says I do a good job if it. It's just right, not too many lumps. The boys swear she does it just to get my help, but really she's taught me how to cook, and I'm glad.

"Are these the famous Brooke mashed potatoes?" Aunt Kenderly comes into the kitchen.

"I don't know about famous, but they're my mashed potatoes." I smile, pounding the masher into the pot.

"Yeah, well, your sister-in-law raves about them." She leans on the snack bar.

"Well, that's sweet of her. I'm glad she enjoys them." I add some seasonings to the pot and continue mashing.

"What can I do to help?" Aunt Kenderly asks.

"We're fine," Mama tells her. "Almost time to eat."

"You're too sweet, Mama Bennett." Aunt Kenderly gives my mama a hug. She's been calling her Mama Bennett since Kenzie and Remy got engaged, and of course my mama just eats it up.

"Where is that brother of yours?" Mama shakes her head. "Dinner is ready and as usual he's not here yet."

"Start without him." My father comes into the kitchen. "The boy's going to be late to his own dang funeral."

Mama shakes her head. "I should have known when he was the only child of mine that was born late." I can't help but chuckle. Keaton is always the last one here and he's always late. It drives Mama crazy, and no matter how much she lectures him on the issue, he still arrives late with some lame excuse. You know how there's always one troublesome kid in the family? Well, that's Keaton. "Dinner is ready." Mama sets out plates. Now that we're so big, we all make plates in the kitchen and then take our seat in the dining room.

Kenzie, Remy, Aunt Kenderly, and Uncle Jasper all lead off the line for food, making their plates and heading into the dining room. Dawson and Kayla follow, and I help Becky make her plate. I can see the agitation on Mama's face that Keaton still has not shown up. Mama begins to pace. She acts angry, but she's really worried. "Lord help that boy if he doesn't walk through that door any minute now. He better be close to dead or I'm going to put him six feet under myself for worrying me." My father tries to calm her but it's not really working. "Today is supposed to be about Kenzie, not him, and my mind is on his late ass."

He comes running through the door. "Sorry I'm

late, Mama," he pants, out of breath.

Mama walks over to him, hugs him, he kisses her on the cheek, and then in true Mama fashion, she slaps him off the back of the head hard.

"Ouch."

"That's for being late and making me worry," Mama growls at him. It's actually funny to witness because Mama is so much smaller than Keaton, but she certainly has no problem putting him in his place.

"I said I was sorry, Mama." He rubs the back of his head. I laugh as I get Becky set up at the snack bar.

"Auntie Brooke, is Uncle Keaton in trouble again?" She looks up at me, her eyes filled with curiosity.

"Yeah, but you know what? That's never going to change. He's a big kid."

"Nana needs to put him in timeout." She crosses her little arms. "It's boring in timeout and it always makes me behave." Her brows shoot up. She's dead serious.

"That's a good idea, sweetie, but I don't think timeouts are going to work for Uncle Keaton. He's a little old for that." I put her plate down in front of her with her food all cut up.

"Thank you, Auntie." She digs in and says nothing more about Keaton being late.

The remainder of our meal is enjoyed in silence. Keaton sits on one side of Becky and I'm on the other. I don't know what his problem is, but I can't get into it with him when Becky is sitting between us, so it's best to leave it be for now. I finish eating rather quickly and begin the process of cleaning up. The women are gathering in the dining room soon to discuss the wedding, and god knows what the guys are going to do.

Mama comes into the kitchen with her empty plate as Keaton finishes his. He usually goes for seconds, but Mama stops him. "Go grab all the empty dishes from the dining room, Keaton."

"But I wasn't done, Mama." She whips her head around and gives him the glare. It's the glare we all feared as kids. The glare that tells him he best put his plate down and do it.

"Yes, ma'am," Keaton mumbles. He puts his plate down and hurries off to clear the table. He comes back a few minutes later with a large stack of plates. He puts them in the sink and sighs in disappointment when he sees Mama put the leftovers into containers already. He's now all out sulking and I think it's hilarious. Since there's no more food out for him to eat, he puts his plate in the sink and goes to sulk in the living room, where the guys are starting to gather.

"What's wrong, Keaton, Mama hurt your feelings?" Remy busts his balls.

"Fu—" He stops himself before Mama yells at him for cursing. "Screw you, mama's boy!"

"Remy, leave your brother alone," my father intervenes. Dawson is the calm one of the four of us. For some reason he never cared to pick on or mess with any of us, but Remy, Keaton, and I, we were always fighting and picking on each other as kids.

I put the final dish into the dishwasher while

Mama wipes down the counter and sink. "There, all done. Thank you for your help, Brooke."

"You're welcome, Mama. Shall we join our guests in the dining room?" She nods her head and smiles.

Kenzie has a binder out and she's flipping through it when we take a seat next to her. She's chosen her dress. Lilly, Kayla, and I all have our dresses taken care of, our church pastor is coming here to marry them, Remy's friend is a DJ and he's taking care of the music, and Mama has arranged for a caterer. "Kenzie, dear. Have you decided on the menu yet? I need to let the caterer know soon," Mama asks her.

"We have, but we can't seem to agree on the cake." Kenzie rolls her eyes. "I think maybe we should do a variety of desserts and call it done, but Remy wants to cut a cake to stick with tradition."

"Why don't we schedule a cake tasting with you guys?" Aunt Kenderly suggests.

"Remy, can you come here?" Mama calls into the other room. Kenzie shows Mama some of the cake options from a bakery she was referred to when Mama realizes Remy never answered her. "Remington Scott Bennett, come here, please." They heard her this time and we all know it's because Keaton messes with Remy now because Mama used his full name. Mama never uses Rem's full name.

"Yes, ma'am." Remy practically runs into the room.

"We are going to schedule a cake tasting. Is there a day or time that's better for you?" Mama looks up at him from her seat.

"No, I have plenty of leave time. Just give me enough notice so I can submit a leave slip to my commander and it should be fine." She nods at him and he exits the room.

"I'll make an appointment and email everyone the dates as well as the menu we've chosen." Kenzie makes a reminder in her notebook.

"What are you doing about flowers?" I ask her.

A huge smile lights up her face. "Remy took me to this open field not too far from here when we first started dating. It was surrounded by the most beautiful wildflowers you could imagine. He even sent me a bouquet of them when I tried to push him away." Her smile slips slightly. "It wouldn't be right to have anything but those same wildflowers." She bites her lip. "He used to tell me they reminded him of me."

"Awww, that's so sweet," I gush. "I hope I find me a good man like that someday." I nudge her with my shoulder.

"I'm sure you will." She winks at me.

It's getting late. Dawson has already called it a night. He needed to get Beau and Becky home to bed. I'm getting tired and I have a final this week, so I need to call it a night as well.

When I get up to my room, I sit on my bed to check my phone and notice a text from a random number. I realize once I read it that it's from Vaughn. He's asking me about helping him pick a dog. I really want to help him, but with my clinic hours and a final later this week, I'm not really sure I can.

Brooke: I'm more than happy to help, but can we do it next week? I have to study for a final later this week on top of working.

Vaughn: Of course, sorry to bother you.

Brooke: It's no bother. I really want to help but I can't do it right now.

I wait for a response that never comes.

Chapter 5

Brooke

It's graduation day and I'm nervous as hell, but I don't know why. All I have to do is walk across the stage, shake someone's hand, and walk off. No big deal, right? Wrong. What if I trip and make a fool of myself? This place is going to be packed with students, faculty, staff, and family. I shake my head checking my appearance one last time. My hair is curled to perfection. I've applied enough makeup to look natural and have my eyes pop. I apply one last coat of lip gloss and run down the stairs. I'm wearing loose, flowing slacks that almost look like a skirt with a sleeveless top that hugs my curves. It's comfortable and professional. The nude sandal heels I'm wearing are already killing my feet.

"Are you ready, sweetie?" my father asks as soon as I'm downstairs.

"Yes, let's get this over with." I step out the door he's holding open for Mama and I.

My father drives us off toward the campus, but

because I'm running a bit late, there's already traffic and parking is tough. My father groans at the people driving like lunatics, trying to get a spot. He finally finds one. It's a bit of a walk, but we consider ourselves lucky to even have a spot. "I have to go, but I'll see you guys at the end." I quickly hug my parents and race inside the building to find my seat.

No sooner do I sit than a gentleman takes the stage. He asks everyone to find their seats and announces the ceremony will begin shortly. I turn in my seat to see if I can spot my parents, but it's no use, there are far too many people here. There's a program on every seat. Opening mine up, I discover there are a few guest speakers and the valedictorian that needs to give a speech. I internally pray they don't drag the speeches on forever. It's the most boring part of the ceremony. We're all so excited to be graduating the last thing we want to do is listen to people talk for hours on end. This is a difficult program, and we've all worked hard for this moment.

The ceremony finally begins, and they announce the first guest speaker. Before I know it the speeches are over. Luckily they did not drag on forever with their well wishes and bits of advice. We finally begin the never ending process of handing out the degrees. Of course it's alphabetical order, so I don't need to wait long to get mine, but I still have to sit and wait while the rest of the graduating class gets theirs. This guy Jack is on one side of me. He's cool, but we didn't really talk much, although we had a lot of classes together. On the other side is this girl, Kim. We studied a lot together but never really hung out outside of school. We all hug to congratulate each other when we get back to our seats and then we sit quietly as we anxiously wait for this to be over with. At this point we want to meet up with our families for pictures and celebrating. The class only has about sixty students, so although it feels like it was going to take forever, it really doesn't take too long.

They've finally announced the last name and we are officially graduates. I'm so excited I hurry off to find my parents, passing a few friends along the way. We congratulate each other and hug before we continue looking for our families. My parents are in the entryway anxiously waiting with their camera handy to take my picture. They snap a few quick shots and we wander around. I introduce them to a few friends that happen to walk by. "Mom, I'm really not interested in hanging around. Are you guys ready to go? We can take more pictures at home if you want."

Mama smiles. "It's your day, sweetie. Whatever you want."

I hug my parents and thank them for all the support they have given me over the years. I'm truly lucky to have such amazing parents. We walk back toward the car and there's a pep in my step. I'm officially Dr. Brooke Bennett, DVM. When we finally arrive back at the car, my dad has a huge smile on his face. "What?" I ask him.

"I'm so proud of you. You have worked so hard for this moment, and to have graduated in the top ten in your class is such an accomplishment."

"Thanks, Dad." He hugs me one more time before we head home.

We pull up to the house and I'm completely shocked. I knew my parents were inviting some family over, but half the town is here, and there's a huge banner outside that says '*Congratulations, Dr. Bennett*' on it. I'm so touched. "You guys didn't have to do all this." I jump out of the car as soon as it stops, my parents right behind me. They each wrap their arms around me and congratulate me one more time. Kenzie is there with a camera capturing the moment before she comes over with Remy to give me a hug. Mama takes the camera and snaps off a picture of the three of us with me still in my cap and gown.

The pictures continue when Dr. Kramer and Courtney come over to congratulate me. He hands me a bag and asks me to open it. I dig inside to find a brand new lab coat with my name on it. **'Dr. Brooke Bennett, DVM.'** I gasp tears welling in my eyes. "Dr. Kramer, thank you so much."

"You're most welcome. Congratulations. I'm so proud of you." They both hug me one more time and I continue on greeting people and thank them for coming.

Aunt Kenderly and Uncle Jasper break my thoughts when they come running over. "Sorry we're late." She wraps me in a big hug. "You look beautiful, dear."

"You're not late, and thank you so much for being here." It's a beautiful day and I'm getting a bit warm in my cap and gown.

"We wouldn't dream of missing it." She smiles

and gives me another hug.

"Excuse me a minute. Mama, are you good with pictures? I want to take this off." She nods. I quickly strip. I've spent the last thirty minutes or so greeting and talking with guests and I'm ready to move on to something to eat. Mama has already told our guests to get started.

No sooner do I lay my gown over my arm than a voice comes from behind my back. "You look gorgeous." His voice sends a shiver down my spine and I instantly know it's him. My face lights up as I spin to see him looking down at me with a huge grin on his face. "Congratulations." He looks deep into my eyes.

"Thank you." My words are barely a whisper. A blush creeps up my body, this man does things to me. My body responds to him simply being close to me.

"You're welcome. Do I get a picture too?" He looks at me with a slight grin and one eyebrow raised.

"Of course you do. With or without the cap and gown?" I question.

He laughs. "Without is fine." He leans in next to me, pulls his phone out, and snaps a picture of the two of us. We both have huge goofy smiles on our faces, but it's a great picture. "Thanks," he whispers close to my ear. My body once again shudders. "Want to get something to eat?"

"Sure." His eyes tell me he's leery on how to proceed, like he has fears of overstepping some boundary.

"I'm going to put my cap and gown inside first."

I take his hand and pull him toward the buffet of food my parents have set up along the back of the house. He waits there while I run into the house to hang my stuff. I don't want it to get ruined.

"You two look quite intense." My brother Remy leans against the doorframe with his arms folded

I jump. "You scared the shit out of me, Rem." He shakes his head at the use of my nickname for him. "I really like him, Rem. I have for a while now. When we were at the bar dancing it was like we had a connection. I felt it as he looked into my eyes, but then I hadn't heard from him until the other day. Now here he is and it's like he wants to ask me out but isn't sure he should." I look down to the floor. It feels weird to be talking to Remy about his friend.

"Listen, he's a great guy. Take it one step at a time, don't force anything. Trust me, he wants to ask you out, and if it is meant to be, it will happen." He hugs me. "Congrats, sis. I'm proud of you." He walks out to the backyard, leaving me to my own thoughts. I watch as he shakes hands and man hugs Vaughn. They exchange some words and Remy walks off to make his plate while Vaughn stands there waiting for me.

I better get back out there. I run down the back steps. "Thanks for waiting for me."

"No need to thank me. My mom raised me right." He hands me a plate and places his hand at the small of my back, setting my skin on fire. We walk down the food line picking our favorites and I can't help but notice we like a lot of the same things. "Where would you like to sit?" he asks when we get to the end of the line. All the tables are taken but there are a few open seats here and there.

"Do you mind if we sit with my brother and Kenzie?" My back is practically pressed to his front when I look up over my shoulder to his gorgeous hazel eyes.

"Not at all." I take his hand and we make our way to their table. "Are these seats taken?" he asks and they welcome us to join.

We take a seat next to each other and begin to eat. There's a lot of tension at the table as we all figure out what to say. I figured this would be an easy place for him to sit, but apparently it's not.

"How's things at the shop?" Remy finally breaks the silence.

"Crazy, actually. We're so busy and I have a few rookie mechanics right now. Two of them were working on a routine oil change not too long ago and screwed it up. Nearly blew an engine."

"Shit." Remy's brows shoot up in shock.

"Tell me about it. The MPs and my commander would have had my ass."

"What did you do?" He leans back in the chair, far more comfortable now than when we first sat down. Kenzie and I continue eating while we listen to his story.

"I chewed them a new asshole for making a silly mistake, and then made the entire team work overtime while they fixed it." He places a napkin on his lap. "At the end of the day I lectured everyone on how these mistakes happen because we rush instead of following protocol and doing things one step at a time." He shakes his head. "The two kids

63

felt awful that the entire crew had to work late because of them and they got their balls busted for it, but you know shit happens. They bought a round of drinks the following Friday to apologize, and of course all is forgotten."

"You know how it is, man. These kids learn best from the mistakes they make. I guarantee you they will never pull that shit again." Remy leans forward so his elbows are on the table. "I had one guy who nearly caused a huge firefight from bad intel. He wanted to show off, trying to be the hero that figures shit out, and it nearly cost him his career." Remy throws his napkin onto his plate. "We can't screw around with shit like that. The kid still gets his balls busted for it."

"I bet it brought him back to reality though, didn't it?" Vaughn relaxes.

"Fucking right it did." Remy nods his head.

"Remy, language," Kenzie scolds him, slapping him on the arm.

"Sorry, sweetie. I forgot where I was for a minute." I giggle at my brother getting reprimanded. He hardly ever curses in front of Kenzie or the family. Unlike Keaton, he always minds his manners.

Kenzie nods at him. "Make it up to me. Let's go mingle with the family."

Remy visibly cringes, because he's not one to mingle. He would be perfectly happy sitting here for the remainder of the afternoon, but their wedding is approaching and Kenzie apparently has the need to get to know the people. He grumbles a "fine" and gets up to follow her. He adores Kenzie and would never disappoint her.

"Have fun." I wave watching Remy follow Kenzie around the yard.

"She's going to torture him, isn't she?"

I laugh. "Nah, she just wants to get to know everyone more before the wedding, and this is a good chance for her to do that." I cross my leg and lean in a bit closer to him. I want to apologize for blowing him off with the dog search. I feel like it hurt his feelings and that's why he hasn't touched base with me since the last text he sent me. "I want to apologize." I place my hand on his arm.

"For what?" he questions, but if I'm reading him properly, he knows exactly what I'm apologizing for.

"I feel really bad that I had to push off helping you find a dog. I know you really wanted to do this and I need to explain."

"You have no need to explain." His voice a bit harsh.

I slip my chair closer to him. "Helping you find a dog is important to me, but I had to remember that finishing school was just as important. I wanted to be able to give you my undivided attention, you deserve it. When you asked me, I felt like I couldn't do that, and that wouldn't be fair to you."

He looks at me with a small grin on his face. "Really?"

I nod. "Vaughn, I like you, and I didn't want any distractions to be in the way of us not only finding you a dog, but maybe having dinner?" My voice rises a little, hopeful he won't reject me.

He leans forward. "I'm sorry too. I shouldn't

have gone silent. I guess I thought you really didn't want to help me and just said you did to be nice." He looks down for a minute and then his eyes come up to meet mine. "I like you too. I have for a while now, but never pursued an opportunity with you because of your brother."

I laugh. "I knew it." I shake my head. "Let me rephrase that. I had a feeling you liked me but weren't saying anything because of my brother."

He smiles brighter and his hazel eyes light up. "I've talked to him, and although he's threatened my life if I ever hurt you, he's cool with me asking you out."

"He is, huh?" My left eyebrow raises. "And what if he wasn't?"

He shrugs. "I would have figured it out, but he didn't, so what do you say? Can I take you to dinner?"

"Under one condition." I slip on a serious look.

He narrows his eyes. "What's that?"

"You let me help you pick a dog." My brows shoot up.

With a grin he stares into my eyes. "Why are you so intent on helping me pick a dog?"

Shit, do I tell him that I believe he needs it? Do I tell him I want to help train the dog to be more than a companion but a service dog as well? "I believe it would be good for you to have one. From what I've heard, you've been through a lot." He breaks eye contact and suddenly looks really uncomfortable. "Please don't shut me out."

"I don't exactly like discussing my past." He pulls away sitting back in his chair.

"I'm sure. We went through it with Rem and I understand. I'm not asking you to talk about it. I'm asking you to let me help you pick a dog." He finally looks back at me. "Please, I've already researched a few in the area for you and I have one I'd like you to meet."

He chuckles and shakes his head. "You're not trying to get me to adopt some lap dog, are you?" I can see he's trying to recover and I can tell from his reaction he's glad I'm not forcing him to talk about it.

I laugh. "I would never do that. You're not a lap dog kind of guy. You need a dog that's smart, strong, and responsive. He's young, but not a pup, which I think will be good for you."

"Where did you find him?" He rests his chin in his hand.

"He's at a shelter. His owner recently passed away and not one of the family members wanted to keep him, so they brought him in." I don't point out that he's had some training in the area of responding to situations. I truly think he'll be a good match for him.

"All right. When do I get to meet him?"

I clap my hands, excited that I've convinced him. "I'll make us an appointment and text you the time. I'll make sure it's at night, so it doesn't interfere with work."

He shrugs. "I have plenty of leave time saved up, it won't matter either way. If it's a day appointment, I would need time to put in a slip."

"I can't wait for you to meet him. He's adorable and fun. I think you two will be perfect together."

"Now does this mean I can take you out? I can't wait to explore how perfect we are together." I feel a blush creep up my cheeks. He's so dang sweet.

"Sure, I'd like that." I bite my lip.

Our conversation is interrupted by some guests who are taking off but came over to congratulate me and wish me luck with my new job. I hug them and thank them again for coming. As I do, Dr. Kramer and Courtney come over to say goodbye as well. They both tell me they'll see me at work on Monday, and that's when I notice the yard emptied out. I hadn't realized how long Vaughn and I have sat here chatting. I take my seat and he goes right back into our conversation. "Now that you're done with school, is your schedule more flexible?"

"Yeah, Dr. Kramer is taking me on as a full time vet, but I'll mainly work days. I'll be on-call periodically to take care of emergencies for him, but that will only be a few nights a week. I'll only have to go in if there's an urgent need."

"Great. Do you have plans for tomorrow night?"

I look up to the sky, trying to pretend like I need to think about my schedule. Tomorrow is Saturday and the clinic is closed. I have zero plans, but he doesn't know that. When I look at him he's staring at me with both eyebrows raised and I can't help but laugh. "I'd love to go to dinner tomorrow night."

He stands from the table, taking my plate along with his. He throws them in the barrel set up not too far from us. "I'll pick you up at six," he says when he returns. Taking my hand, he pulls me from my seat and kisses me on the cheek. "I've got to go, but text me later." I nod, not having any words. He leaves, and as soon as he does, I miss him. I pull my phone from my back pocket and immediately text my friend, hoping the dog is still there. When she replies that he is, I tell her we'll be by tomorrow.

Chapter 6

Vaughn

I keep thinking about the text message banter between Brooke and I last night. She's so fun and easy to talk to, but I have a feeling she's up to no good. Her final message to me last night was asking me if I can pick her up at four instead of six, and even after I told her that wasn't a problem, she wouldn't tell me why. I have a feeling she's taking me to see this dog she's so excited about, and I have to admit I'm nervous. What if I don't think the dog is right for me? I don't want to offend her. I feel like I'll know when I see the right dog, and I hope she won't be hurt if I say he's not it. I take a few deep breaths, trying to calm down before I send myself into another panic attack. Once I have it under control, I check my watch. Shit. It's three-fifteen.

I need to get going if I'm going to pick her up on time. I hate being late and I don't want to give a bad first impression. I flip on the little lamp by my front door and grab my keys before locking up. There shouldn't be a ton of traffic at this time of day, but I don't want to chance it. When I start the car and turn on the radio, Charlie Puth rings out through the speakers, and it reminds me of the night we danced at the bar. She felt good swaying in my arms to the music, staring into each other's eyes. My gut instinct kicks in, telling me this is going to be a great evening.

I arrive at her house ten minutes early, and in Army time, that's perfect. If you're not ten minutes early, you're late, is our motto. I climb out of the car and the door opens before I can even finish climbing the steps. I'm greeted by her father. "Good evening, Dr. Bennett."

"Good evening, Vaughn. You do know that Remy no longer lives here." He has a hint of a smile on his face, telling me he's busting my balls.

"Yes, sir. If it's okay with you, I'm here to take your daughter out."

Before he can even answer, I hear Brooke's voice. "Oh Dad, stop messing with him and let him in."

He steps to the side and allows me in the house, but not before he looks me dead in the eye. "I like you, Vaughn. Please don't make my opinion of you change."

"No, sir. I won't, I promise." I maintain eye contact. He nods and steps out of the way.

"I'm sorry, Vaughn. Dad's having some issues with his big girl growing up. Especially now that he knows I'm looking for a place of my own."

Mrs. Bennett comes over and gives me a hug. I

71

kiss her on the cheek and bid her good evening. I'm trying to be a perfect gentleman because I know this family well, and as her father said, the last thing I want is their opinion of me to change. "Are you ready?" I slip my hand into hers. She nods and tells her parents she'll be home late.

I can feel her father's eyes staring at me as we walk down to my car. I'm trying hard not to turn around. I respect her father, but I don't want to let on that he's making me nervous. I open the door for Brooke and she slips herself inside. I run around the other side of the car and start it up, turning the air conditioning on to cool the car down. It's quite warm today. "Okay, where to?"

She turns to me with a bashful smile. "You know where I want to go, don't you?" She bites her lip to stifle her giggle.

"I have an idea, but I'm not sure which one."

"Claremont Street." She buckles her seatbelt and I pull out of her parents' driveway. I knew it. She's taking me to meet a dog. The shelter she's referring to is well known in this area and has a great reputation. I know because when I started to investigate dogs, I did research on the local shelters. I glance over to see her staring out the window. "What's wrong?" I place my hand on her knee and give it a gentle squeeze.

"You're not mad that I set this up, are you?" she asks, her voice full of concern.

"No, not at all. I'm nervous, I'll admit. I don't want to hurt your feelings if I feel this dog isn't right for me, but I'm not mad. Actually, I'm excited, and I appreciate the effort you've put in."

Her face lights up and I can see she visibly relaxes.

We pull up to the shelter and I can tell she's excited because she jumps out of the car before I even take the keys from the ignition. She looks gorgeous in her white jean shorts. They hug her gorgeous round ass, and her pink top shows off her curves. She's showing me just enough to make me want her. She takes my hand and pulls me into the shelter. There's a counter in front of us where we're greeted by a woman whose name tag tells me she's Cindy. She clearly knows Brooke. "Brooke, how are you, darling?" She walks around the counter and gives Brooke a huge hug.

"I'm well, how are you?"

"I'm great." She turns to me. "You must be Vaughn." She holds her hand out to me.

"Yes, ma'am." We shake and she tells me to follow her.

"Now listen, Brody is a great dog, and I think he's the perfect age for a new dog owner, but you have to feel like he's right for you. If he isn't a good fit, don't let guilt lead you to adopt him." I nod and we walk through a room lined with kennels. There's probably about twenty to twenty-five dogs in total here. She opens another door and says, "Wait here, I'll bring him in." She exits the room and we both sit quietly.

The door opens again a minute later and in comes this gorgeous Golden Retriever. He's so happy and full of life. I squat down in front of him, hold my hand out for him to sniff, and he instantly jumps on me and starts licking my face, causing me to burst into laughter. I pet his face and body trying to calm him down. "Wow, he really likes you." Brooke squats down beside me.

"Brody is being incredibly shy with those who have thought about adopting him. They say the pet chooses the owner, and I think he's chosen you. I'll leave you two to visit with him for a bit."

"Thank you, Cindy," Brooke tells the woman as she scoots out the door.

I'm sitting on the floor with the dog lying before me. "You want to come home with me?" My voice has gone from grown man to a silly baby voice in two seconds flat. Brody barks his answer and I'm already in love with him. "I'll take that as a yes."

We spend the next few minutes playing with him and getting to know him. "I want to thank you for asking me to help you with this. I know you think I was blowing you off when you first asked me, but I wasn't. I truly wanted to help you and I'm sorry I had to ask you to wait."

"Again, you don't owe me an apology, Brooke."

"Maybe not, but I need you to understand where I was coming from." Brody puts his head on Brooke's lap. "I dated a guy not too long ago. Remy didn't like him and tried to warn me, but I didn't listen. He became a distraction. He would get mad at me if I told him I couldn't go out because I had to study. I had to work hard to get into vet school and I didn't want to chance not getting in because of my grades. He didn't take my decision to go to school seriously, and it caused problems between us. I didn't want that for us. I really like you."

I smile happily that she shared her past with me. "Thank you for that. I really like you too, and I'd like to see where things go between us, if you're good with that."

A smile spreads across her gorgeous face and there's a twinkle in her eye. "I'd really like that." I lean in to give her a gentle kiss and our moment is interrupted by Cindy's return. She starts telling us about the dog. He already knows basic commands and responds to my voice. "Brody, sit." He sits and wags his tail against the floor. She tells me about Brody's previous owner, an elderly man who was ill. His children couldn't be around to care for him all the time, so they got him the dog, who they trained to press the button on an emergency machine if his owner was in distress. He did as he was taught, but his owner didn't make it. He was too old and didn't have any fight left. Cindy's voice is a bit sad and Brody whimpers as if he knows we're talking about the man.

"Come here, boy." His ears perk up and he comes running to me, practically knocking me over. "What do you say we blow this joint?" Brody again barks his answer. "What paperwork do I need to fill out in order to take him home?"

"Come on. I'll show you." We all make our way out to the front. Brody is on his leash and Brooke takes care of him while I fill out the paperwork. I'm lucky I have the email on my phone stating I'm allowed to have a dog, or she wasn't going to let me take him home today. I pay the adoption fee and turn to my new buddy with a smile on my face. "You're all mine, buddy. Let's go get you some stuff from the store." I take his leash from Brooke and walk him out to the car. I open the back door and he jumps right in.

"The closest pet store is up around the corner on Coldwell Ave." I pull out of the spot and she instructs me on how to get there. She's right…it's literally up the street.

I take his leash and walk him into the store. "Now, since he's already pretty trained, you won't need a crate for him, or puppy pads, or anything like that. We need to get good dog food, a dog bed, and maybe some toys for him."

"What about treats?" I see a counter with dog bones, and it makes me realize I want to reward him for being a good boy.

"Oh yeah, you can get him some treats, but don't overdo it or he'll gain too much weight." She pushes a cart through the store while I walk with the dog. He's sniffing other dogs wagging his tail happily. I can't stop smiling and I've only had him for ten minutes. We get to the dog food aisle and Brody begins sniffing the bags while Brooke tells me about the different types of food available. Of course, knowing nothing about dogs or their food, I pick the one she recommends. I buy a small bag to start in case he doesn't like it and refuses to eat it. If that's the case, I'll donate it to the clinic or the shelter and move onto another bag. She also makes treat recommendations. We let him pick a toy, and when I say we let him, I mean that we were in the aisle and he picked one up in his mouth, making it his. We both burst into laughter and agreed that he should get to pick, since it's his.

Brooke's stomach growls and I realize that between the shelter and being here, it's starting to get late. "Well, I was going to take you out for dinner, but given this is his first night in my home, it's probably not a good idea for me to simply leave him there. What do you say we take him to my place, get him settled, and we'll order some takeout?"

"Sounds perfect. Trust me, I knew if you fell for him, we wouldn't be going out tonight, so I'm perfectly fine with that." She runs her hand down my chest.

When we get to the checkout, she takes the leash from me so I can take care of my purchase. We've bought a ton of stuff and I'm excited to get his bed set up in my room, along with all his other stuff. I haul all Brody's stuff outside and load it into the trunk of my car while she gets Brody settled in the back. I can't help but notice my car is already covered in dog hair. "I should have gotten a blanket for the back of the car." I watch my new buddy snuggle up on the backseat.

"You can order them cheaper online. You have the necessities for today." She pats my leg.

We pull up to my place about forty-five minutes later. "Can you grab Brody? I'll get the bags from the trunk." She nods and opens the back of the car, grabbing his leash. I open the door and he practically drags Brooke inside, excited to check out his new surroundings. I laugh at her reaction because she really didn't expect it.

My place isn't huge, but I have a two bedroom apartment with two bathrooms, one in the master, and one in the hallway. It's a pretty open layout. My kitchen is a decent size with a small dining area off to the side, and the living room big enough to comfortably seat five people. The master bedroom is pretty big and has a large walk-in closet, where the second bedroom has a smaller double door closet. It's not my ideal living conditions, but it's home.

"Sit, Brody," Brooke calls to him and he listens, but I can tell he's excited and struggling to stay still.

"Good boy, Brody." She drops his leash and walks away. His bum starts to come off the floor, but I look at him and hold up my hand, telling him to stay, and he does. After a few minutes of him sitting, he lays down and relaxes a bit. I'm proud of my buddy already. I place his dog bowls down in the kitchen by the back door while Brooke grabs his bed.

"Where do you want this?" She holds it up.

I shrug. "My room?" It's more of a question than an answer, but she does as I ask without trying to change my mind.

We really got a lot of stuff. I have a dog brush, shampoo, treats, food, toys—lots of toys—and a basket to put them in. I toss a few of them on the floor near him and he begins chewing on the one he chose, while I put the remainder in the basket in a corner of the living room.

Brooke comes back into the kitchen. "You have a nice place."

"Thank you. It's small, but it works for now." I toss the bags into the trash and try to figure out where I'll store his food.

"You're really going to want to get him on a feeding schedule. What time do you leave in the morning?" She leans on my counter top.

I go through the morning routine I've created with Callen. She's happy to hear about our run, she tells me it'll be good for him. He's a high energy job. She tells me to feed him as soon as I get home from our run and take him out right before I leave. That should eliminate any accidents during the day, since he's already trained…or at least I'm hoping. Then I need to feed him again as soon as I get home. Grabbing a cup from the cabinet, I give him the amount of food she recommends and fill his bowl with water.

"Now, what would you like to eat?" I ask, pinning her to the counter top she's leaning against.

"I'm not a picky eater." She looks up at me, biting her lip. I stare into her eyes, thinking about how much I've wanted to bite that lip. I slowly lower my lips to hers, pausing as our noses are about to touch. My intentions clear, she releases her lip from her teeth, closes her eyes, and I gently press my lips to hers. I glide my tongue across the seam of her soft, full lips and she instantly opens for me. Our tongues collide, meeting for the first time. She tastes heavenly. I run my hands up her arms and into her hair, tipping her head just enough for me to deepen the kiss.

We suddenly feel a tail smacking us in the leg, breaking our moment. I press my forehead to hers and chuckle. "I think someone's already jealous."

"I think you're right." I rub my nose on hers and gently kiss her one last time before I step away to pet Brody.

"There are take-out menus in the drawer right

beside you." She pulls them out and we flip through them, deciding to share a pizza and some breadsticks. We both typically eat pretty healthy, but agree we deserve the splurge from time to time.

While we're waiting, I send off an email to the apartment management office, letting them know that I did, in fact, get a dog, and that I'll be by on Monday with his papers and the check for the deposit.

A short time later the doorbell rings. It's the pizza guy. Brody starts barking and I tell him to calm down, it's okay. He answers the door with me, tail wagging. Brooke grabs his collar to control him while I pay the guy.

"That's some attack dog you have there," the guy pokes fun.

"Scared the shit out of you." The guy chuckles handing off the pizza and runs down the porch. "Good boy." I pet him and he runs back into the living room with us.

I set the box down on the kitchen counter while we get plates. "There's water and beer in the fridge."

She opens the refrigerator door. "I'm going to have water. What do you want?"

"Water is good. I have to bring you home later."

She pulls two bottles of water from the fridge while I place pizza and breadsticks on some plates for us.

We take a seat on the couch to eat while we watch some TV. Brody lies at my feet, calm and relaxed. We begin talking about shows we enjoy and different things we like to do. We learn that neither of us watch TV much and would rather be out doing stuff. I put my plate on the coffee table when I'm done. I've left a piece of crust there that I was too full to eat.

"Bad idea," she warns. "Dogs are quick. Always keep food out of his reach. The last thing you want is for him to get used to people food."

"I wasn't even thinking."

"Having a dog around takes getting used to, but you don't want him to eat something that could make him sick." She's right. I take both our plates and scrape them into the trash. When I get back, she's petting him while he relaxes in the same spot he was in when I left. I take a seat next to her.

She leans in close. "Thank you for dinner." She presses her lips to mine.

"Thank you for finding me the perfect dog." I slip my hand into her hair and kiss her again. This time our tongues meet and the kiss becomes more intimate. She climbs onto my lap. My hands run up her back under her shirt, feeling her silky soft skin.

"You have no idea how long I've been waiting for this." She grinds her pussy against my cock. I didn't realize she has wanted me as much as I've wanted her, and she doesn't give me the opportunity to question it. Her mouth crashes back down on mine. I flip her so she's beneath me on the couch. I rub my hard cock against her squeezing her breast through her bra. She moans into my mouth. Trailing kisses along her jaw toward her ear, I bite down gently on her earlobe. This time she whimpers, and it causes a reaction from Brody, who jumps up and puts his front paws on my ass.

I turn to my dog. "What? She's fine. Look." He licks her face and she bursts into laughter.

I sit up, pulling her with me. "Is this what my life is going to be like now? You interrupting my time with Brooke?" I pet his head. "Go lay down," I tell him but he doesn't budge. He sits there staring at me like I'm crazy.

"It's getting late. Maybe I should head home. What are you doing tomorrow?"

"Nothing. I'll be with this crazy guy trying to adjust."

"How about I show you two a really great dog park not too far from here." She looks so excited and I think it's fucking adorable.

"That sounds good to me." I look at the dog. "What do you think, buddy? Should we go to the dog park with Brooke?" I lower my head and pet his face. He licks me, full of excitement. "Well, I guess that makes it a date." I hook his leash back onto his collar and we all head out to take Brooke home.

Chapter 7

Vaughn

What's that noise and why is my face all wet? I jump up. "Shit, Brody. I'm sorry, bud. Need to go out?" he whimpers again. I hurry out of bed and throw on some shorts. I grab his leash on my way to the back door. I'm trying to hurry. He had a rough night sleeping in his new bed, and I don't want him to have an accident. No sooner do we get out to the yard than he starts sniffing around. I lead him over to the far corner of the yard where I would like him to go. He digs around a bit but then does his business like a good boy. He's really excited, he starts jumping around and running as far as the leash will allow him. "Tomorrow we'll go for a run, buddy." I tug his leash gently, telling him it's time to go in. "Come on, Brody. I have to shower before Brooke arrives." Brody lights up at the mention of Brooke's name and runs for the door. I laugh. "Okay, okay, calm down." We get inside and he goes straight to his bowl. I pour his food in and head to my room to get in the shower.

When I'm done getting ready I realize that I never called the gate to let them know I was expecting a guest. I grab my cell phone and quickly dial the number, hoping I get to them before she gets there. I told her to be ready with her ID because they won't let her in without it. They tell me it's all set, and that she hasn't tried to get in yet. While I wait for her, I pack us a picnic for lunch. Nothing too crazy, just sandwiches, chips, fruit, and some carrots and hummus. I stick everything in the fridge to keep it cold until she gets here. I gather some essentials like bottled water for both us and the dog, a plastic bowl for his water, a couple of his toys, and a blanket for us to lie on.

I have everything together in the living room when there's a knock at the door. Brody runs to the door, barking like crazy. "Brody, calm down. It's Brooke." Unfortunately my thought that those words would calm him are wrong. He starts jumping like crazy. I grab his leash and open the door to find Brooke laughing at Brody's reaction. "Did you hear him? He got louder when I mentioned your name."

"I know. I could hear him going crazy through the door." I shake my head. She steps through the door and stops to pet him. She calms him down and tells him to go lay down. He listens and takes a seat in the living room. "What's all this?"

"Well, since we're going to the dog park, I figured we would have a picnic. I think I thought of everything for Brody, but can you make sure I'm not forgetting anything?"

She presses her lips to mine. "I love how concerned you are." She looks through my pile of things I have aside for Brody. "I would add a small baggie of treats to reward him for good behavior. We don't know how he's going to react to the other dogs, and it's a good opportunity to teach him your expectations."

I laugh. "I've always loved dogs, but I've never owned one. What are my expectations?"

She bursts into laughter. "Well, for starters, we have to get him to calm down a bit and control his excitement. I have a feeling he's going to be overjoyed when we get there, but we'll see."

"Okay, shall we find out?"

"Let's roll." She calls for Brody, who comes running with excitement. She puts her hand down in front of him and he slows, but still wags his tail like crazy. "Sit, Brody." He listens and plops his butt on the ground. She clips his leash to his neck. "Stay." She walks away, leaving him sitting there.

"How do you do that?" I'm amazed by how well she handles him.

"First, I'm a veterinarian. I know a lot about animals. Second, I spoke with the woman at the shelter before bringing you to meet him. I wanted a dog that was already pretty well trained for you. He's young, but was taught well." She scoops up the blanket and his stuff while I finish tossing our picnic into the cooler.

"We'll take my car. It'll be easier for us to get back on base after." I grab the cooler and Brody's leash.

When we get out to the car, Brody jumps right

into the backseat like a good dog, and I load everything else into the trunk. Brooke and I get settled in the car and she leans in to kiss me. As soon as our lips meet, we get licked by Brody, who is very excited to be going out today. We both laugh and I set the GPS to the coordinates of the park. It'll take us about twenty minutes to get there.

When we arrive it takes us a minute to find a spot, because it's quite busy. There are trees scattered throughout, creating nice, shady spots. "Look, there's the dog playground," I point out.

"Too bad Brody is far too big for that one."

Brooke climbs out, grabbing Brody while I get the stuff from the trunk. "Look, Vaughn. There's a perfect tree right over there. Let's start there."

"Sounds good." I push the button to lock my car and we head over to set up our picnic. Brody is so excited he's pulling Brooke. "Brody, slow down." Brooke giggles.

"Easy boy." I try to calm him down. There are dogs everywhere. I can tell he's itching to run free, but we won't let him. He's a bit bigger than some of these dogs and I'm worried he'll hurt them. Plus I don't trust that he'll come back to me when I call him…not yet, anyway.

I get busy setting up the blanket and placing the basket down while Brooke introduces Brody to some other dogs. I love watching her interact with the dogs. She looks so happy kneeling in front of them, talking to the other dogs' owners. She's amazing.

She catches me checking her out in her fitted jean shorts and purple shirt. I didn't think it was possible, but her smile grows even bigger when she catches me watching her. She stands biting her lip and holding Brody's leash. She walks toward me, but Brody never budges. "Brody, come," she says, never breaking eye contact with me. Lord help me, this woman makes my pulse race.

Brody sits at our feet as she looks up into my eyes. "Were you just checking me out?" She smirks.

"Guilty as charged." I try to fight my grin but fail.

She grabs my shirt and pulls me down for a kiss. "My ass best be the only ass your eyes are on." She looks at me with one eyebrow raised.

"You better believe it." I place my hands on either side of her face and press my lips to hers one more time. Brody barks, letting us know he wants our attention. "We really need to work on that with him." She giggles and the sound is music to my ears. We both take a seat leaning up against a huge tree trunk and Brody lays beside us. I put the bowl out for him with some water and he begins lapping it up.

"I bought him a treat." Brooke digs into her bag and pulls out a Frisbee. "I'm not sure he's ready to use it yet, because I'm not sure if he'll run wild when we take him off the leash. I would recommend we try it while we're together, so if he tries to take off, we can catch him."

"Do you really think he'll take off?" I ask, because realistically, I think he's a great dog, and although it's only been one night, he seems really happy with me.

"Test him. Walk away while I sit here next to

him." She scoots over closer to his leash when I get up.

I look down to see his ears perk up and he watches to see what I do. He starts to get up, but I stop him. "Sit." I hold my hand out and he stops, but his eyes never leave mine as I walk the area. "Come here, boy." He comes running full steam at me, but stops at my feet. "He's trained pretty well." Leaving his leash on the ground, I begin to walk away. "Come on, Brody." He walks alongside me.

We're both impressed. Brooke hands him a treat and praises him for his behavior. Once he settles, we both decide to dig into our lunch. "How's the new job going?" I ask, curious to see what's changing now that she's an actual veterinarian.

"It's great. I'm doing a lot of the things I was doing before, only now Dr. Kramer isn't looking over my shoulder when I do them." She bites into her sandwich. "Legally, he couldn't allow me to do anything on my own because I wasn't licensed, but now that I've finished school, and taken my license exam, we can work on separate animals." Her face glows with pride as she talks about it.

"You really love what you do, huh?"

She nods. "I do."

"How about you? Do you love being a mechanic?"

"Yeah, I went to a trade school to be an auto mechanic, but at the last minute I decided to join the Army straight out of high school." I take a minute to pet Brody, who quietly lies beside me.

"Why?" She turns to look at me with her head rested against the tree trunk. Her hair pulled back into a ponytail showing off her beautiful face.

"Well, in New York you can get job placement straight out of high school if you go to a trade school like I did. The problem was the jobs I was being offered weren't going to pay me shit for money. I loved my job, but wanted more than a minimum wage job. I worked hard in school to finish top of my class, hoping to get something decent and I got shit. That's when I decided to be a mechanic in the service. This way I could do what I love and serve my country."

She grins at me. "How much time do you have left?"

"My time is about up. I don't know if you know this, but I met Remy in boot camp. We were separated for a bit, and then hooked back up later on. We've always stayed in touch."

"I didn't know that. He mentioned he's known you for years, but didn't really say how you guys met. What are you going to do when your time is up?"

"Well, Callen finishes right after me. We've discussed opening an auto shop of our own and working it together." I shrug. "Give the local folks the small hometown shop they all love." She grins. "It's one of the things I love about the south, everyone loves to take care of the small town mom and pop places."

"It's so true. You guys would do great down here."

"There's that and then there's the fact it would keep me close to you." I lean in and rub my nose on hers. She slips closer to me, places her hand at the back of my neck, and pulls me in for a kiss. She instantly opens to me and our tongues meet, tangling together in a passionate kiss.

After a minute I pull away, not wanting to get out of control in public. "Stay with me tonight." It's more of a demand than a question, and I can't believe I just made it. I never, and I mean never allow a woman to stay at my house. What if I have a nightmare and scare her away? I stare into her eyes, because despite my fears, I really want her to stay. She looks at me like she can read my hidden fears, but she finally nods. I press my lips to hers one more time. "Thank you."

"Let's pack up this mess and get Brody running around a bit before we leave. Then he'll be good and tired when we get back to your place." She wiggles her brows. My sexy girl is thinking dirty thoughts and a ton of ideas come to mind. My dick twitches, and I mentally tell him to chill the fuck out. She picks up the frisbee that she brought. "Brody, you want to play?" She shows Brody the frisbee and he jumps up, ready for some fun. She throws it near me, hoping he'll run to me and pick it up. He does. I try to get him to give the frisbee to me, but he runs it back to her. She pets his head and she throws it again. He grabs it up and runs back to her. The next time she throws it, I scoop it up before Brody can grab it.

He barks at me, letting me know he's not happy I took his frisbee. "Is this what you want?" He jumps up and barks again. "Go get it." I throw the frisbee toward Brooke and he runs after it. We continue on like this for a good thirty minutes. We probably would go longer, but clouds are rolling in and we don't want to get caught in the rain. I call for Brody, who runs to me like a good boy. I tell him to sit, and he listens. He sits still while we gather the remainder of our stuff.

No sooner do we get everything into the car than the sky opens up and it pours. "Looks like we'll be spending the rest of the day inside." Brooke pouts.

"I wouldn't be too sad. There's a lot of fun things we can do inside." I pull out of the parking lot and head straight to my place.

When we get back, I grab the umbrella to take Brody out. He hasn't gone since the park, and I don't want any accidents. When I get back inside, I find Brooke in the kitchen unpacking the picnic leftovers. She's so busy she isn't paying any attention to me as I lean on the doorway watching her every move. She's busy opening cabinets and trying to figure out where things go. "What are you looking for?" She jumps.

"Holy shit, Vaughn! Don't do that! You scared me." She puts her hand on her chest.

I take the few steps needed to close the gap between us. "I'm sorry. I didn't mean to scare you."

"Well, you did." She smacks me on the chest playfully. I pretend to be wounded, and it makes her laugh. I take the cooler bag from her hands and put it down on the floor. I wrap her ponytail around my hand and pull back, exposing her neck. I can see her breathing has already changed. I lick up the vein in her neck to her ear, gently biting down on her lobe, I then lick her earlobe and whisper, "I want to taste every inch of you." She whimpers when I step away. "First we have to figure out dinner."

"That's easy. Take out."

"Or I can cook." I pull some chicken sausage from the freezer and set it on the counter to defrost.

"Okay, Mr. I Can Cook. What are we having?" She places her hands on her hips and awaits my response.

"You'll see. I promise it'll be good, but first while that's defrosting, let's see if there's a movie on."

We both take a seat with Brody at our feet, and we scroll through Netflix looking for a movie to watch. We settle on *How to Lose a Guy in Ten Days*. She tells me that she and Courtney have watched this movie a few times over. "This reminds me of the movie *Twister*. I made my brother watch that movie with me like a hundred times."

"No way. When's the last time you got him to watch it?"

She giggles. "When he first moved back to Georgia."

My eyes go wide. That wasn't all that long ago. This girl has her brother whipped and I can't wait to bust his balls over it.

We sit watching, with her pointing out her favorite parts. The movie was a bit girlie for me but she's happy and there were some funny parts. "Are you hungry?"

She shrugs. "A little."

"I'm going to start dinner." I pull some tortellini noodles from the cabinet along with a jar of white sauce. Once the water is going on the stove, I grab the broccoli from the freezer. "This is my version of chicken and broccoli tortellini. It's quick, easy, and tasty," I explain, since Brooke looks totally confused.

"Can I help?"

"Sure, can you grab an onion?"

"Sure, where are they?"

"In the fridge." She makes a funny face. "I know some people keep them in a pantry, but I don't have one, and I grew up with my mom leaving them in the fridge." She shakes her head but gets one from the fridge and we begin making our dinner together, flirting as we do. We bump hips, fling water at one another, she even spanks me when I lick the spoon to see how it tastes. "What? I have to test it."

"You could have let me test it."

"No way. You don't get to taste it until it's done." I strain the noodles in the sink and dump them back into the pan, adding the sauce to finish it off while Brooke puts the frozen garlic bread in the oven. I point to a cabinet. "Can you grab plates?"

She hands me the two plates. "Here you go."

"Thanks." I start putting tortellini with chicken sausage and broccoli onto plates and by the time I'm done, the garlic bread is ready. "Look at that, only took about twenty minutes, and dinner is served." We take a seat at the table and Brody sits in the middle of the kitchen whimpering over our food. "No, go eat your dinner." I point to his dish but he doesn't budge. "You can't eat this." I place our plates down on the table and we dig in.

"I need to find a place." Brooke puts a napkin on her lap.

"Okay, do you know where you want to look?"

"Yeah, closer to the clinic, which works out good, because it puts me closer to you as well."

"We can do some research if you know what you're looking for."

She takes a bite, her eyes close and she moans. "This really is good." She continues eating and then adds, "Well, I'm thinking I would like to rent a house if I can find one that's reasonable. Nothing too big or too fancy, because I want to save as much as possible to buy a house."

"Why do you want to rent a house? Why not an apartment?"

I shrug. "An apartment would be the natural first step, but I would love to have a dog too, or be able to have Brody over, and if I rent a house I can have a yard to do that."

"In my opinion, either way is fine. You have to go with what your gut tells you."

"I'm not good with gut instincts."

"I am, and mine tells me it's time for dessert." I quickly scrape our plates into the trash and then dump the leftovers into a container and place it in the fridge. By the time I'm done with that, Brooke has put our dishes into the dishwasher. She's washing her hands when I come up behind her, placing my hands on her hips. I lean in and smell her hair. I love the way she smells of coconut all the time. "You smell delicious," I tell her between kisses. Her head rolls to the side and I press my lips to that sensitive spot just below her ear. I slip my hand up over her shirt between her breasts to her neck, where I gently grab her throat and hold her still while I continue tasting her. She rolls her hips, pressing her lovely ass against my already hard cock. My other hand goes under her shirt to cup her tit. I press her back to my chest. She rolls her head back onto my shoulder, pressing her breast into my hand as I massage it. She's biting her lip and moaning while I play with her nipple. The sounds she makes shoot straight to my cock. "I need to taste more of you." I pull away. Taking her hand, I lead her down the hall to my bedroom. I stop myself, remembering I told her we'd go slow. "Am I going too fast for you?" She shakes her head no, and before she can say more, my hands are on the button of her shorts and I have both her shorts and her thong down at her ankles. She slips off her sandals and steps out of them. "Lay down in the middle of my bed."

She crawls on, showing me her ass, which I playfully slap. "No worries, baby. I'll claim that at some point too." Her head shoots back to look over her shoulder at me. She starts to lay down, but I've changed my mind, so I grab her beautifully round cheeks, stopping her. I pull them apart to expose her soaking wet pussy. She lowers her upper body so her face presses against the pillow while I lean in to lick from her clit to her ass. She sucks in a deep breath as she begins to pant. "I promise you this will be good." I continue lapping up her deliciously sweet juices. "Fuck, you taste amazing." Using my thumbs, I attack her hardened clit. She presses her hips back into my face as I fuck her pussy with my tongue and rub my thumb over her clit. Her muscles tighten telling me she's getting close, but I'm not ready to taste her release yet. It's time for her to see

95

how good it feels to have me devour her ass the same way. Again, I lick a path from her pussy to her ass, this time I stay put, my tongue poking at her tight hole, she's whimpering and panting as I eat her up.

"Vaughn, please." She's begging for release. My name rolling off her tongue sounds amazing. Slamming two fingers into her soaking wet pussy, I continue to eat at her ass as I fuck her tight little hole. "Oh my…" She screams out before biting my pillow. I quickly remove my fingers and lap up her release as she grinds her hips against my face, riding out her orgasm.

She starts to laugh, because Brody barks outside the bedroom door. He probably heard her scream and is worried about her. "Brody, I'm fine. Go lay down." He whimpers and we hear him plop down on the floor against the door.

I escape to my bathroom to grab a warm facecloth. When I return she's still in the same position. I gently wipe her up and collapse down on my bed.

"That was intense," she mumbles.

I chuckle, sitting on the bed next to her. I stretch out and her hand glides up over my leg. Her eyes are closed, but she still manages to go straight for my hard cock. My eyes close when she gently squeezes it through my jean shorts. I feel the bed move when she sits up and begins to unbutton my shorts. "What are you doing?"

"You're not the only one who wants dessert." She wraps her hands around my cock, freeing it from my shorts. She looks up at me licking the full length of my cock and then wraps her luscious lips around the tip. She slowly sucks me deeper and deeper into the back of her throat. It's taking all of my might not to grab her hair and fuck her mouth hard.

"Shit, that feels so good, baby." She slips her hand between my legs and massages my balls sucking me harder. "Fuck, I'm going to lose it."

"Please do. I want to taste you." She hollows her mouth and takes me almost all the way to the root, and then hums as she pulls back off. The vibration shoots straight to my balls. Thank god she never lets my cock leave her mouth because the second she sucks me back in, I explode. She instantly sucks me deeper, swallowing every drop I give her. Fuck me that was the most intense orgasm I've ever had. Once she's sure she's gotten every drop, she pulls away, licking her lips. To be funny though, she runs to the bathroom and comes back a minute later with a warm washcloth to clean me up.

"Oh, someone thinks she's funny." I grab her up and slam her on my bed, tickling her. She laughs and screams, causing Brody to bark.

"Ha, you better be nice or your dog will have to come protect me."

"Yeah, how fucked up is that? He's my dog." She laughs and runs back to the bathroom. I grab her a t-shirt to relax in and a pair of my lounge shorts. We open the door to let the dog in and he runs straight to his bed. We decide to watch TV in here with him for the night.

Chapter 8

Vaughn

It was so nice having Brooke in my bed last night. I'm not sure what it was, but it was great to sleep all night without a nightmare. I may have to have her stay over more often. She would be a beautiful cure to my problem. Today's my first day to work since I brought Brody home and I want to take him to meet Callen for our morning run. Brooke is staying back to make coffee and get herself ready for work as well. She'll need to leave shortly after I return.

Brody did a great job keeping up with us, although I did ask Callen to go easy today. I needed to see how he does before we work him too hard, and I have to say I was proud of him—he did great. I'm willing to bet he'll have no problem keeping up with us even at our normal pace.

When we got back, Brooke was standing in the kitchen all dressed for work sipping her coffee. She looks beautiful in her business attire with her hair pulled back. She's wearing a lab coat that says the clinic's name on it. I walk into the kitchen, her eyes rake me over, and she licks her lips like she wants to devour me. I give her a quick kiss. "I have to shower."

"I have to get going," she responds, dumping her coffee into the sink and putting her cup into the dishwasher. "I'll talk to you later?"

I nod and watch her pet Brody quickly before she walks out the door, locking it behind her. I can't help the smile that spreads across my face as I make my way to the shower. "You like her, huh, buddy?" I pet him. "Yeah, me too."

Now that I'm set for work. I grab my keys and kneel down to pet Brody one more time. He's lying in his bed, pretty beat from the run. I'm hoping this means he'll sleep for a bit and just chill until I get home. "You be a good boy while I'm gone and we'll have some fun after work." He licks his face and closes his eyes. Not even a bark. I chuckle and walk out of the room. I need to get moving. It's Callen's turn to grab coffee, but I still don't want to be late.

When I pull in, I discover I'm the first one here. For me, that's a good thing. I can get to my office and get through some emails before I brief the guys on what we have to accomplish this week. Summer is upon us, and that means even more missions, and more missions mean more preventative maintenance, and more breakdowns. I settle in and boot up my computer. While I wait, I decide to send Brooke a text.

Vaughn: I hope you have a good day at work.

As I hit send, there's a knock at my door. "Good morning, sir. What can I do for you?"

The Major steps into my office. "I know it's early and the guys aren't even here yet, but as soon as they get in, I need you guys to head out to recover a broken down Humvee. There's hell to pay because it's been sitting since early this morning." He leans on my door.

"Yikes." I shake my head. "Whose head is rolling for this one?"

"Not my problem." He laughs. "It's not my ass and it's not anyone in our section. Just make sure it's recovered as soon as possible."

"Yes, sir. Any idea what's wrong with it?"

He shakes his head. "None. It was a brief email stating it wouldn't start. They gave us the location with orders to recover it as soon as possible. I promised them you'd get someone on it immediately."

"No problem, sir. If it's okay with you, I'm going to go out on this one and leave Callen here with the rest of the team. I want to observe the guys and see how Callen handles the shop."

"Your team. It's your ass if he screws up."

I chuckle. "He won't screw up, and we'll figure out what's wrong with the vehicle and report back to them on a return date immediately." I scribble a note on the pad sitting on my desk. This is going to be a job for Callen.

"Thanks." He nods and walks out of my office. I hear a faint "good morning, sir," in the distance. It sounds like Callen just got here, but I pay it no mind because I have emails I need to respond to, and I need to get the location of that vehicle so we can recover it.

"What was the Major doing here? He never comes in here at this time of day." He peeks his head out the door to make sure no one is lurking.

"We have to recover a Humvee. He didn't say why, but they need it back ASAP. That means you have to drop what you're doing and check out what's wrong with it. They said it won't start."

"God only knows with the MPs on this base," he mumbles under his breath as he walks out of my office. I chuckle and shake my head. My phone pings to notify me of a text.

Brooke: So far, so good. I hope you have a good day as well. Call me tonight. I want to know how both your and Brody's day was.

Vaughn: Will do.

I put my phone back into my belt clip and go into the bay to see if everyone is here. We don't need a ton of guys to do a recovery on base, but I want to observe one of my specialists do a recovery. That means it's going to be me, Max, and Liam on this mission. Callen usually goes with the guys for this stuff, but I want him to stay back and keep an eye on things here and help Nolan and Tommy.

"Good morning," I call out to the guys. Callen hands me my coffee and I thank him. "Gather around here for a minute." The guys all do as I ask

101

and settle down. "The Major was in to see me this morning. It appears one of the MPs has a broken down Humvee that we need to recover here on base. We need to get it off the side of the road immediately because someone's ass is on the line. It was abandoned early this morning." The guys start laughing. "All right, all right, listen up. Recovery will be handled by myself, Liam, and Max." I turn to Callen. "Callen, you're in charge here while I'm gone. You'll work with Liam, Nolin, and Tommy on getting one of these vehicles done and out of here so we can check out the Humvee as soon as we get back. I've promised the Major that we'd get on it immediately and let them know when they can have it back."

Max and I grab a truck. He jumps into the driver's seat and I tell him where the vehicle is. "Hey, Sarge, are you going out with us on Friday?"

"Yeah, why wouldn't I?" My brows furrow confused.

"Callen says you have a girl now. He thinks you're going to stop hanging with us."

I laugh. "He does, does he? Don't you say anything to him, I'll fix his ass."

Max laughs as he drives in the direction of the Humvee. "So, what's up with the observation?"

"Come on, guy, you know how this goes. Of my three E-4s, you've been here the longest. That means I need to make sure you know your shit. I'm promotable, as is Callen. That could mean you make sergeant in the near future, and for that to happen you need to prove you can handle everything you need to without help. This is your mission, you tell me what to do, and I'll do it." He shakes his head. "You got this. I know you know what you're doing, now it's time to prove it. But do me a favor, no shortcuts. You do it by the book." He nods and I can see the wheels are spinning while he drives. He's going over the steps in his head. I sit in silence the remainder of the ride so he can process everything.

***

Brooke

I've had a really long day. I'm beat and my feet are killing me. It's five thirty and Vaughn should be calling me any minute now. I run up to my room to change into some comfy clothes, no longer wanting to be in my work clothes. Dr. Kramer is adamant that we dress in professional attire. He's usually in slacks with a button down shirt and tie with his lab coat. Now that I'm an actual vet, I've been wearing slacks and dress shirts, but it's so hot for that. I need to figure something out because I do not like wearing skirts. No sooner do I slip on a t-shirt than my cell phone rings. It's Vaughn. "Hey, big guy. How was your day?"

"It started out okay and got progressively worse."

"Oh no, what happened?"

"Well, first I had to recover an abandoned vehicle. Then I get it back to the shop to look at it and the thing is a mess. We don't have the part we need to fix it, and then to top it all off, Brody tore up the house. I have trash everywhere." He sighs into the phone. "I totally didn't expect this and I don't know what to do."

"He's looking for attention. He missed you and was probably lonely. He went from being in a home where he was with his owner all day, to being in the shelter, to spending an entire weekend with you. He didn't expect to be alone all day. I'm not telling you it's okay that he did it, but I want you to understand."

"That's fine, but what do I do now?"

"What did you do when you walked in the door and saw the mess?"

He lets out a deep breath. "I yelled at him and sent him to his bed. He whimpered and ran off." He sounds so sad and it breaks me.

"Do you want me to come over?"

"No, it's fine. I think I need to handle this on my own. I'm going to clean up and then take him for a walk."

"Are you sure? We can go for a walk together." I'm trying to cheer him up because I have a feeling he's just as sad as Brody right now. He chuckles into the phone, telling me my sing song voice works. "I'm not taking no for an answer. You better let the MPs know I'm on my way." He starts laughing and cuts the call. My man and his dog have had a rough day and they need some cheering up. I shoot him off a quick text telling him I'm grabbing dinner on the way, but he never responds. He's probably trying to clean Brody's mess.

I pull up to Vaughn's house almost an hour later. I had no problem getting on the base, which means he listened and called over to the gate. I picked up some chicken, mac and cheese, and corn on my way over. I'm hoping he will like it. The place I got it from is fast and the food is good. I climb out of the car to find Vaughn at the door with a much happier Brody. Too bad Vaughn still has a look of defeat on his face. He grabs Brody's collar and opens the door for me. "You have good timing, I just finished cleaning up."

"Good, we can eat and take this bad little boy for a walk." I pet Brody's head talking to him in a baby voice. He barks at me and wags his tail. "Go lay down while we eat."

He follows us to the kitchen and sits at our feet. "Brody, go lay down." Vaughn points to the living room and he takes off. When he lays down outside the kitchen as he was asked, Vaughn rewards him. "Good boy." He pets his head. "Now stay and we'll go out soon." The dog stays and Vaughn heads to the sink to wash his hands before we sit down to eat. He finally joins me. "Before I forget, do you have any plans for Friday?"

"No, why? Do you have something in mind?"

"Would you and Courtney be interested in joining us guys for a night out again?"

I shrug my shoulders. "I can ask her. She could use another night out. She broke up with her boyfriend a few months ago and is having a hard time of it. She found out he cheated on her and it's the second time she's been cheated on. She swears she's never going to find the right man."

"Well, she and Callen seemed to hit it off pretty good, and the guys and I make it a point to get

105

together at least every other Friday. We try weekly but stuff often gets in the way. We usually go to that bar I saw you at to have a beer or two and grab some food."

"That's cool."

"Yeah, it's a good way for the new guys to feel welcome and we've all become friends. Plus, the guys on base get bored. I have three guys who don't get as much freedom as Callen and I do." He digs into his plate.

"How come?" I have no idea what military life is like. Why would some guys get more freedom than others? That's not very fair.

"While you're a lower enlisted soldier, you have restrictions, plus the kids can't usually afford a car. It's expensive to store if they get called on an overseas mission or if your duty station changes, it can be hard to transport your vehicle to the new location, so most of them deal without one. The base has stuff for guys to do, but after a little while it can get old. The guys live in the barracks, and hanging there gets old, especially if you're with guys you don't get along with."

"I can't imagine that's easy."

I shrug. "That's why I try to get together with them. It boosts their morale, and for a short time we're just a bunch of guys hanging out."

"You're so sweet." I lean in and kiss him on the lips. His tongue darts out, licking across the seam of mine. I open to him and our tongues explore one another. He tastes of Vaughn and fried chicken. Not a bad combo.

"Let's clean up and take him out before we get

out of control."

"Good idea. I can't stay too late. I have to get my clothes ready for work tomorrow."

"Yeah, me too. I have no idea what I'll wear." He laughs mocking me.

"You'll pay for that." I toss my dirty napkin at him. He throws it back, missing me completely. Brody jumps up and starts to bark but never sets foot into the kitchen. I run over to calm him down. "It's okay, boy." I pet the top of his head and he sits back down. We quickly pack up the leftover food and get it into the fridge.

When we're about done, Vaughn pulls the dog's leash from the drawer and hands it to me. "Can you get him hooked up for me?" He grabs our dishes and starts to rinse them for the dishwasher.

"Sure." I hook up his leash, and because he knows we're going out, he gets excited.

Vaughn dries his hands and comes over, patting his head. "Are you excited to go out? You need to be a good boy tomorrow while I'm at work, though. No more playing in the trash." He takes the leash in hand and my hand in the other and we take off on our walk.

"So, what's up with Courtney?" he asks as we walk down the street hand in hand.

"Like I told you, she's been cheated on a few times. The first time he had given her a key and she showed up at his place to surprise him and found him in bed with two other women."

His brows shoot up. "Holy shit. That's messed up."

"Tell me about it. She had just started working at

the clinic with me. I felt so bad for her. She was a mess for the longest time. She dated a few guys and said it wasn't working out. Then she met Ted. He was really nice to her and treated her well, or at least she thought. Her friend Tiffany sent her a picture of him kissing another girl on the sidewalk outside a restaurant."

He shakes his head. "What is it with men? It kills me. Guys like that give us a bad name." Brody pulls us to the side of the road where he finds a tree to do his business. "Thank god he didn't leave me any messes like this to clean up." He bends over with the bag wrapped around his hand to clean the mess. Being an apartment community, there are receptacles set up to dispose of things like this. I can't help but giggle at the face he makes when he ties off the bag. We turn the corner to head down the next street. "That's where Callen lives." He points to Callen's building.

"Cool. What's the plan for Friday?"

He shrugs. "We usually meet up around six. I'll try to get the same big booth we had last time."

"Sounds good. We'll plan to meet you about the same time. I'm on-call this weekend, so I can't go too far in case there's an emergency."

"Does that mean I won't see you this weekend?"

"I honestly haven't thought far ahead, but I'm sure we can do something." We walk back up to his place, he opens the door, and Brody darts into the house. I pause on the porch. "Listen, I think I'd best be going." He smiles down at me. "I think it'll be good for you spend the rest of the night with your buddy, and maybe tomorrow he'll be a good boy for you."

He nods but he looks concerned. I press up on my tippy toes and grab his shirt. He lowers his lips to mine and I instantly open to him. He moans into my mouth and the sound awakens the butterflies in my belly. I pull away. "I'll talk to you tomorrow."

"Drive careful."

"I will." He and Brody stand by the door, watching me get into my car. I wave and drive off, feeling a little bit better. He still seems a bit off, but owning a new dog can be overwhelming. I can tell he's really happy with Brody, though. They'll be fine. My phone chirps and when I pull up to the light I see it's a text from Vaughn.

Vaughn: Thanks for coming over and bringing dinner. I'll talk to you tomorrow.

I smile and put my phone in my purse to finish my ride home.

Chapter 9

Vaughn

A yawn escapes me as I pull up to the house after a long ass week. I need to hurry so I can take Brody out. He's gotten a lot better as the week has gone on. He's no longer making a mess in the kitchen with the trash. Now he just takes his toys out of their bin and scatter them around the house. That I can handle. We've started to create a nice routine, and he seems to be adjusting nicely. He's smart as hell too. He sensed me having a nightmare the other night and jumped up on the bed and began licking my face to wake me up. Just thinking about it makes me smile.

I open the door and I'm instantly greeted by my boy. "Hey buddy. Do you need to go out?" He whimpers, telling me he does. I run to the drawer to grab his leash and hook it to his collar. "Come on, buddy." We head out and my mind drifts to the other night. I was dreaming about a mission we were on, it was rough. We were losing guys left and right. Vehicles were breaking down and we had lost a bunch to mortar attacks. Thanks to my new buddy, that's as far as it got. I thanked him for waking me, he jumped off the mattress, and went back to his bed. We both fell back to sleep, and that was the last of the nightmare for that night. I do still need to catch up on a bit more sleep, but I'll work on that this weekend.

Brooke is spending the night, but we can't go far because she's on-call this weekend. I'm sure we'll hang here and take it easy. Brody is finally done doing his business. I clean up his mess and we both head back into the house. I need to shower and get changed out of this uniform. Brooke is meeting me here and then she's taking a cab with Callen and I over to the bar. We both agreed not to be out too late, but neither of us wants to drive after having a beer or two. Unhooking Brody's leash, I head straight for the shower, washing off the day's grime. Rubbing soap all over reminds me of Brooke's hands on my body as she wrapped her warm, wet lips around my cock. It instantly stiffens as I stroke myself, it's been a while, so it doesn't take me long before I'm shooting my load down the drain of the shower. It was helpful, but didn't feel nearly as good as her mouth, and I can't wait to be buried in that tight pussy of hers.

The water runs cold. I shut it off, quickly dry off, and tie the towel around my waist. I go straight to my closet in search of something to wear, I need to hurry up. I'm finishing up tying my shoe when there's a knock at the door. Brody starts barking and jumping around the entry. "Down, boy. It's

Brooke." I grab his collar and open the door to find her standing there in a gorgeous sundress, her long blonde hair is curled, and she has just a touch of makeup on. Damn, she looks fucking hot. I pull her into the house, closing the door and pinning her to it. My mouth crashes down on hers and our tongues explore each other's mouths. Her hips grind against my now fully erect cock. Fuck, I don't even want to go out now. I want to pick her up and carry her fine ass to my room. Our kiss is interrupted by a knock at the door. Brody starts up his barking yet again. I press my forehead to hers as we both try to calm our breathing. "Fuck me." I'm panting.

"I was hoping for a bit of that tonight." She bites her lip.

I press my lips to hers one more time and then grab her hand and pull her away from the door. I open it to find Callen standing there with his arms crossed. When he sees Brooke next to me, a smile spreads across his face. "Did I interrupt something?" He's trying to fight his laughter.

"Fuck you, man. Get your ass in here." He steps inside and begins petting Brody to calm him down.

"Dude, your dog acts so vicious but he's such a softy."

"Yeah, well, I don't need an attack dog…" my words trail off. I almost say more but I bite my tongue and he gives me a look like he knows what I need but he drops it. "Come, Brody." I take him into the kitchen to feed him.

Callen and Brooke follow behind me. "I already called for the cab. It should be here any minute."

"Courtney is meeting us at the bar."

"Nice. She's hot. Can you hook me up?" Callen rubs his hands together.

"Listen, she seems to like you, but she's been through some shit. She needs a good guy, and it's going to take her a while before she trusts anyone," Brooke warns him.

"It kills me when guys pull shit like that. It gives us all a bad name." Callen shakes his head. "Maybe we can all hang here or at my place one night. Ya know, have like a game night."

"That sounds like fun. Then she can get to know you a bit and give her a chance to get comfortable with you." She looks up at me and I shrug my shoulders. I don't care what we do. I'm cool with hanging with Callen. "Let's see how tonight goes and we can make plans."

"Thanks." His smile grows.

We hear a horn, and when I look out the window I see the cab in the driveway. I tell Brody to be good and we run out the door.

When the cab driver pulls up outside the bar, I let him know that I'll be calling him in a few hours for a ride home. He tells me it's no problem and pulls away. We walk into the bar. It's early, so the table we want is still free. We head straight over to it and the waitress from last time comes over. "Back for more?"

"Yeah, we have more people joining us, but we'll take a round of beers, please," Callen tells her sliding into the booth.

"Who's coming tonight?" Brooke leans into me.

I wrap my arm around her shoulder. "Well, you've already met Max, Liam, and Callen. Tonight

Nolin joins us, and I believe he's bringing his girlfriend, Vicky."

"He said they were coming. He told me he talked to her about it when I told him Brooke and Courtney were coming," Callen adds as the waitress drops our first round of beers.

"Do you want to wait for your friends to get here before you order?" The waitress has a pad in her hand.

"Nah, we've already agreed to split the bill. Can you order us nachos, two cheese fries—one with bacon and one with chili—onion rings, potato skins, boneless buffalo wings, and mozzarella sticks." The waitress nods at me as she writes it all down.

"Sure, I'll put everything on a few large platters to save space for you guys on the table.

"That would be awesome. Thanks." Callen sips his beer. She winks at him and walks away.

Courtney arrives next, and Callen's face lights up when he sees her. She looks cute wearing a pair of capris and a light weight purple top. She has her hair pulled back and she, like Brooke, keeps her makeup light. "Hey, guys."

"Hey, gorgeous." Callen checks her out as she slips into the booth.

Courtney instantly blushes sliding into the seat next to him. Looking to the floor she says, "Hey," and gives him a shy smile.

"Can I get you a beer?"

"Yes, please." The waitress comes over and Callen orders her a beer, but before she can leave Max and Liam join us. She takes their drink order and walks off to get three more beers. The guys say hello and slip into the booth. "Can I sit next to Brooke?" Courtney asks Callen. He promptly gets out to switch with her. The girls quickly hug and begin chatting.

"We already ordered a bunch of food and it should be out soon," I tell everyone.

"Thanks, man." Liam sips the beer the waitress just dropped off. She told us our food will be out any minute. It's a pretty big order, so she went back to check on it, but I imagine it would take some time.

Courtney and Brooke are chatting next to us about animals in the shelter, and the guys are talking about the shop. There are always rumors flying around about the MPs and the shit they pull on base. The guys who abandoned the Humvee we recovered are in some serious shit, and the latest rumors are all about why they abandoned it and what's going to happen to them. The guys burst into laughter as Nolin and Vicky arrive. He looks pissed, and she has a fake smile plastered on her face. It appears they're late because of a fight, and I'm hoping it doesn't dampen the night, because everyone is having a great time.

"Hey guys. This is my girlfriend, Vicky." He goes around the table giving names until he gets to Brooke and Courtney. He looks at me.

"This is my girlfriend, Brooke, and her friend, Courtney." The girls each hold out their hand and shake with both Nolin and Vicky. Nolin finishes the intro with Callen and they take a seat next to Liam and Max. Just as they're getting comfortable our waitress arrives with another following her. They're each carrying a tray of food. The waitress puts down plates and gets us one more round of drinks.

Brooke's leg bounces under the table as we make our plates. I place a gentle hand on her knee and give it a squeeze. "What's wrong?" I whisper close to her ear.

She turns to me with a smile on her face. She bites her lip for a minute, and then whispers back, "I'm itching to get back to your house."

"Hey, you two going to keep whispering to yourselves all night?" Courtney teases. We both chuckle.

I press a kiss to her lips. "Busted."

We all start laughing and eating. Nolin and Vicky look like they're in a better place. Callen is talking with Courtney, who has a huge smile on her face. The food is delicious and in no time it's almost all gone. I'm glad we ordered enough. We were slightly concerned we would need to order more, but decided to start with this and add on if we needed to. After a short time the music kicks up a notch, and *Your Body is a Wonderland* by John Mayer begins to play. My hand glides up the inside of her leg. Her skin is warm and soft. I feel her body shiver slightly at my touch, but no one else notices because they're all so engrossed in conversation. My thumb glides over her pussy, her breath hitches, and she turns to me.

"Are you ready?" Her voice is soft and needy. I nod my head.

The waitress comes back over. "Can I have the bill?" She nods and walks away. "Listen, guys. We're going to take off. Callen and I are splitting

the bill to this point, but you're on your own now."
The waitress comes over and hands Callen and I
each a slip. We each hand over a card for her to
swipe, and she runs off one more time, telling us
she'll be right back. I call the cab driver, letting him
know we're ready.

As soon as she comes back with the cards, we
head outside to wait for our ride, my fingers
interlocked with hers while we wait. When the cab
pulls up, I open the door for her and she slips in.
There's so much sexual tension flowing on the ride
home it's almost painful. I'm thankful my place
isn't far, because just thinking about what I want to
do to her has my cock thickening.

When we pull up to my apartment, I quickly pay
the guy and take Brooke's hand. I pull her into the
house, slamming the door shut behind us and
locking it. Brody comes running to see who it is.
We both quickly pet him and tell him to go lay
down. As soon as he runs off, I slip my hands into
her hair, and my mouth crashes down on hers. She
pulls my shirt from my shorts and runs her hands up
my back. Her touch sets my skin on fire. I rest my
forehead on hers. "Come on." I take her hand and
pull her toward my room. When we get there, she
pulls the straps from her sundress off of her
shoulders and it slips down her body, pooling at her
feet. My jaw drops at the beautiful sight before me.
She's wearing a white lace bra and matching
panties. She's stunning. I step up to her, running my
hands up her bare arms. She shivers, and
goosebumps spread across her body. I slip my
hands up over her shoulders and into her hair,

pulling slightly so she's forced to look at me. "Are you good with this?" She bites her lip and nods. I press my lips to hers in a much softer, gentler kiss. She wraps her hands around my hips and presses my body against hers.

Grabbing her hair, I pull it, exposing her neck, and kiss up her jaw to her ear. I whisper, "It's time for dessert," and then I lick down the vein in her neck. Her pulse is rapid and her breathing has picked up. I back her up until the back of her legs bump my bed, and then I gently push her down onto the center of the mattress.

I pull my shirt over my head and unbutton my shorts as her gaze rakes over my body. She's hungry for more, so I drop both my boxers and my shorts to the floor, revealing my cock, it's hard as nails. She licks her lips—and what mighty fine lips they are, the way they feel wrapped around my cock is heavenly—but right now I want to taste her. After that, my cock is going to experience that sweet pussy of hers. I slip her panties down her legs, and then climbing onto the bed, I settle myself between her legs. I gently bite the inside of her thigh and then kiss it better. Her legs are spread wide for me. She thrusts her hips forward, wanting my tongue on her pussy. I chuckle licking up her pussy to her clit, sucking it into my mouth and rolling my tongue over it. She whimpers when I suck it even harder. She tastes so damn fine I could devour her all fucking night long.

"Yes, Vaughn, that feels fucking amazing." I can't help but laugh that she just said fuck. Brooke doesn't typically curse like that, it sounds funny coming from her mouth.

Slipping my tongue deep inside of her pussy, I start fucking her with it while massaging her clit with my thumb. I peek up to see her eyes are closed and she's grasping the sheets. I know she's getting close because I can feel her muscles tightening up.

"Shit, I'm going to…" her words trail off as I pinch her clit and send her over the edge. Her legs tighten around my head and her body shakes. My tongue is still deep inside of her, enjoying every last drop of her release. Kissing my way up over her hip, she giggles, and the sound is so beautiful it makes me smile. I continue my way up her body to her perky breasts. I take one in my mouth and massage the other. Her back arches, pressing her tit into my face. I scrape my teeth along her hardening nipple, causing her to hiss.

Sitting up, I grab a condom from the night stand. I rip the package open with my teeth and slide the condom over my cock. I line myself up and gently begin pressing at her opening. "Holy shit, babe. You're so tight."

She presses her hips forward. "Just give it to me."

"Easy, babe. I don't want to hurt you." I look into her eyes slowly slipping my cock deeper and deeper inside of her.

"You're not going to break me. It's just been a little while. I want to feel you fill me up." Her hips are meeting my thrusts. I grasp her shoulders and slam myself the rest of the way in. She whimpers.

"Are you okay?"

"I'm fine. Give me what I need." I begin rolling

my hips as she meets my thrusts. We find our rhythm as we pick up the pace. She's so tight there's no way I'm going to be able to last long. I start pounding her harder and deeper. "Yes!" The word comes from her lips in one long moan.

"Fuck, babe. I'm not going to last." I keep going, fighting my release until she finally finds hers. Her pussy tightens around my cock, squeezing it. My balls tighten and I find my own release. I pound deep inside her a few more times before I plant myself balls deep, shaking as I empty myself into the condom.

I rest on top of her as we both try to calm our breathing. "Holy shit, that was amazing." She presses a kiss to my chest.

"Fuck yeah, it was." I smile down at her and then kiss her forehead. "I need to get rid of this condom. I'll be right back with a warm washcloth." I grip the end of the condom and slip out of her. I run to the bathroom to throw it in the trash. I turn on the warm water and let it heat up while I grab a washcloth. When I get back, she's lying on top of the comforter with her eyes closed. "Are you okay?"

She smiles. "Yeah, I'm great. I'm just tired."

Chapter 10

Brooke

We both fell into a comfortable sleep while holding each other after an amazing night of sex. God, the things this man does to my body. He can just look at me a certain way and my panties are wet. Now I'm lying in his bed listening to him whimper. It sounds like he's starting to have a nightmare and I'm not sure what to do. He's never mentioned having a problem with nightmares before. He starts flinching slightly and beads of sweat are forming on his forehead. Suddenly Brody jumps up and starts growling at Vaughn's side of the bed. "Sshh, Brody. Go lay down." He doesn't listen. He continues to growl as Vaughn starts to thrash around in bed. I need to do something, but I'm not sure of the best way to wake him. Brody jumps up on the bed and starts licking his face. I'm trying to get Brody off the bed, but he won't listen.

"Thanks, buddy. I'm okay now." Vaughn pets Brody's head, he barks, jumps down, and goes back to his bed. He turns to me, looking embarrassed. "I'm sorry I woke you."

"It's fine. Want to talk about it?"

He shakes his head. "It's still early. Let's get back to sleep." He kisses me on the cheek and rolls back over, and I'm left with my mind reeling. How many of these nightmares does he have? Did something bad happen to him while he was away and he can't get the memory of it out of his head?

I roll over onto my side and watching Brody sleep in his bed. Every move I make, his ears perk up just a tad more, and it's in that moment I know we made a good decision in adopting him. I think it's amazing how he knew something was off with Vaughn and he came to his rescue. Even now, he's listening to see if he needs him.

I can't seem to fall back to sleep. I've been lying here watching Vaughn for almost an hour now, my mind drifting in different directions. I can't help but wonder if he has anything else that he's keeping from me. I want him to know he can talk to me. I want to help him. I've liked Vaughn for a long time, and now I'm falling for him. It will kill me if he doesn't let me in. I need to figure out how to get him to let me help. It's almost six a.m. and I'm debating if I should get up and make us some breakfast. I'm on-call all weekend, so we're just going to hang out. We need to make plans with Callen and Courtney for a game night...maybe next weekend. I also want to take Brody to the beach. I need to stop thinking so much.

A yawn escapes me, but I know I won't fall back to sleep. I roll back over to face Vaughn, his back is still to me, but he seems to be falling back into a deep sleep. I want him to know I support him and I'm here for him. I scoot myself closer, wrapping my arm around him and pressing my front to his back. He flinches, reacting to my touch. His elbow flies back and he nails me in the stomach. Holy shit, the pain is fierce. I lose my breath and Brody starts to bark. I'm out of the bed and on my feet before Vaughn even realizes what just happened.

"Brody, calm down." He turns over to see me holding my stomach.

"What's wrong?"

"Nothing. I'm fine." He jumps up with a look of fear in his eyes. I can see it clear as day. I stand up straight, trying to shake it off. I don't want him to push me away any more than he already has.

"Don't tell me nothing. What happened?" His raises his voice to me...something I've never heard him do.

I close my eyes as I contemplate my words. "I tried to snuggle up to you but you reacted, elbowing me in the stomach. I'm fine." He runs his hands through what little hair he has and his eyes are all over the place, but he won't look at me. I can see he's panicking. He has no idea what to say or do. "Vaughn, look at me." His eyes stay on the floor. I take a slow step closer to him. I want to be careful because I don't know where his head is at right now. "Look at me." My voice is soft, and because I'm shorter than him, he doesn't have to lift his head much to look in my eyes. "Let me help you."

"You can't help me. I'm fucking broken, Brooke." He shakes his head, holding onto his last

123

ounce of control. "I've tried so hard to fight this, to be the same guy I was before…" his words trail off and his breathing has picked up.

"Take a deep breath. We don't have to discuss this now." I close my eyes. "I just want to be there for you. You mean a lot to me, Vaughn. I don't want to lose what we have."

He nods. "I don't either, but I'm fucked up, Brooke, and I'm not sure that's ever going to change."

I nod my head. "Why don't you shower? I'll go make us some breakfast."

He wraps me in a hug. "I'm sorry. Please know I would never intentionally hurt you." I can feel his heart beating out of his chest.

"I know you wouldn't." He kisses the top of my head and walks off to the shower.

I throw on a t-shirt and some shorts and head for the kitchen. I find everything I need to make my man breakfast. I search the cabinets for the right pans and set the bacon to defrost in the microwave. While I preheat the oven and heat some oil up in a pan, I cut some onion and potatoes and toss it with the hot oil, adding some salt, pepper, garlic, and other seasonings to the pan. I stir it and let the potatoes start to cook. When the microwave is done, I lay the bacon out on a pan and slip it into the now hot oven. I stir the potatoes and grab another pan to start on the eggs when Vaughn comes into the kitchen. "Damn, it smells good in here." Vaughn looks like he's feeling much better after his shower.

"Well, I hope you're hungry, because I'm making eggs, and there are potatoes in that pan, and bacon in the oven."

He's about to say something when Brody whimpers from the back door. "I'm starved, but clearly I need to take care of my buddy." He grabs Brody's leash and takes him outside while I finish breakfast. I peek in the oven to check on the bacon that is now almost done.

When Vaughn comes back in with the dog, he takes his leash off of him and tells him to go lay down. Brody listens and Vaughn steps up behind me. He presses a kiss to my lips and holds it there. I can tell he's struggling. What I thought was him feeling better was simply a mask he slipped into place so I wouldn't worry. Now is not the time to press him, so I'll hold off, but we need to talk about this at some point. "You smell like breakfast and sex. That's a pretty crazy combination. I'm not sure whether to eat you or fuck you."

I burst into laughter. "Well, how about I feed you first, and then we can see where the day goes." I wiggle my brows. "You're stuck with me unless I get called in."

"Stuck is not the word I would use, and that sounds like a good plan. My stomach is growling." He rubs his stomach.

"Why don't you check those potatoes while I take care of the bacon?" I grab an oven mitt to take the bacon out. He opens the door for me and steps aside.

Once I have it out, he closes it for me and stirs the potatoes. "These are done." He puts a cover on them and shuts the burner off. I quickly make us each two eggs and serve up breakfast. He makes us each a coffee while I put our plates on the table, watching that Brody doesn't help himself. I'm sure smelling the bacon is killing him, but he's being a really good boy, sitting at the door without complaint.

Vaughn turns around with our two cups of coffee in hand and starts to laugh. "Think he's itching for some bacon?"

"I know he is, but that's a bad habit to form. That said, he's your dog."

"Nah, you're right." He looks at the dog. "Be a good boy and I'll give you a treat when we're done eating." Brody collapses to the floor like he's now heartbroken, but we ignore him and take our seats.

"What should we do today?" I ask as we both dig into our breakfast.

He shrugs. "I don't know, maybe we can take Brody for a walk? It's supposed to rain later, and I'd rather not take him in the rain."

"Okay, after we're done eating, I'll shower, and then we can take him for a walk."

We both finish eating in silence. I feel like there's a bit of tension in the air, and I'm not sure if it's because I feel like he's hiding from me, but I don't like it. I need to figure out how to get him to open up to me, and I will if it's the last thing I do.

I'm so deep in thought I hadn't noticed that he's finished eating until I'm done. I look up to find him at the sink cleaning up. "I can do that." I want him to relax a bit.

"I've got it. Go shower so we can go out." I sigh but do as he asks. I don't want to make things worse.

I put my plate in the sink, kiss him on the cheek, and head to the bedroom to grab the bag I packed. When I get into the bedroom, I see the light flashing on my phone. I scoop it up to see it's the clinic. "Fuck," I whisper to myself and hit the dial button. Sure enough, I have to go in. We have an emergency.

I walk back out to the kitchen. "What's wrong?" Vaughn looks concerned.

"I'm sorry, but I have to shower and go to work. A cat was hit by a car and they think we can save him."

He closes his eyes and takes a breath. "Go. Hurry."

"I'm sorry." I run back to the room, shower in record time, and quickly dress.

When I'm done, I find Vaughn in the living room, placing the leash on Brody's collar. I can't help but wonder if he was going to leave for his walk without saying goodbye, and to be honest, the thought of him doing that stings a bit, but I have to have a clear head if I'm going to save this animal. I press a kiss to his lips, and promise to call him later before running out the door to my car.

***

Vaughn

She's gone. Just like that, she's out the door to go do emergency surgery on a cat, and I miss her already. "Let's go, boy." I walk Brody to the door, grab my keys, and head out with him for a walk around the neighborhood. We didn't even get to discuss making plans with Callen and Courtney, and after what I did to her this morning, I can't help but wonder if I should. I can't believe I hurt her. Fuck, this was one of my biggest fears, and now I have to figure out what to do. I tried really hard to slip my mask into place during my shower. I needed her to see that I'm okay, but I honestly don't think she bought it. I feel like she sees right through me. This is why I don't get close with anyone. This is why I haven't dated in years. Women need a strong man, someone who can help them deal with their shit, not give them shit to deal with. I'm supposed to be there for her, be strong for her, and I'm so fucking weak. And God help me if Remy finds out. He's my boy, but if he knew that I hurt her, he would fucking kill me.

Brody pulls me to the side of the street so he can take a piss on the same rock he uses all the time. I need to get my head on straight. Remy and Kenzie's wedding is just around the corner and I'm supposed to be in it, but if I can't pull my shit together, I'm going to have to back out. I turn the corner and walk past Callen's house. His car is in the driveway, but I don't bother to stop. I don't feel like talking, and if he sees me, he's going to know something is up. The guy knows me too fucking well. Apparently better than I thought, because before I get to the end of his street, my phone rings. "Hey, man. What's up?"

"I thought Brooke spent the night. What happened?" He's trying not to sound concerned but I know my boy just as well as he knows me.

"She did, but she got called in to work. Something about a cat and surgery."

"That sucks. What are you up to today?"

"Not a hell of a lot. Probably going to take a nap and chill."

"Want to play some *Call of Duty*?" I chuckle into the phone. He knows when I'm fucked up I sometimes bury myself in video games. It takes my mind off things and lets me live an imaginary life for a while. I get to pretend my brain isn't fucked from the real live shit I've witnessed.

"Sure, why the fuck not?" I cut the call and slip my phone in my pocket. Callen shocks me when he runs up behind me. "Dude, were you talking on the phone from behind me the entire time?"

"Yeah, I saw you walk by and you look like shit. I could tell something was up and didn't plan on taking no for an answer."

"Asshole." I shake my head and he pats me on the back.

When we get back to my place, Brody goes off to play with his toys and Callen sets up the Xbox. I need a drink. "Want a beer?"

His brows shoot up. "Dude, it's ten in the morning."

I shrug my shoulders. "We're not working, and it's after five somewhere."

"Fuck it. Sure, why not?" I pull two beers from the fridge handing one to Callen. We both take a seat and start playing the game.

It's been hours since Callen first came over and we've done nothing but drink beers, eat chips, and play video games. We've played *Call of Duty*,

Wrestling, *Football* and more *Call of Duty*. He told me a little about his time with Courtney last night. He asked her out on a date. Brooke thinks Callen will be good for Courtney. Courtney is definitely Callen's type. He used to be a bit of a player. Not that he slept with more than one girl at a time, but he's always told them he was a no strings attached kind of guy. I think Courtney may be able to change that for him.

"Earth to fucking Vibe. Come in, Vibe."

"Fuck, sorry, man."

"Is Brooke coming back here?" He stares at me waiting for a response.

I shrug my shoulders. "I don't think so." I haven't even bothered checking my phone, so I have no idea if Brooke has tried reaching me, but I can't talk to her right now anyway. I have a nice little buzz going and I don't need her freaking out on me. "I think it's best if she sleeps at home tonight."

"Why's that?" he questions, never taking his eyes off the TV.

"I don't want to talk about this shit right now." I take out two enemy guys that were just about to shoot Callen. "Saved your ass again."

"Fuck you. It's about time. I'm always saving your ass."

"Like hell you are." This guy sucks at this game, and to prove it I let him get shot. He dies and throws the remote. "Break another one of my remotes and you're fucking buying me a new one."

"Sorry." He picks up the remote and starts fighting again.

After another couple hours of video games and pizza, I kick Callen out of my house. I'm tired and I want to go to bed. I grab my phone and head to my room, leaving the mess we made right where it is. I'll clean this shit up in the morning. "Come, Brody." I call my buddy, who follows behind me. He plops down on his bed and I take a quick shower. When I finally slip into my bed, I'm pissed because all I can smell is Brooke's coconut scent on the pillow, and it makes me wish I had called her. I sigh, grabbing my phone. I wonder if she's thinking about me as much as I am her. When I unlock it, I find a few missed calls and text messages from her.

Brooke: How was your day?

Brooke: I miss you.

Brooke: Why aren't you answering me? Are you okay?

Brooke: Vaughn, you're worrying me. Please answer me.

The phone beeps in my hand one more time.

Brooke: I'm really worried about you. I've called several times and sent numerous texts. This isn't like you. Please respond or I'm sending Remy over there to check on you since I can't get back in.

"Fuck," I shout out causing Brody to jump.

131

"Sorry, boy." He whimpers and lays back down.

Vaughn: I'm fine. I'm sorry I scared you. I was hanging with Callen and my phone was on silent. I just saw all of this now. I'll call you tomorrow.

Brooke: Fine.

Now I've really pissed her off. I shake my head, put my phone on the charger, and lay down to try and sleep. I hope I can keep the nightmares at bay tonight.

Chapter 11

Vaughn

It's been an entire week since I've seen Brooke. We've spoken over the phone a lot and got back into our routine of sending multiple texts a day, but we haven't been together since last weekend. It really fucked me up to think I hurt her, and I've had several nightmares about it since. Thank god for Brody, who wakes me from them night after night. I swear this dog deserves some sort of doggie award. I feel bad that we haven't gotten together all week, but I'm tired and I'm trying to catch up on some sleep. At least we made some plans for today. All week she's been talking about spending the day with me and the dog. There's a beach about an hour away from me that she loves. Says it's the perfect place to take Brody. She even called to confirm they would allow the dog on the beach. With all of her excitement, I didn't have the heart to tell her that after spending countless months in the desert, I'm really not a fan of the beach, so I'm going to suck it up and take her there. Then, we're coming back to my place to freshen up and drop off Brody before heading to her parents' house for dinner. Remy's wedding is next weekend, and his mom wanted to have everyone over for dinner tonight.

I'm already in my swim trunks and I have the cooler ready to go along with a separate small bag for Brody. Brooke said she's bringing a blanket with some beach towels and plenty of sunscreen. She knocks at the door and I shout for her to come in. She opens it to Brody greeting her with excitement. I swear to god this dog loves my girlfriend just as much as he loves me. Maybe that's a good thing. It would suck if he was a pain in her ass every time she came over, especially considering I really like her and care about her. Maybe that's his way of telling me he accepts her too.

"Hey, babe." I kiss her on the top of her head.

"Are you ready to go?" Her voice is full of excitement. I just wish I was with her on this.

"Sure. Let me start the car and get it loaded, and then we'll bring Brody out. It's hot and I want the car to cool down a second." She smiles and starts petting the dog.

"I'll take him out while you do that." She grabs the leash from the top of the bag I packed for him and takes him to the back while I run out to start the car and get the air conditioning going. By the time I'm done loading the trunk, the car has cooled down.

"I think we're ready." She takes Brody to the car and I lock up. When I get outside, she has the GPS programmed on her phone to get us to the beach. I pull out of the driveway and follow the directions the female voice provides. I'm focused on the road and she's looking out the window. The tension in the car is thick. I know she wants to say something, but she hasn't, and I'm actually quite glad. I have no desire to discuss my military past or my nightmare issues with her.

"What time do we need to be at your parents' house?" There, an easy question to try and break the tension in the car.

"I told my mom I would be there by five. I want to help her get things together. My father is going to grill, but she still needs to put sides out and dessert."

I nod. "That's fine. We have plenty of time to get to the beach, have some lunch, and come home. Who's going?"

"My brothers and their families will be there, Kenzie's aunt and uncle, and I believe Lilly." She shrugs. "Shouldn't be too many people." She turns her head to look back out the window.

The remainder of the ride is quiet. I want to ask her why she won't talk to me or look at me, but I'm afraid. What if she's pissed because I haven't said anything about my nightmares? I'll be forced to talk about it. I decide it's best to stay focused on the road and not say a word.

When we finally pull up to the beach, the gentleman at the gate tells us we have to go to the next lot down because of Brody. There's a separate area of the beach for people who want to bring their dogs. I take a right in the parking lot and go down to the area he's talking about. We find a spot to park. It's busy, but not overly full. This could be a good thing. This end of the beach may be quieter and have less people because of the dogs.

Brooke storms out of the car and grabs Brody's leash while I grab the rest of our stuff. She takes the beach towel bag from me and storms off toward the beach. I take a deep breath. I'm trying hard not to get frustrated, but I'm at a fucking loss here.

When I finally catch up to her, she has the blanket already down and Brody lies on one corner of it. He's already panting from the heat, so I pull out his bowl and pour some water in it. I place it in front of him and he instantly laps it up. "Will you tell me what's wrong?"

"Nothing. I'm fine." Her famous lines. She's always fine, yet she's not. Fuck. What am I thinking? I'm doing the same thing to her. I'm always telling her I'm fine, but am I? Of course I am. I'm a soldier. I can fucking handle anything.

"Okay." I stay calm. I can turn this day around. I peel my shirt off of my body, grab the sunscreen, and spray my chest and arms before reaching behind me to spray my back.

"Give me that." She takes it from me and sprays my back again and then rubs it in. "I don't want you sunburned for my parents' house later."

"Thank you." I turn, wrapping my arms around her waist. She softens just a little, wrapping me in her arms as well.

"You're welcome." She plops down on the blanket and I rub sunscreen all over her amazing body. She feels so fucking good my cock starts to stir, and that's not what I need right now.

"Are you good with just relaxing for a bit?"

"Yeah, that's cool." She grabs my hand and we both lay back, using our towels for blankets.

My eyes are closed and I'm relaxing as I look forward to soaking up the sun's rays. Damn, it's fucking hot out here. I wipe my forehead with the back of my arm. I'm already sweating like a motherfucker. Suddenly the ground starts to shake. I open my eyes, trying to gauge what the fuck is going on. We're surrounded by people. They're everywhere, and there's no telling who's friendly and who's not. I'm scanning the crowd for my boys, and I can't see them anywhere.

"Callen," I call out, but I hear nothing. "Eagle Eye, where the fuck are you guys?" Fuck, this is not good. How the hell did I get separated from my men? That's when I see her. She's here in the middle of the fucking desert, calling my name and searching for me. She's scared, and no matter how loud I call out to her, she can't hear me. I run at her full speed and tackle her to the ground just in time. A shot rings out, but she's safe now. I saved her. Out of nowhere this dog starts jumping on me and licking me.

"What the fuck?" Shit, it's Brody, but why is he barking?

"Get off of me. What is wrong with you?" I look down to see Brooke underneath me in the sand.

"Shit. I thought…" my words trail off. How the fuck do I explain this to her? I'm so fucked right now. I want to run, but I can't just leave her here, we're an hour from home. "Brooke, I'm so sorry. I have no idea what came over me. I was having a nightmare." I can't even look at her. I'm embarrassed and people are staring at us. "I need to go cool off." I run straight for the water, and when I'm deep enough, I dive under, trying to cool my body and gain some sense of control. Brody is behind me, swimming and enjoying the water. I love my fucking dog. He's by my side, making sure I'm good at all times. I knew coming here was a bad idea. I'm such a fucking pussy I should have just told her. Being on the beach in this fucking sun has fucked me all up. Maybe I should tell her we need to eat and get the fuck out of here.

When I walk back up the beach, I see her pacing with her phone to her ear. She has tears in her eyes and I can see she's trying to hold it together. I'm really fucking this up and I don't know what to do. I stop dead in my tracks, watching her, with Brody still by my side. I'm not sure I want to hear the conversation she's having, and I don't want to eavesdrop and piss her off more. She suddenly cuts the call and drops her phone into her bag. She plops down on the blanket and wipes the tears from her eyes. She rolls over onto her stomach, turning her back to me. I sit down next to her. "I don't know what to say. I'm sorry."

"You know what to say but you refuse to say it. I want to help you and support you, but I can't because you won't let me in."

"I've ruined the day and I'm sorry." I look at my watch. "Maybe we should eat our lunch and head out." She closes her eyes but nods in agreement.

We leave the beach thirty minutes later without saying so much as a word to each other. It's an awful feeling. We were only at the beach a few hours, and I feel terrible that she didn't even get to enjoy her time there. The entire ride home she stares out the window. The look of hurt on her face fucking kills me, but I need to focus on the road, ensuring we get home safely.

When we pull up to my house, she storms out of the car and into the house. She drops her bag at the door and goes into the bathroom. When she comes out, I can see her eyes are red and she looks so hurt.

"Brooke, please understand. This isn't something that's easy to discuss. I don't want the ugly things I've seen stuck in that beautiful head of yours. Shit, I wish they weren't stuck in mine."

She closes her eyes and a tear runs down her face. "I guess I can respect that, but if you can't talk to me, then you need to talk to someone. You scared the shit out of me today. The look on your face was blank. You were lost out in space somewhere, and no matter how much I called to you, there was no getting through. I had no idea what to do."

Yup, just when I thought I couldn't feel any worse. "I'm sorry. I didn't mean to scare you. I don't realize I'm having a flashback until it passes. Brody snapped me out of it."

She licks her lips and sighs. "I need to get ready for tonight. I'm going to go home to shower and I'm going to try to cool off. I hope you'll still come to dinner tonight." Her eyes are hopeful and the thought of canceling is now gone.

"Do you really want me there?" I'm not sure I want to hear the answer, but if she wants me to stay home, I understand, and can definitely respect that. Maybe deep down I'm even hoping she'll say yes. I have no idea how I'm going to face Remy after this. We are brothers and I just attacked his sister on the beach.

"Yes, I want you there, and I know Remy does too. You're like a brother to him."

I nod my head. "Then I'll see you there."

I'm not sure why, but she softens a little. Pressing up on her toes, she kisses me on the cheek. "I'll see you in a little bit." I stand watching her walk out the door, closing it behind her. My house instantly feels cold and lonely. Fuck, I can't lose her.

Chapter 12

Brooke

I pull up to my parents' house and cringe when I find Remy's car in the driveway. That means I have to face him about what happened with Vaughn. I was freaking out at the beach and didn't know what to do. Remy was the first person I called. I grab my bag from the backseat and head into the house. I try hurrying up the stairs to avoid my brother, but I'm not fast enough.

"Freeze." He stops me dead in my tracks.

"Rem, I really don't feel like doing this right now." I turn to look at him from halfway up.

"I get you don't want to discuss it, but I need to know that both my sister and my friend are okay." His expression is serious. I can tell he's not going to let up.

I take a few steps down. "I'm fine. He scared me and I needed to know what to do."

"If you're fine, why are you here without him? I thought you two were going to get ready at his place and then come here together."

I lick my lips, trying to figure out what to say. "I needed a little space. He scared me, and not just because he had a flashback or whatever he called it, but because he won't talk to me." I look down to the ground. "I'm falling for him, and I want to help him, but he won't let me."

"Wait, he admitted to having a flashback?" His voice is now laced with concern.

"Yeah, why?"

He shakes his head. "I'll talk to him. You go get in the shower."

"Remy, I think he's already afraid you're going to be pissed at him. He was concerned you wouldn't want him here."

My brother nods, but says nothing else. "Go." I run the remainder of the way up the stairs to my room. I go straight to my closet to pull out a sundress for the party. I want to look good for my man tonight. I need to show him that I lo—I stop my thoughts. "Do I love him?" I whisper. I thought I was falling for my ex and he was a total ass. He didn't treat me nearly as good as Vaughn does and our chemistry was all off. I shake off my thoughts. Either way I need to show him I still want to be with him despite the fact he's broken, as he calls it.

I jump into the shower, and as I wash my body I think about his hands on me. He's so strong, yet so gentle, and then I see the look he had on his face just before I left. It said so many things, but most of all I saw fear, that is until I turned back to pull the door shut. His shoulders were slumped over and he looked so defeated, so broken. My tears well yet again for the man I want to help fix. I take a deep breath and decide I need to pull myself together. I'm a mess and we have people coming over shortly. I step out of the shower, dry off, and slip on my robe. It takes me about forty-five minutes before I'm ready and feeling a bit more confident than earlier.

I run downstairs to find Mama in the kitchen, busy getting things ready. "Hey, Mama." I kiss her on the cheek. "What can I do to help?"

"Can you finish making the potato salad?" She nods toward the cooked potatoes. I nod and get busy adding ingredients to a bowl. We're both incredibly quiet and the silence is killing me, but Mama finally breaks it.

"You got a phone call yesterday that I forgot to tell you about."

"Oh?"

"Yeah, it was a guy about a house you wanted to rent."

Shit. I hope she's not mad. "Yeah, I called to inquire about it. I want to buy a house, but I thought about renting for a little bit first. I need to get a place of my own and I'm not sure where I want to start."

"I don't think renting is a bad idea, Brooke. As a matter of fact, I think it's smart."

I smile at my mom, feeling good about my decision. "I keep looking at the pictures. It's really cute and it's not far from home, work, or Vaughn. I can't wait to see it."

"Do me a favor. Be sure you take one of your brothers to look at it with you." Mama gives me a stern look.

"Look at what?" Remy asks walking into the kitchen.

"A house I want to rent."

Remy's expression changes to one of concern. "Are you sure that's a good idea? I mean, you living by yourself?"

I put my hands on my hips. "Not too long ago you wanted Daddy to kick me out. Now you're worried about me living on my own? I'm a grown woman, Remy, and I'm going to look at this house with or without you."

His brows shoot up. "Okay. I'm sorry." He puts his hands up in a defensive manner. "Keaton and I will both go. I'll make sure it's safe and he'll make sure the house is in good condition. Let us know when." He starts back out the door but turns back. "Just so you know, I'll always worry about my baby sister." I shake my head as he joins my father back on the deck with a fresh round of beers.

My two other brothers have both arrived and are sitting on the back patio with my father. Kenzie comes in from the yard and offers to help Mama, while Kayla keeps track of the kids. "Why don't you two go relax outside? I've got this." Mom gives us a warm smile. I walk out to the back deck and take a seat next to Remy, and Kenzie greets Lilly, who walks into the backyard. I can't help but watch for Vaughn, who should be here any minute now.

"When do you want to go look at that place, sis?" Remy bumps my shoulder.

"As soon as I can. I'll call the guy tomorrow and set up a time. Maybe he can let us see it one night

144

this week." I take a pull from my beer.

"My big girl is moving out." My dad shakes his head. "What's the place look like?"

"It's a two bedroom house with two baths. It has a nice size eat-in-kitchen and a small living room. The place isn't huge, but it's big enough for me, and the rent is reasonable. I'll be able to continue saving to buy a house when I'm ready."

"It sounds nice." Remy smiles at me.

"It looks it, and what's better is it comes partially furnished, so I won't need to get a ton of stuff to start out with. There's a sectional sofa, TV stand, coffee table, and end tables in the living room. There's also a small table in the kitchen. I just need to get a bedroom set."

"Even better." My dad looks proud. I clap my hands, excited to see the place.

"Excuse me, I have to check on the food." My father gets up from his spot on the bench. Kenzie and Lilly jump in it.

"Is your dress all set?" Kenzie's face lights up when she asks about the wedding.

I smile. "It sure is. It's hanging in my closet, all ready to go." I'm in the wedding, and I'm happy to talk about it. It's a nice distraction from the issue I'm having with my boyfriend.

"I'm so excited. Lilly is obviously walking with Dawson, since they are best man and maid of honor. Brooke, I have you walking with Vaughn." She wiggles her eyebrows, not knowing what kind of day we've had. "And Kayla, you'll walk with Keaton." I give her a tight smile, not wanting to give any signs of our misunderstanding today. It's a

Fourth of July wedding, and this year the fourth is on a Saturday, so it worked out perfect. "The rehearsal dinner is Friday night, and you'll all need to be here at six. We'll do a quick walk through with the priest and then we'll enjoy dinner."

"I can't wait." Lilly claps her hands, full of excitement.

Aunt Kenderly and Uncle Jasper walk into the backyard. Kenzie jumps up to give them a hug. I sigh, forgetting Remy is beside me. "He'll be here. If not, I'll kick his ass," he whispers in my ear.

I look up at him and I try to smile, but it doesn't quite work. "I'm worried about him."

"Let me go say hi to Kenzie's aunt and uncle, and then I'll text him if he's not here."

I bite the inside of my lip. "Maybe you shouldn't."

"Up to you." He gets up to go say hi and he talks with them for a few minutes.

"Dinner is ready," Mama calls out putting the remainder of the food on the table next to all the meat my father has pulled off the grill.

I stand up to get a bottle of water, and then get in line to make my plate. I'm not really hungry, but I don't feel like spilling my guts, and if I don't eat everyone is going to wonder why. This entire party is killing me, and it pisses me off because I should be happy for my brother and future sister-in-law. Instead I'm sad and depressed because the man I love is not here. I close my eyes and take in a breath as the 'L' word just flew through my mind yet again. "Auntie Brooke, will you eat with me?" Becky pulls on my dress.

146

"Sure, sweetie. Let me get my plate and I'll go sit on the blanket with you."

"Yay," she cheers and runs off to sit on the blanket her mother set up. Becky always eats on a blanket when we eat in the yard. She loves sitting in the grass. Funny thing is I was the same way when I was her age. I never cared to sit at the table with the adults. I didn't even care if I ate alone. As long as I had a soft blanket and grass to sit on, I was a happy little girl.

It's finally my turn. I grab a plate and start picking at some of my favorites, making sure I don't take too much. As soon as I'm done, I make my way over to the blanket where Becky is set up with her baby doll. She has her sitting and she's pretending to feed her. "What's the baby's name?"

"Katrina," she answers simply without even looking at me. "Auntie Brooke, are you sad?" Holy shit, even my little niece can tell I'm off.

"No, sweetie, Auntie is fine."

She takes the spoon, brings it to the baby's mouth, and then eats it herself. "My baby really likes the macaroni."

"I bet she does. It's good stuff." I giggle at her innocence. I'm picking at my food and watching her play and eat.

I glance up to see Vaughn walking into the backyard. He looks good, but I can tell he's still off from this afternoon. He's wearing a nice pair of khaki shorts and a purple polo that shows off his muscular arms and chest. Remy gets up and walks straight up to him. They shake hands and man hug. Remy pats him on the back and I can see his mouth

147

moving as he whispers something to him. Vaughn nods and slaps him on the back. They look at each other and silently exchange some words. Vaughn's mask slips for just a second—I almost missed it, but it definitely slips. I can't help but wonder if Remy caught it. Remy walks back to his table and Vaughn's eyes scan the yard. He gives me a nod and I offer a small smile in return. He walks over to the food and makes a plate, but instead of sitting with me he sits with Remy and my parents. I won't lie, I'm a bit crushed. I know he's my brother's friend and all, but I would think he would come sit with me for a bit.

"Becky, Auntie is going to clean up. You be a good girl."

"I will, Auntie." I get up from the blanket, grab my plate, and run into the house to throw it away. Then, I go out to the food table, grabbing the empty platters and bring them into the house to wash up. I can't stand to be out there watching him laugh with my brother while he pretends like nothing happened between us. I dry the platters and put them away before going outside to see what else I can clean up. It's warm out, so I grab the remainder of the salads, put them into smaller containers, and stack them in the fridge. I'll do anything to avoid being out there right now.

I dry my hands, and when I turn around, I'm startled by Vaughn standing at the door. "Holy shit, you scared me!" I slap him on the chest.

"I didn't mean to, but I wanted to check on you. I saw you run off and I wanted to make sure you were okay."

I shake my head no. "You came in here pretending like I didn't exist. What would make you think I'm all right?"

"Brooke. You ran out of my house telling me you needed space. I screwed up today, and I know I have to figure out how to fix it, but you can't tell me you need space in one breath and then be mad at me when I give it to you in the next."

My brows shoot up in shock. "That's not what I meant, and I'm sorry if that's what you thought. I just meant I didn't want to argue with you, and I wanted time to pull myself together before the party."

He nods, taking in my words. "Hey Vibe," Remy calls out and Vaughn turns around.

"Vibe?" I question.

"Yeah, it's my nickname from the service."

I chuckle and shake my head. "Go. See what he wants. I'm fine."

"No, you're not. It appears we both have thoughts we need to square away." He kisses me on the cheek and walks out. I gasp thinking about his words. The man I've wanted for years is finally mine and I can't bring myself to tell him how I feel about him. Maybe that's why he won't open up. He's afraid because he doesn't realize what he means to me. I guess he's right. I do have my own thoughts I need to square away, but I can't do it down here. I grab my phone and run up to my room to send both Remy and Vaughn a text saying I'm sorry and that I've turned in for the night.

Chapter 13

Brooke

I groan to myself realizing the god awful noise is my alarm telling me I need to get up for work. I roll my stiff neck and jump out of bed. My body is stiff and aches because I haven't been working out much lately and I'm definitely feeling it. After a few quick stretches, I go straight to my closet to figure out what I'm going to wear today. I'm really tired from the crazy dreams I kept having last night. I feel like I hardly slept. Every time I would fall into a deep sleep I would envision Vaughn on the beach looking lost and scared. His expression was pained, and I have no idea what brought it all on. My big strong, independent soldier was scared, and then to make matters worse, I walked out on him. He scared the shit out of me. At the time I felt like I did what I needed to, but how am I going to get him to open up to me if I walk out on him when he needs me? He must feel like he can't trust me. I close my eyes and take a deep breath. As much as I want to figure this all out, I need to focus on getting myself ready for work.

I grab my favorite floral print jumpsuit and lay it out on the bed. It's bright with fun colors and it makes me smile. Plus, it's really comfortable, and comfort is something I need today. I also need to feel confident, and nothing makes a woman feel more confident than a sexy ass matching panty and bra set. I grab what I need and head to the bathroom to get ready. I can't help but notice the quiet. This house used to be filled with hustle and bustle, and now there's not a sound. My mom is on vacation from school. She's probably still sound asleep in her bed while my dad is already at work. Dawson, Remy and Keaton have all moved out, and now I'm about to move too. I'll need to have music or something going in my house. I'm not sure I can handle this quiet.

Forty-five minutes later I walk out of the bathroom dressed, with my hair in a twist, and my makeup done to perfection. I make a smoothie for breakfast, throw a lunch together, and run out the door. When I get to the car I realize I haven't checked my phone yet this morning.

Vaughn: I think Brody is sick.

I wonder what could be wrong with Brody. He's only had him a few weeks, but you can tell he's totally attached to his dog. You can tell by the way his face lights up when he sees him that he adores him.

Brooke: Why do you say that?

I put the car in drive and take off toward the clinic. I need to see what we have going on today. I want to be prepared to squeeze him in if need be.

Vaughn: Are you sure you want to talk about my dog's shit this early in the morning?

I'm driving now, so I can't text him back. I hit the call button on the screen to dial him instead. "Hello."

"I can't text you anymore. I'm driving to work, and yes, I want to hear about his shit. I'm a vet, it's what I do." I roll my eyes.

"Fine. It was runny, and he went twice this morning, barely making it out the second time." I hear his chair creak. He must be in his office. I can picture him leaning back in the chair with his leg crossed at his ankle, looking all sexy.

"Are you in your office?" I bite my lip.

"Yes." He sounds confused.

"You're leaning back in your chair, aren't you?" I need to stop picturing him shirtless, looking all sexy. My panties are getting wet.

"Ummm, yeah. Why?"

I shake my head. "Never mind. Back to the dog. Did he eat anything he shouldn't have?"

"Not that I saw. There was no trash on the floor when I got home."

I pull up to the red traffic light and pinch the bridge of my nose. "It could be a number of things. Keep an eye on it, and if he doesn't improve, call me and I'll have you bring him in." He could be upset he saw us fight. He could be worried about what he saw on the beach with Vaughn. I don't tell him that because I don't want to cause added stress, but I'm really hoping it's just nerves.

The person behind me beeps their horn, letting me know the light has changed and I need to wake the hell up. "What was that?"

I sigh. "The guy behind me. I'm tired and wasn't paying attention to the light."

"You need to focus on driving. I'll let you go." He sounds sad.

"Call me later and let me know how he is." And how you are too. I don't say that last part, but I want to. I'm afraid if I push him too hard, he'll continue to push me away. He sounds so tired, I'm sure he's not sleeping any better than I am. I again try to push thoughts of Vaughn out of my head for now. He's right, I need to focus on driving, and I can't do that if I start to worry about him all over again.

I pull up to work with about ten minutes to spare of us opening. Dr. Kramer and Courtney's cars are already here. I climb out and unlock the front door, letting myself in. "Good morning," I call out, trying to figure out where everyone is.

"Hey." Courtney comes to her desk carrying a cup of coffee that she made in our one cup brewer. "Are you all right?" she asks, looking concerned.

"Yeah, I didn't sleep too well last night, but I'm okay."

"Do you want to do lunch today and we can talk?" She gives me a warm smile and I can tell she's hopeful that I'll lean on her.

"We'll see how the day goes." I give her a small smile and head to find Dr. Kramer. I walk to the back to find him with one of our many pets. "How is Pretty Kitty?" Yes, someone named their pet Pretty Kitty. I can't help but giggle at some of the names people chose for their animals.

He pets her head and scratches her chin. "Much better today. I think it's time she goes home."

"Oh good. I'll have Courtney place the call to notify the Harrisons that they can pick her up."

"Thank you." He looks up with a small smile.

"Dr. Kramer, are you okay?" He looks extremely tired and very pale. I press my hand to his forehead and he instantly pulls away.

"Don't you start too. I just had to endure Courtney's rambling on about my health. I'm fine, just a bit tired."

With my hands on my hips, I give him a look that tells him I'm not buying it, but I say nothing, giving him a chance to speak up. When he continues working and ignoring me, I have no choice. "Dr. Kramer, we have worked together for a few years now, and I've known you since I was little and I brought that sick stray cat into your clinic. Do you really think for one second I'm buying your 'I'm fine' line?"

He sighs. "Okay, so I'm not feeling too hot today. And before you say anything else, yes, I very much remember the little blonde girl that strolled into the clinic crying because the kitty was sick. The care and concern in your eyes told me you would be treating animals someday, and here you are, but what am I going to do? Tell the animals not to be sick today?"

"Really? I *am* a veterinarian now. You have no excuses. I've been helping you treat animals long enough that I would think you trust me at least a little."

"Oh dear, it has nothing to do with trust. I trust you with these animals wholeheartedly, but it doesn't mean I don't want to be here to treat them just the same."

We can hear patients coming in with their owners as we wrap up our conversation. Courtney must have opened the doors. "Fine, but I'll be keeping an eye on you, and you will take a lunch break today," I demand, not caring if it upsets him. This man is like a second father to me, and I'll be damned if I don't take care of him.

After a few hours of seeing our furry little patients, I tell Courtney to order us lunch in. We can sit in the break room and chat, that way I'll be able to keep an eye on Dr. Kramer, who happens to be moving a bit slower than usual today. I asked him to please make an appointment to see my father, and he said he would if he wasn't feeling better in a few days.

"Lunch is here," Courtney calls into the back. We both peel off our gloves from working with a dog and toss them into the bin.

"Thanks, Courtney. Come on, Dr. Kramer. I ordered you your favorite soup." He turns to me with a smile.

"You're a stubborn girl, Brooke, but thanks." We walk into the break room together. He takes his soup and crackers from the table, thanking

Courtney. "I'm going to eat in my office. I have some paperwork to take care of. I'll see you ladies shortly." He walks out of the kitchen.

I shake my head. "I'm worried about him. He doesn't look good."

"I know. You didn't look too hot yourself this morning. What's going on?"

I turn back to her. "I'm sorry, what was that you said?"

"Really? What is with you? One minute we're supposed to be getting together for a game night, and the next I've heard nothing more from you about it and then you come in looking exhausted."

"I know. I'm sorry." I look down at the salad in front of me, and as delicious as it looks, I'm losing my appetite. "I'm not sure how much I should tell you, but I'll tell you this. It appears Vaughn has some issues settling back in after his last tour." The look on Vaughn's face flashes through my mind.

I'm so deep in thought when Courtney talks I'm not hearing her. "Hey! I said is there something I can do to help?"

"Sorry." I shake my head. "I don't know. I haven't figured out what to do myself. I feel so bad and I need to figure out how to fix it."

"What do you have to feel bad about? You didn't send him over there." Her brows are furrowed.

I swallow a bite of my salad, trying to fight my loss of appetite. "I walked out on him after one of his flashbacks. He scared me and I didn't know what to do. I told him I needed space and he would see me at dinner. Now he'll never trust me to open up."

"Oh Brooke, don't be so hard on yourself. It's not an easy situation to deal with. You need to apologize and explain to him that you didn't know what to do. He'll understand."

"I don't know. He showed up at my mom's for dinner and sat with my brother the entire night. I know the dinner was for my brother and future sister-in-law, but it felt like he was ignoring me." I lean my head in my hands. "I think I've fallen for him." I let out a slow breath. "I've liked him for so long now it didn't take much once we started connecting, and now I fear I'm going to lose him."

"Have you told him?"

I shake my head no. "What am I supposed to say? 'Hey, I've had a secret crush on you since the first time we met years ago and I now I think I love you.'" I close my eyes. "God, I sound stupid."

"No, you don't, and I wouldn't be so sure he doesn't feel the same."

"I have to get back to work. My next patient will be here soon." I get up, toss my salad, and storm out of the kitchen to the bathroom.

***

Work has dragged by today. I couldn't help but keep an eye on the clock because I'm really excited to go see this house I'm hoping to rent. I hurry on my way to meet Remy, Keaton, and the landlord. This was his grandparents' house, and now that they've moved on, he wants to rent it until he decides if he's going to sell it or move into it himself. He's promised me the house is mine for at least a year, maybe longer if I so choose. The location is perfect. It's about fifteen minutes from Mama, fifteen minutes from work, and twenty minutes from Vaughn. Now I just have to pray the house is in good condition.

I pull into the driveway to see Keaton's truck already here. He and Remy must have driven together because they're standing on the lawn talking to the landlord and Remy's car is nowhere to be found. I jump out of my car and hurry over to introduce myself. "Hi guys." My brothers each hug me and I hold out my hand to the gentleman. "Hi, I'm Brooke."

"Hi, Brooke, it's good to meet you. Your brothers were just introducing themselves and asking a little about the house."

I smile up at my brothers. "Thanks, guys."

Remy puts his arm around me. "We were just explaining that we want to make sure our baby sister is well taken care of." Good Lord, I blush. They act like I'm a kid and not a grown woman.

Mr. Daily comes to my rescue. "Come on, let me show you around." He opens the door to the house and we step inside. "I updated the furniture in the living room and the dining room table is new." Both sets are nice. The living room has dark furniture, not really my style, but seeing how it requires me to only furnish my bedroom, I'll take it. The dining room table is small but seats four. The kitchen is an eat-in kitchen, it doesn't leave room for a table much bigger than that. I'm looking around the kitchen when I hear Keaton ask him to see the attic space. Mr. Daily walks off with him and Remy stays with me.

He leans on the counter next to me. "What do you think?"

"It's cute. I love how open the living room and kitchen are. The small snack bar separating them are perfect for extra seating, and yet I can talk to guests while I cook."

He pulls away from the counter. "Let's go check out the bedrooms. There are two of them back there." I follow Remy to the back of the house where, sure enough, there are two bedrooms and two bathrooms. One bathroom is in the hallway and it's a full bath with a shower tub combo. It's not big, but it's nice. There's a shower curtain already hung up with a liner.

"You can change that if you would like, I thought it showed nicer with a curtain hung." I jump, not realizing Mr. Daily was behind me.

"It's fine. I'll leave it up to you. If you want to take it down to save it, you can. I don't mind buying one." He smiles but says nothing.

The guest bedroom is small, but would work as an office or kid's room. I chuckle at my thoughts. Vaughn and I are barely talking and kids come into my brain. Yikes. I sigh, saddened by the thought that I miss him. I move onto the master, which is a bit bigger than the second room. It has a walk-in closet and its own bathroom. Again nothing overly huge, but it will work until I decide to buy or build a house. This is a cute starter house, but not where I would want to stay...not unless Keaton could do some serious adding on.

Keaton comes walking into the room. "Mr.

Daily, will you give us a few minutes."

"Certainly. I'll be in the kitchen." He walks out of the room and Keaton closes the door.

He turns back to me. "The house is in good shape. The windows are outdated, as well as some of the flooring, but I don't see anything that would say don't rent from him. I wouldn't recommend you buy the house without planning on doing renovations, but to rent I think you're fine."

I sigh. "The location is great and the price is right. It's not the house of my dreams, but I think I could make it home. The question is, do I keep looking, or do I take it, because I haven't seen much else out there to rent."

"Listen, sis, there's no rush for you to get out of Mom and Dad's house. I mean, I get you're a grown woman and you want to be on your own, but it's not like you have to be out by a certain time." Remy leans on the door. "Why don't you tell him you're going to take the weekend to think it over and you'll get back to him on Monday?"

"Good idea. Then it will give me a chance to browse around a bit more too to see if anything new has popped up. If it were a bit bigger and a little less outdated I would be all over it, but I don't want to be locked in here for a year and be miserable."

"Exactly." Remy pulls the door open and the three of us walk out to the kitchen where we find Mr. Daily sitting at the kitchen table on his phone.

He looks up when we approach. "Thank you so much for your time. The house is lovely, but before I make any decisions I'd like to sleep on it. Can I get back to you on Monday?"

He stands up holding his hand out. "You can, but I'm not holding it for any one person. I've had others look at the place too and the first person to say they want it and pass the background check gets it."

"I understand. I'll be in touch. Thank you again for your time." We all shake hands with the guy and start to head out the door.

Mr. Daily stops Keaton. "Can I ask, did you find anything I should be concerned with?"

He sighs. "Not really. The floors in the kitchen and the windows are outdated. The windows especially will need replacing soon. They're getting drafty and need new insulation. The attic seemed to be dry and well insulated, that's always a good thing. It's a fine home. I'm just not sure Brooke feels it's the home for her."

"I understand. Thank you for your input and for coming to see the house."

I hug my brothers goodbye and head home for dinner with my parents.

Chapter 14

Brooke

We have a busy few days ahead of us. Everyone in the bridal party will be here shortly for the rehearsal dinner and I have to say my body is racked with both nerves and excitement. I'm really excited for Remy and Kenzie's big day tomorrow, but I haven't seen or spoken to Vaughn much, and I know he'll be here tonight. We've managed a few text messages throughout the week, but that's it. I can't help but feel like he's avoiding me. We really need to talk or I need to move on, and that will crush me. I'm hoping he at least gives me the chance to tell him how I feel about him.

"Hey, sis." Keaton walks in the door and for once he's early. Actually, now that I think about it, he hasn't been late since that family dinner when Mama yelled at him and smacked him hard on the back of the head. I guess she's finally gotten through to him.

"Hey, Keaton." He kisses me on the cheek and

hugs me.

"Look here," Mama calls out, picking up her camera and taking a photo of my brother and I. Mama has become quite the photographer. I heard her telling my father she wants to take some photography classes when she retires to give her something to do. I can't really see her giving up teaching, she loves her kids, but I can tell she'd also make a great photographer, so maybe she can combine her loves and photograph children. "Keaton, can you go help your father with the chairs around the yard?"

"Yes, ma'am. I'm just going to drop my stuff upstairs first." She nods at him and he runs off.

I point over my shoulder with my thumb. "What's up with him?"

"Whatever do you mean?" I give Mama a look. "To make up for scaring me, he promised to help with the setup today. He apologized, and now he's trying to be better about being on time."

I nod. "Good. What's with the bag?"

"It's hot, dear. The man will need a shower before the party starts later."

"I'm glad he's here to help."

"Me too. Now come here and help me with this mac and cheese. I'm surprising Kenzie with it as part of dinner."

My eyes go wide. "Is that her mama's famous recipe?"

Mama smiles. "It is. I managed to get it from Aunt Kenderly."

"Oh, you sneaky woman, you. You love this dish. Did you do it for Kenzie or so you could have it too?"

Mama gives me a side grin. "Brooke Leah Bennett, I did this for Kenzie. Now if that happens to mean I have the recipe for future use, well, I guess I'm a lucky woman, but I will always give credit where credit is due." She gives me a stern look.

"Yes, ma'am." I nudge her jokingly with my shoulder and she giggles, but we both get busy following the directions for the recipe, hoping to do it justice. I have no doubt it will be delicious, Mama is an amazing cook, and the recipe isn't hard to follow.

Keaton comes running through the kitchen and out the back door to help my father get the backyard set up. We aren't doing any decorations because people will be here early tomorrow to set the yard up for the wedding, and we don't want a ton of cleanup at the end of the night. Mama is having some of today's food catered to make life a bit easier. She's ordered pulled pork, fried chicken, shrimp, and a vegetarian dish. We're busy making the sides to go with it all. I made potato salad yesterday and Mama is boiling eggs for deviled eggs. As always, she's over doing it, but that's the way Mama is. I keep trying to remind her that the caterer will have tons more food tomorrow, but she won't hear it.

Everyone is due here in a couple of hours and Keaton just ran up to shower. That means I'll need to go next. I throw the green bean casserole into the top oven to get it going. "I'm heading upstairs to get my stuff ready."

"Okay, dear. Thanks for your help." I kiss Mama on the cheek and run upstairs to get ready.

I pass Keaton in the hallway. He's walking toward his room wearing nothing but a towel. I shake my head. He's always doing that and it used to annoy the hell out of me. Of course, he's lived alone for a while now, so he probably thinks nothing of it. I grab my clothes and run to the bathroom to begin the process of getting ready. I'm making quick work of it. I want to be back downstairs when Vaughn gets here. I feel like it's been forever since I've seen him and I'm hoping to spend some time with him today.

I make it back down before any of our guests arrive, but Kenzie and Remy are here, along with her aunt and uncle. I quickly say hello and go back to the kitchen to see what I can help Mama with. When she tells me she's all set, it leaves me feeling antsy and lost. I need to keep myself occupied or I'll go crazy waiting for him to get here. I begin wiping down the island in the kitchen where Mama and I had been working earlier. "I already did that, dear, but thank you." I nod my head and dry it off. I'm starting to wish I took longer to get ready when Dawson comes in carrying Becky, and Kayla has Beau.

"Hey guys." I take Becky from my brother. "Hey pretty girl." She giggles and squirms from me tickling her.

"Dad's out back. I'm going to go take her into the yard." I walk out back with her and put her down in the grass. She runs to the bin my parents have with her yard toys in them. When I get back inside, Remy is holding Beau, playing with him.

"We should all go outside. People are going to be arriving soon." We all step back outside, and sure enough Lilly is walking into the backyard.

We're now waiting on Vaughn and the priest to get here to go through the rehearsal. The caterer is talking to my mom about the food they have to set up and where she wants it. While she's handling that, Keaton is playing with Becky in the grass and my father sits enjoying a beer. "Are you excited, Kenzie?"

"I'm so excited. It's funny because I thought I would be nervous, but I'm really not. I can't wait to get the ceremony over with and have some fun."

"You may be nervous in the morning." Aunt Kenderly nudges her shoulder.

"Maybe, but I don't think so." She smiles at her aunt.

Remy comes over and kisses her on the cheek. "She'll be fine. She's such a strong, confident woman, I have no doubt she'll get through it no problem."

"Awww, what did you do wrong that you have to kiss up, Rem?" I bust my brother's balls.

He puts me in a headlock and starts to noogie me. "I didn't do anything, brat."

"Hey, stop. You'll mess my hair."

"Don't mess her hair, dude. You'll never hear the end of it." I hear Vaughn's voice and instantly smile. He lets go of me and shakes hands with his boy. "What's up, man? Sorry I'm a bit late. Things are really crazy at work."

"Don't stress it, man, just glad you can be here."

I smile shyly at him. It's weird being with him with my family around. We haven't spent much time together in front of them and the last time we were together at my parents' we actually didn't spend much time together, he hung with my brother more. He gives me a small smile, but I can tell he's still keeping his distance. The smile looks slightly forced and it breaks me a bit. I need to hold it together through the wedding tomorrow and then I can discuss our relationship and where it's going, if anywhere. It may even be time that I'm honest and tell him how I feel about him.

The priest shows up and he pulls Kenzie and Remy aside to go over the details of the wedding. When they are ready, he makes a quick announcement, and in no time we've managed to practice walking down the fake aisle that will be set up in the morning. The archway is already in place but it hasn't been decorated yet. Mom had it delivered today, that way we could see where it would be and have an idea on how we would be walking through the yard.

As soon as we're done, Mom announces that dinner is ready. Everyone walks over to the buffet that is set up on the deck to make our plates. I'm sweating and my stomach doesn't feel well from the tension rolling off of Vaughn. We have to walk down the aisle together, and I know it was set up that way because we're dating, but now I wish it weren't. His touch lights my skin on fire, and right now I'm not sure I affect him the same way he does me.

I make a small plate and make my way down to

the table to sit with Mom, Dad, Aunt Kenderly, and Uncle Jasper. I take a seat and Aunt Kenderly smiles at me. "How's the new job?"

"It's amazing. I absolutely love what I do." I smile at the easy question.

"It has to be hard some days," Uncle Jasper says.

"Of course. There are days when I'm on-call and I have to go in for emergencies, or we have to put a pet down, but I think the hardest part for me is when someone doesn't pay attention to their animal and they end up eating something that can seriously hurt them. One woman told me she watched her cat eat something because she was afraid to reach into the cat's mouth and take it out. We had to operate to remove a piece of her kid's toy from its stomach." I shake my head. "It's hard to not let my emotions and my personal feelings get in the way."

"That's awful."

"I know, and we had to give the cat back to her. Lord only knows what she'll let the cat eat next." I shake my head. The conversation continues on with crazy stories my father and I have experienced, he in the human medical field and I in my pet world, and before I know it, we've been talking for well over an hour.

I excuse myself to throw my plate away, and that's when I notice Vaughn is no longer in the yard. He'd been sitting with Remy, Kenzie, Lilly, and Keaton. I can't help but wonder where he's gone. I'm standing by the food table, scanning the yard, when Remy walks over. "Hey, have you seen Vaughn? I'm a little worried. He disappeared about twenty minutes ago."

168

"I'll find him." Dropping my plate in the trash, I head into the house to use the bathroom. The downstairs bathroom is empty, but I run to the upstairs one to leave it open for guests. When I get there, I see him.

"You've been avoiding me." I stand behind Vaughn, checking out his muscular body through the fitted t-shirt he's wearing.

He flinches slightly, then turns to face me and his eyes go slightly wide. "I wouldn't call it avoiding you. I've just been busy." His voice is snippy, like he wants no part of this conversation.

My brows shoot up. "I would call it avoiding me. Why? Why can't you simply talk to me?"

Sudden frustration flashes across his handsome face. "Because I'm broken, Brooke. I'm not the same man you met all those summers ago. You have no idea what my life is like. The things I've seen, they haunt me in my sleep. The roadside bombs I've watched wiping out half a convoy; the gunfire that takes place while we try to recover men and a few broken down trucks; or how about this…have you ever seen one of your guys drop as he's standing right beside you, dying at your feet from his battle wound? These things haunt me on a daily basis. For a short time, I thought I had it under control, but I don't, and I don't know what to do." He pauses, but he's panting, and part of me wants to respond, but part of me wants to let him continue. I decide to give him a minute. "I can't even fucking stay for the fireworks tomorrow night because I'm afraid I'll either have a flashback or a panic attack, and I don't want to embarrass you or your family."

169

A tear rolls down his cheek. "I'm standing here torn, Brooke. When you're not with me…" his words trail off as he tries to calm himself down. "When you're not with me, I'm a mess and I fucking miss you. When you're with me, I fear I'm going to hurt you or embarrass myself again. I don't know if I should push you away and fight the pain I feel in my chest when we're not together, or hold you close and try to love you, risking it all." I assume when he says risking it all, he's referring to losing both myself and his friend, but Remy would never turn his back on Vaughn.

He's leaning against my bedroom door, staring inside with tears running down his face. I get it now, he came up here to think about me, to think about us, and now I know what I have to do. I wrap my arms around his waist, pressing my face to his chest, and inhale his scent. "Oh, Vaughn, you may be a broken man, but you're my broken man, and you need to see that love can heal many things. I made a mistake when I walked out on you the other day. I should have shown you that I would support you and be there for you, and instead I ran. I'm so sorry."

He sniffles and kisses the top of my head. "You have no idea how much I've missed this, holding you in my arms. I feel like it's been forever."

"I've missed it too." I plant a kiss on his chest.

He let's go to wipe away his tears. "I've never thought I needed help before. I always told everyone I was fine. Shit, even at my evaluation after my last deployment I told them all I was good. I lied about the nightmares because I thought I

170

could handle it, I didn't think it was a big deal, but now I'm starting to think different. I've been home for quite some time now and the nightmares have gotten worse again. I had a panic attack the other day in my office." I rub his back, encouraging him to continue speaking. "I'm so thankful I was in my office and not in front of my guys. I was able to calm myself down, but it took me a while, and then Callen walked in toward the end. He knew something was wrong and told me I needed to get fucking help." He shakes his head. "Dude finally fucking yelled at me."

"You've been through a lot and always have guys leaning on you. It's time you lean on someone else. I'm not saying you have to regale me with stories of your past, but let me help you. I want to be there for you. I love you." I gasp. I don't want him freaking out at those words. I've been holding back because I wanted him to admit he needed help, and I wanted to wait until I knew it wouldn't cause him to push me away even more out of fear, but the words came out so naturally

He pulls away and looks into my eyes, searching. I'm trying to show him I mean it. I've had a crush on him for so long now that I think I've loved him from the minute he first kissed me. "God, I love you too, Brooke." His lips crash down on mine, hard. I can taste his tears mixed in with the beers he's had.

When he pulls away, we're both panting. "Go use the bathroom right there and wash your face. My brother is worried, but I told him I would look for you." He nods and wanders into the bathroom to clean up while I wait for him by my bedroom.

When he comes out he looks a lot better, but I can still see concern on his face. "Listen, I promise to help you through this."

He gives me a tight smile and kisses me on top of the head one more time. "Thanks, Brooke."

"Come on. Let's get back outside." He puts his arm around me and we make our way back downstairs. When we get there we find everyone picking up the yard in preparation for the big day.

We both start folding up chairs and setting them aside when Remy comes over. "You good, man?"

"Ya know, for the first time I'm starting to think I will be." He winks at me and I know he's slipping his mask back into place so he won't worry Remy the night before the big day, but I won't give up and I'll stay on him. I have to. I love him and I want to see him get better.

They hug it out. "I'm glad to hear it. Remember, no matter what, Vibe, I'm here for you."

"Thanks, man. Listen, do you guys need more help? If not, I think I'm going to head home and try to get some sleep before tomorrow."

I give him a warm smile. "Go, we're fine, but you have to do me a favor."

"What's that?"

"Give Brody a hug for me."

He laughs. "You got it. He's a good boy and is feeling so much better. Thank you for helping me find him. I'm not sure where I would be right now without him."

"Drive careful." I press up on my toes to give him a kiss.

"I will. Good night, beautiful."

"Good night." I watch him walk out of the yard with his head down. I can almost see the wheels turning as he heads toward his car.

My brother puts his arm around me. "Is he really as good as he says he is?"

"Not yet, but I won't give up on him, and he's made the first step. He's admitted that he needs help, now we just have to help him get it." He kisses me on the head.

I look up to see a pained expression on his face. "Please make sure you let me know if I can help in any way. That's my boy and I want to be there for him."

"I will, now go get some rest. You're getting married tomorrow." He chuckles and runs into the house. He's spending the night here and we're all getting ready at their place tomorrow. It's going to be a gorgeous day for a wedding.

Chapter 15

Brooke

We're all at Kenzie's and we've been getting ready all morning. We just have to help her slip on her dress before the photographer gets here and she'll be ready to go. Her dress is exquisite. She's wearing a beautiful strapless dress with a sweetheart neckline. "Look at this." She pulls out two garter belts, one that says **'Army Wife'** on one side with **'Bennett'** on the other, and the other says **'You're Next.'** She slips them both into place under her bathrobe.

"Those are so cute, but you know what's even cuter?"

"What?" she asks, confused.

"This. Remy asked me to deliver it to you today and told me to have you wear it around your neck." I open the box that displays a white gold necklace that holds a single white gold dog tag he had made special for her. It has a solid diamond on the tip of it and it's engraved with 'Bennett' on one side and on the other it says 'Near or far you're always on my mind and in my heart.'

Her hands are shaking as she pulls the box from me. "It's beautiful."

I smile at her. "No crying now."

Lilly hands her a tissue to dab her eyes. "It's gorgeous. Let me help you." Lilly pulls the necklace from the box and places it around her neck. It lays perfectly on her chest. "Let's get you dressed, the photographer will be here any minute, as will the limo, and you promised Remy you wouldn't be late." She takes a deep breath, trying to maintain control over her emotions. She's done well up until this point. We girls are all dressed and ready to go. Kayla and I are wearing red halter dresses, with some embellishment below the breast to dress it up slightly. Lilly is wearing the same dress but hers is blue to go with the patriotic theme for the military wedding that's about to take place.

"Let's do this." She finally stands and slips off her robe to reveal a beautiful white corset and thin white stockings. I grab her dress from the hanger and Lilly and I get busy helping her into it.

"The photographer is here," Kayla shouts to the back room.

"We'll be out in one minute," I shout back.

Lilly tells Kenzie to hold her dress in place while she zips up the back. Once she's dressed, we sit her down and we each get busy helping her put on her shoes. She thought it would be funny to wear boots for the wedding, so without Remy knowing, my mom took her on base and got her fitted for a pair of women's boots. It's funny, but in reality probably smarter than heels. It's July 4th, and with the wedding being outside in the south, she would only sink into the grass, causing her to worry about falling. Once her boots are laced up, we all walk into the living room, and as soon as we do, she picks up the dress, revealing her glamorous shoes. The photographer bursts into laughter and starts snapping pictures. She also gets a close up of her new necklace.

The photographer is a hoot. She has us doing all sorts of silly things. She takes a fun picture of us checking out her camouflage garter with shocked looks on our faces. We also take a shot pretending to help her with her boots, and then she takes some serious shots of us as well. When Aunt Kenderly and Uncle Jasper arrive, she takes some nice photos of the three of them, as well as some of her and Uncle Jasper alone. He's giving her away today since he's the only family she has left, and she's close to him. Poor guy got choked up when she asked him at one of our family dinners.

It takes the photographer a little bit to take every shot that Kenzie had requested, but she does it in her allotted time. As she's finishing her last shot, the limo pulls up to the house. It's silly she got a limo when we're only going from her house to ours, but it's what she wanted, and Remy told her she could have anything she wanted. My understanding is that was their compromise. He wanted a backyard wedding and she wanted a limo. "You ready to do this?" Lilly asks Kenzie.

"Let's get out of here." She walks to the door and the photographer is behind us snapping pictures as we help her into the limo. Uncle Jasper and Aunt Kenderly follow right behind us and the door is closed with the five of us seated inside.

When we pull up to my parents' house, I'm totally shocked. It almost doesn't look like their house. There's a sign out front with rings on it that says **'Congratulations Remington and McKenzie.'** There are wildflowers and decorations all over the place. There's no way that you could mistake which house the wedding was taking place at. Kenzie has a huge smile on her face as the limo comes to a halt. "Wait here. I want to make sure they know you have arrived before you get out of the car," Uncle Jasper tells her as he climbs out. The limo has pulled into the driveway. It's the only car in front of the house. Mom and Dad have valet parking set up to move cars away from the house so the caterers and everyone else can do what they need to, plus she didn't want anything to take away from the decorations or the sign she had put up.

"Well, in a few minutes we'll all be getting out to start this amazing ceremony. Are you ready?" Kayla asks her.

She takes another deep breath. "I'm excited. Is that weird?"

"No. I was excited on my wedding day, but I felt like I didn't breathe until after I said 'I do,' and then it was all a breeze from there." She gives her a warm smile.

She chuckles. "That's kind of how I feel. I keep taking deep breaths, like I'm gasping for air, but I'm excited, not really nervous." She rubs her hands together and suddenly the door opens.

"They are ready for you." Uncle Jasper gives her a huge smile and we all pile out of the air conditioned limo.

"Damn, it's a hot one today," Lilly fans herself.

"Come on, girls. Let's get you into place before you all melt in this heat." Aunt Kenderly ushers us to the side of the house where we're supposed to wait for the music to start so we can make our entrance into the backyard. The honor guard stands by the entrance we are to walk through, as we enter there's a white path telling us how to get to the archway set up in the shade toward the back of the yard. I peek around the corner to see the yard is filled with people, most of which are our family. There are teachers from the school, and I believe one of Kenzie's cousins made it.

The air is sucked from my chest when I spot them. Remy and Vaughn are standing together in uniform and they look amazing. They hug it out and Remy takes his spot at the altar with Dawson by his side. The music begins and Kayla begins her walk down the aisle. I turn to Kenzie. "You look gorgeous." I give her a quick hug and begin my walk down next with Lilly following. When we're all lined up, I can't help but glance around the yard at all the decorating that was done today. There are white tablecloths on each table with red and blue napkins. There's a huge chalkboard set up with the schedule for the day in military time. Vaughn catches my attention and winks at me when the music changes and Kenzie walks down the aisle holding on to Uncle Jasper. I can't help but giggle at her boots peeking out from her dress and I know the minute Remy catches it because he bursts into laughter. As soon as she's at the altar and Uncle Jasper has given her away, he pulls her in and tells her she's amazing. He's about to kiss her when the priest reminds him that it's not time for that yet and we all laugh.

The priest says his speech and they go through their vows, both my mom and Aunt Kenderly light the candles, and they light their unity candle, which I absolutely love. It's white with camouflage wrapped around both the single tapers and the bigger one that they lit together. They once again take their place, and after a few more words from the priest, he's finally announcing them husband and wife. The honor guard has taken their places at the altar again, lining the aisle. Remy and Kenzie finally turn to their guests. "I'm honored to introduce to you for the very first time, Mr. and Mrs. Remington Scott Bennett." Everyone in the yard claps and cheers for my brother and his wife. My eyes well with tears of joy. I'm so happy for my brother and I'm excited to have a new sister-in-law. The honor guards raise their swords up in the air and Remy and Kenzie step down to walk under them. When they get to the end guys, their swords drop, stopping them in their place. Remy leans in and kisses Kenzie sweetly while the photographer snaps a dozen pictures. The swords go back up in the air for the rest of us to walk under. Lilly walks down with Dawson, I walk down with Vaughn, and Kayla walks down with Keaton.

When Vaughn links his arm with mine, I can't help but look up at him. "You look mighty fine in that uniform, Vibe," I tease.

He chuckles grabbing my arm and walking me out to the front of the house where we're going to take a few pictures. "Yeah, well, you look delicious in that red dress." I bite my lip and fight the blush that creeps up on me. The photographer starts snapping pictures of Remy and Kenzie as we follow behind them, honor guard included.

When the photographer announces for everyone to stand around the bride and groom in any order, we all bunch in. Vaughn being tall is toward the back, and I stand in front of him. The photographer gives a few directions and then hands two of the honor guard guys each an end of a sign that they hold up for the shot. She tells Remy and Kenzie to kiss, and as soon as they do, she starts snapping pictures. She tells us to look at her and smile, then she tells us to turn our heads to face the bride and groom with excitement. When we're done, we get to see the sign says 'Mission Accomplished.' I can't wait to see these photos.

It takes a while, but we finally manage to get through all of the photos that Kenzie and Remy wanted of their bridal party and family. Luckily, the catering staff had been walking around with appetizers, because we're starving at this point. We finally make our way to the backyard, where there's a reserved table for the bridal party, as well as the honor guard. Once we're seated, the photographer takes a few more pictures and the DJ announces that it's time for the first dance. We all watch Kenzie and Remy take to the dance floor that was set up in the yard. They sway to *Wanted* by Hunter Hayes, staring into each other's eyes Remy sings to her and she can't stop smiling. They look absolutely blissful together.

Their song comes to an end, and when it does, wait staff appear by the table with plates of food for us. They're holding them up with covers on them, waiting for Remy and Kenzie to take their seats. As soon as they do, the plates are placed in front of us and the covers removed. The wedding is set up buffet style, but Kenzie wanted her bridal party served. We all put an order in for what we wanted off the buffet and the staff served it. I told her I didn't think it was necessary but she disagreed. The caterers send the honor guard up to get their dinner and then start sending the remainder of our guests.

I look over to Vaughn, who sits beside me. "How's your food?"

He wipes his mouth. "This is so good. I love southern barbecue food."

"For a New Yorker you certainly fit in down here."

"Good, because I don't plan on leaving." He has a grin on his face. "Listen, will you stay with me tonight?"

"Is that what you want?" I'm so excited, but I'm really trying not to show how eager I am.

"Well, you know Brody really misses you, and I think it would be good for him if you spent the night," he teases. My jaw drops and I smack him playfully. "I'm kidding. Yes, that's what I'd like. I meant it last night when I said I miss you."

"Then yes, I'll stay with you."

Dinner is finally over and I'm thrilled, because

that means we all get to change. Remy doesn't know it, but we all had t-shirts made up and they're in my room for us to change into. "You ladies ready to get out of these clothes?"

Remy looks at Kenzie, shocked. "What do you mean out of these clothes?"

"We were smart enough to plan a change." She wiggles her brows at him. "I warned you."

He laughs. "Okay, let's see what you have in mind." We all hurry up from the table and run into the house. Once we close my bedroom door, we all start stripping out of our dresses and into our shorts, olive green sneakers, and camouflage shirts. "Kenzie, catch." I toss her the shirt that says **'Army Bride'** on it with dog tags. All of ours say **'The Bride's Crew'** with dog tags on them. We can't help but giggle at our appearance. We all still have formal makeup on with our hair all done up, but we're now wearing kick ass t-shirts with sneakers. Kenzie is still in her boots and she has her garters on for Remy to toss shortly. After a quick selfie, we make our way back out to the party. When we do, we find the guys in total shock. Even Kayla, who is very prim and proper, is wearing shredded jean shorts and sneakers. Dawson's jaw drops when he sees her, and I can't help but wonder if baby number three will be conceived tonight.

Everyone starts clapping when they notice us on the back porch. The photographer runs over and snaps some more pictures, asking the Honor Guard to jump in for a few. It's going to make for some great memories. The guys burst into laughter. "You ladies look great! I'm glad we'll match." Remy

182

turns to his guys and says, "Shall we?" They all nod their agreement and head inside as well. This wedding is getting interesting. It went from formal to casual really quick. I'm glad my mom told everyone to dress comfortable for a summer backyard wedding because I would feel bad that we were so dressed down.

Mom and Aunt Kenderly come out a few minutes later, getting their first glimpse of us. "You ladies look awesome."

"Hey, Kayla, did you see the look on Dawson's face when he saw you?"

"Yeah, I thought he was going to fall over. He hasn't seen me dressed like this in years. I have to admit it feels good to let my hair down, so to speak."

Suddenly the music changes and the guys come walking out wearing khakis and white t-shirts that say **'Groom'** and **'Groom's Crew'** in camouflage. We all burst into laughter because we really do match and we didn't even try.

"I think it's time for some fun!" I shout. Vaughn takes my hand and leads me to the dance floor. We start dancing, and next thing we know people are joining us. We're having a great time, Kayla and Dawson are dancing next to us, and even Lilly and Keaton are dancing. They were once a couple, and although I don't see them getting back together, it's nice to see them getting along. *One Dance* by Drake starts and the younger crowd erupts into cheers. Vaughn is behind me holding my hips as we sway to the beat. I'm so thankful my man can dance.

It's starting to get dark, but there are lights

kicking on around the yard lighting up the dance floor. He leans down and whispers in my ear, "You look so sexy like this." I turn to face him, but before I can say anything, he plants a soft, sweet kiss on my lips.

"I love you," I remind him. I don't want him to ever doubt my feelings for him.

He smiles. "I love you too." The song comes to an end and the DJ switches it up to something a little slower. If he only knew how perfect the song he chose was. Charlie Puth's *One Call Away*, starts to play, and I start singing to my man, changing superman to superwoman, and he bursts into laughter, but I don't stop because every word of this song is fitting and oh so true. Once I've sung the entire song to him, he wraps me in a hug and doesn't let me go until the DJ announces that it's time to toss the garter and bouquet. I look up at him with a grin. "You're tall, make sure you catch that garter."

"It's mine." He wiggles his brows.

Kenzie sits while Remy kneels before her and slips the garter off her leg. As soon as he does, he stands, pulling Kenzie up off the chair. He holds her hand and has the garter in the other. "Gentlemen, are you ready?" the DJ shouts. When the men all begin clapping their hands, he begins to count. "One, two, three." Remy throws it, and sure enough, Vaughn jumps up and catches it.

He walks over with it in his hand. "It's all you, darlin'." He kisses me and I run out onto the dance floor. Lilly stands next to me and there are a bunch of girls behind me.

Kenzie waves a bouquet similar to hers but smaller. "Ladies, are you ready? There's a fine military man up for grabs tonight." The hell he is, I think. Kenzie turns around with a smile on her face and again the DJ counts to three and she tosses it. I jump, and thanks to my sneakers, I'm quick enough to snatch the bouquet just as another girl is about to.

I look at her with a smile. "Sorry, but he's mine." I walk over with the bouquet in hand and take a seat in the chair Kenzie was originally sitting in. Vaughn is about to slip the garter on my leg when we hear someone clear their throat. We look up and over his shoulder to see my father standing there with his arms crossed. I giggle and Vaughn drops his head with laughter. He stands up, hugs my father, and whispers something in his ear. My father laughs and they shake hands. Vaughn goes back down on one knee and slips the garter into place on my leg. He takes my hand, pulling me from the chair. I take a quick curtsy and we walk off the dance floor. I note it's almost time for the fireworks, and I know he's been watching the time as well.

When we're back at the table, he pulls me close. "Listen, I'm going to get going, but I don't want to pull you away from the fun. When you're ready, why don't you head over?"

"I'm ready. Let's just say bye to my brother and Kenzie. I'll run in and gather a quick bag and we'll get out of here."

"Are you sure?"

"I'm positive." I squeeze his hand and we walk off to find my brother. Once we've said goodbye, I head toward the house.

On the way, I find my mother. "Hey Mama. Vaughn and I are going to leave, but I'll be home sometime tomorrow."

"Okay, dear. You two have a nice night." I kiss my mom on the cheek and Vaughn does the same. I have to hurry if we're going to be out of here before the fireworks start.

"I'm going to tell the valet to pull my car up." He kisses me and runs out of my room, but I'm not far behind him. I'm actually panicking, hoping it doesn't take them long to bring his car over so we can get out of here. We only have about ten minutes before they start. When I get down to the front lawn, I can see he's nervous. He's pacing, waiting for the car. "It's okay. I'll drive if you need me to." He shakes his head no, but doesn't say anything. "Take a few deep breaths, the car will be here any second now."

"I cut it closer than I wanted to." He tries to breathe deeply. The car finally shows up and the valet jumps out. Vaughn hands the guy a tip and we both hurry into the car. We start pulling away, and when we get up the street from my parents' house, the first round of fireworks burst into the air, causing Vaughn to flinch.

"Are you okay?"

"Yeah, sorry. I'm okay." I can see he's totally focused and I don't want to break his concentration, so I sit quietly. About halfway there, I see him start to visibly relax.

Chapter 16

Vaughn

I'm exhausted after the rough night I've had. I was afraid to sleep, I didn't want to have a nightmare and wake Brooke. Brody typically wakes me but I couldn't take any chances. Now she's lying here beside me looking so beautiful. I want to wake her, but when I turn, Brody comes to check on me. I whisper, "Come on, boy." He follows me out of the room. It's still early, but he's used to going out at this time and I hate to break his routine. I grab his leash and take him to the yard, hoping after he does his business, I can get some alone time with Brooke. When he's done and we get back inside, I tell him to lay down. He listens, and like a good boy he gets cozy out here. I go back to my room, strip my clothes, and gently slip back into bed.

Brooke has a small smile on her face, it makes me wonder what exactly she's dreaming about. I slip my hand into her sleep shorts to find she's not wearing any panties, and her pussy is wet. I stifle a groan. I smear her juices all over her clit as I lean in and lick up the vein in her neck to that sensitive spot just below her ear. Her hips start to move. I'm trying to figure out if she's still dreaming or if she's awake. I'm pretty sure she's still sleeping when I gently lift her ass off the bed to slip her shorts down. I fear I'll wake her, but I don't care, I'm not stopping now. I'm starving for her. Crawling under the covers, I plant myself between her legs, lapping up her juices. If she wasn't awake before, she is now. Using my fingers, I spread her beautiful pink lips wide and devour her clit. She whimpers when I scrape my teeth over her throbbing nub. "Damn, Vaughn," she pants.

"Good morning, love. Are you ready to come?"

I can tell from her moan that she's biting her lip when I dive back in. Her hips roll but I hold her still. I've missed her and I know she wants to come, but I want to savor this. I press two fingers inside of her, gently curling them to ensure I hit that special spot. "Fuck, Vaughn. I'm going to come." She bucks her hips as my fingers pound her tight, wet pussy. "Yes," she screams and her legs tighten around my body. She continues to shake while I suck on her clit, setting her up for yet another orgasm. Pulling my fingers from her pussy, I flip her over and pull her ass into the air. I spread her beautiful cheeks and continue eating her like she's my final meal. I know she loves the feeling of my fingers poking at her ass because she pressing back into me, wanting more. I lick from her clit to her ass, spreading her juices and lubing her up as my pinky continues poking at her. "Fuck, yes,

Vaughn," she screams again, sucking in a breath. My thumb strums her clit as my tongue sinks into her and it's exactly what she needs to fall over. I grip her hips to stop her from collapsing as I suck up every last drop of her release.

"My lord, woman, you taste fucking amazing." She giggles and the sound is music to my ears. She rolls onto her back as I climb up the bed to get a condom from the nightstand. She takes it from me, pulls my boxers down, and rolls the condom over my extremely hard cock. She lines me up with her entrance and I gently thrust my hips forward until I'm balls deep inside of her. I gently begin rolling my hips, gradually picking up the pace, but she wants more. She plants her feet on the bed, thrusting her hips forward to meet me. The rhythm we've created is amazing. "Brooke, I'm sorry, darlin', but I'm not going to last."

"Oh God, that feels so good."

"Come on, Brooke, squeeze my cock." I slam into her a few more times and she does as I ask. Her pussy tightens around me, squeezing me and sending me over the edge as we both ride out our orgasms together. I lay on top of her with my cock still buried inside her pussy while we both try to calm our breathing. I rub my nose on hers. "How did you sleep?"

"Good, but shouldn't I be asking you that?" Gripping the condom, I slip out of her and walk to the bathroom to dispose of it, totally ignoring her question. When I get back she's lying there waiting for my answer.

"What?" I question.

"You completely ignored me. I thought we agreed you were going to let me help you. Don't shut me out the first question I ask." She sits up in my bed, her perky little nipples poking through her sleep shirt.

I sit on the edge of the bed, resting my head in my hands. "Give me a break, Brooke. I'm not used to this." I exhale a deep breath. "I didn't sleep well. I was afraid I would have a nightmare and wake you."

I feel the bed dip behind me as she sits and presses her cheek to my back. "Thank you." She kisses my spine and crawls back into the bed. "Come here." I turn to see her patting my side of the bed. I climb back in, wanting nothing more than to please her. We've had such a nice morning so far. "Let's catch up. I feel like it's been a while since we really talked about everyday life."

I rest my head on her chest. "Okay, what have you been up to?"

"Did you know I went to look at a house for rent?"

"I didn't. Tell me about it." I feel my eyes getting heavy, but I really want to hear about her house.

She's rubbing her hands through my hair. "Well, it wasn't my dream house. Actually nowhere near close to my dream house. The location was perfect, and the size wasn't bad, but it's not what I want. I told the landlord I would get back to him by tomorrow."

"What did it look like?" I question, but my voice is almost a mumble. She's making me tired playing with my hair.

"It was two bedrooms, two baths on one floor. The living room and kitchen were very open to one another, which I liked, but everything was very outdated. Keaton and Remy went with me to look at it. Keaton said there was nothing major to stress over, but all three of us agreed since I'm not on a deadline to move out, I would keep looking." My eyes are closed and my breathing is picking up when I tell her I would love to help her look. "After you rest." She kisses me on the head and continues stroking my hair until I'm asleep.

I wake to the smell of bacon cooking and it smells damn good. I must have fallen asleep on Brooke while she was telling me about the house. I look over to see it's now almost ten. Holy shit, I've been sleeping for a good five hours. I climb out of bed, step into some lounge pants, and head to the kitchen where Brooke gives Brody some peanut butter. "I'm sorry, Brooke."

"Don't be. It was my plan. I was hoping if you fell asleep holding me, you would stay asleep for a bit and get some rest. Brunch is almost done. Why don't you grab yourself some coffee?"

I pet Brody on the head. "Why does he get peanut butter?" I nod my head toward the dog with a smile on my face.

"Because while you were sleeping, we did some work in the yard, and he was such a good boy." Her voice changes to a baby voice for the second half of her sentence.

I sip my coffee. "He is a good boy. I'm so lucky to have him. He wakes me from most nightmares before I even realize I'm having them."

"Are you hungry?" She changes the subject.

I lean in close to her ear. "Why yes, I am." I kiss the spot just below her ear, sending a shiver through her body.

She smacks me playfully. "I mean for food."

"Yeah, well, there's that too," I joke. She pulls bacon from the oven and uncovers two pans, one has scrambled egg whites and the other has potatoes in it. "Wow, you went all out, thank you."

"You're welcome." She grabs the two plates she's pulled from the cabinets and begins loading one up with food. She hands me the plate and starts making hers. I put the plate on the table and fill our coffee cups, that way we can sit and eat together. I take my seat and wait for her to finish taking the bacon off the pan. She turns to me. "What are you doing? Eat."

"I'm not eating until you sit down. My mom taught me better than that."

She grins and takes her seat. "Fine, I'll clean up more after we eat. Your mama sounds sweet. I wish she lived closer. Maybe we can get her to come down here for a visit."

"I'll talk to her and see what I can work out." I dig into my breakfast as does she. "Now, what should we do today?"

"Well, I thought we could do one thing to help each of us."

My brows furrow. "How do you mean?"

"Well, I need to look for a place. I thought maybe we could spend a little time looking for places online, and then after we do that, we can do some research on programs to help you with your PTSD."

Shit. She's really going to push me through this, and I'm not sure if I should be happy or frustrated. It's hard to even discuss it, but maybe we can find something without me having to actually share with her what I went through. "Okay," I squeeze out in between bites of food. I feel bad because I can't even manage to look at her when I say it.

"Hey. Look at me, Vaughn." She can read me like a damn open book. "I'm just asking that we look, not saying you have to necessarily sign up for anything." I nod my head finishing my breakfast. When she's done she clears the table and I begin putting the leftover food in containers. She's a clean cook, we're done cleaning up in a matter of minutes. She sits back down with a fresh cup of coffee. "Do you have a laptop?" I could easily lie and tell her no, but that would be wrong on so many levels, so I go into the other room to grab the laptop I hardly ever use and I boot it up. She slides her seat closer to mine, and as soon as the computer is up and running, she starts searching for houses to rent. There are two new ones listed and she's excited about both of them. She requests a view on them, pointing out that they are only about fifteen minutes from my house.

"You know what that means?" A grin spreads across my face.

"What's that?"

"You're close enough that Brody and I can come spend the night at your house and I'll still be close enough for work."

She giggles. "That was the plan, love." I love how good it makes me feel to think she was purposely looking for something close to me.

Next she opens Google, and after typing in a few searches she finds some self-help tools that actually could help me. There's even an app I can download on my phone to keep with me as a coaching tool. It covers everything from sleep, to anxiety, and even my flashbacks. I jump up to grab my phone and I quickly download the app. While I'm looking through it, she continues doing her research on the computer. "Hey, have you tried doing stuff like this with your guys?" She points out a bowl and dine that's happening on the base. "Or maybe doing some other sports with them?"

I shrug my shoulders. "Not really, never thought to."

"From what I've read, it could be good for you. There's a program that actually organizes sports for veterans with PTSD, but it's like four hours away. I'm thinking maybe if you got into something like that here, it may serve the purpose without it being directly linked."

"I'm not opposed to playing sports. The bowl and dine will be cool for my guys and I because they can get there easily. Two of the guys don't have cars, so it's hard for them to do stuff off of base." She smiles and clicks the button to get more info. When it all pops up on the screen, I send a group text to my guys giving them with the info and wait for a reply to see who's in. A golf event pops up and she gives me a look. I quickly shake my head. "I'm not a golfer at all." She laughs at my expression. "Oh, you find that funny?" My brows shoot up and there's laughter in my voice.

"No, I find the face you made funny. You would think I asked you to make out with Callen." She laughs harder.

Now I have to tease her. "Now that I would do. There's no more don't ask, don't tell."

Her eyes go wide. "That's not funny. You know damn well you don't go that way."

I laugh. "No, I don't, especially after having your sweet little pussy. There's no way in hell anyone else's will do." Holy shit, the blush that creeps up her face is adorable.

I can't believe it's already after lunchtime, but the time flies by because we're relaxed and totally enjoying each other's company.

She gets up to dump her cold coffee and place her cup into the dishwasher. "Listen, I should get home soon. Lord only knows what kind of mess my parents have after yesterday."

"Let's grab a quick shower and I'll get you home." She nods and thanks me.

We pull up to her parents' house a short time later and the banner from yesterday is still hanging in the front of the house. "What are your plans for the rest of the day?"

I shrug. "Head back home and do some reading on that app I downloaded, and then get ready for work tomorrow."

"Can I call you later?"

"Of course." She leans over to kiss me goodbye and then jumps out of the car. I sit watching her run into the house, thinking about how lucky I am. I need to work on pulling my shit together. I don't want to lose her.

Chapter 17

Vaughn

Walking out of my office, I find my guys cleaning up around the shop as our day winds down. "Good work today, guys." They gather around. "Don't forget about bowl and dine next weekend, and you're welcome to bring a girlfriend or friend if you'd like. I know Brooke and Courtney will be hanging with us."

"They need to gather some more friends for us." Max wiggles his brows.

I shake my head. "Sorry, man, my girl's not much of a partier. She spent the last eight years busting her ass in school. I don't think she'll be bringing too many more friends around."

"My girl and I broke up, so it'll be just me." Nolin looks relieved.

"Sorry to hear that, man." Callen slaps him on the back.

Surprisingly, Nolin laughs. "I'm not, she was getting to be a pain in my ass. Always complaining

197

about my career choice. She wanted to hang twenty-four-seven and I can't do that shit. I want to go somewhere with my fucking career and I won't get there with her up my ass."

"But you have such a nice ass." Max slaps him fucking around.

"Okay, okay. I'm out of here. I have to go meet my girl to look at a house. Callen, make sure everything is locked up tight." Brooke called me last night, really excited that she'd heard back from the landlord on the house that she really liked, and asked me if I'd go with her and Keaton to look at it.

He shakes my hand and tells me he has my back. I thank him and run to the men's room to change into civilian clothes before leaving. I don't like going off base in uniform. It draws attention to me, and that's not something I'm comfortable with. Brooke has two houses to look at, but tonight we're only looking at one. This is the one she's most excited about, and when we're done, we're grabbing dinner at a little mom and pop place up the street. I think it's called Joanie's or something like that. She says she's heard that they have awesome home cooked southern meals, and being that I love southern food, she thinks it'll be a good place for us.

I pull up to the address she gave me and as promised, it's not even fifteen minutes from the base. This is going to be awesome. It's a nice house. There's a gorgeous farmer's porch that runs half the length of the house. The outside looks very well kept, from the siding to the landscaping. I can see why she's so excited about this place. Brooke pulls in next with Keaton right behind her.

The three of us get out of our cars. Keaton shakes my hand and gives me a man hug. "How's it going, man?"

"Good. How's the business?"

"Crazy." He hugs his sister and then she comes over to me and gives me a kiss.

The three of us walk up to the house. "How was your day, sweetie?"

"It was good. Nothing too crazy blew up on us," she says as a gentleman steps onto the porch.

"Hello, you must be Brooke." He's a sweet older man.

She sticks out her hand. "Yes, sir and this is my brother, Keaton, and my boyfriend, Vaughn."

The guys all shake hands and exchange pleasantries. "Great, let's head on inside and I'll show you around." He opens the door for us and we all step into a gorgeous kitchen that has light wood cabinets and granite counter tops. I can already see how excited Brooke is about this place. There's a small dining room to one side of the kitchen and on the other is a spacious living room with a slider that leads to a huge backyard.

"Can we check out the bedrooms?" Brooke's face lights up.

"Of course, feel free to roam. I'll give you some privacy." He leans against the countertop while the three of us wander down the hall. Keaton walks off checking out windows and plumbing while we look at the spacious bedrooms. This house actually has three bedrooms. One of them is quite small, but would make a nice office space for Brooke, while the other two are nice size rooms. The two larger rooms have walk-in closets and the master has its own bathroom. The bathroom has dark cabinets and a light granite counter top. It's awesome to see Brooke walking around with a huge smile on her face. I can tell she really likes the place and I'm thrilled for her.

Keaton comes walking into the back room. "Hey, this place is in good shape. You shouldn't have any problems. It has central air too, which the last house didn't have."

"Good, because I love it. Now I just have to confirm one thing with Mr. Jacobson and I'll be good to go." Keaton and I follow her into the kitchen where the owner is still leaning on the counter. "Mr. Jacobson, you have a beautiful house here."

"I'm glad you like it." He smiles with pride.

"I only have one question for you." She links her fingers with mine.

"Shoot."

"My boyfriend has a dog, and it's important to me that he can come here once in a while. Would you be opposed to me having pets in the house?"

He sighs, and I can see the fear in Brooke's face as he contemplates his answer. I'm about to tell Brooke not to sweat it, but he finally smiles. "You're a veterinarian, right?"

"That's correct."

"I assume that means you know how to take good care of animals. I'll tell you what, if you're willing to give me an extra five hundred in your deposit just in case, then I'll allow animals in the house."

She jumps up and down, clapping her hands, she's so excited. "That's fine. I know there won't be any damage. He's a great dog and I promise to keep the house really clean."

The gentleman smiles. "Well, I'll run your background check, and as long as everything comes out good, we have a deal." He holds out his hand and they shake. I hold mine out next and thank him for agreeing to the pet, and for his time. We all walk out of the house, and when I get to the front lawn, Keaton hugs his sister goodbye and shakes my hand.

"Are you ready to get some dinner?"

"Yes, I'm famished." She steps closer, grabs my shirt, and pulls me down for a kiss. "Thank you for being here today."

"Angel, there's nowhere else I'd rather be. Come on, I need to feed you."

I walk her to her car and open the door for her, but she quickly turns to me. "Speaking of feeding, who has Brody?"

I love that this woman cares so much for my dog. "Callen has Brody." A huge smile spreads across her face and she climbs in. "I'll follow you." She nods and I close her door. I jump into my car and we head off. She's right, the place isn't far at all. It takes us maybe ten minutes to get there.

We pull into the lot and manage to find two spots side by side. She meets me at the back of the car, our fingers instantly interlock, and we walk into Joanie's BBQ hand in hand.

As soon as we're through the door, we're greeted

by a young hostess. "Two?" she questions.

"Yes, please," I respond.

She smiles and says, "Right this way." We follow her to a corner booth. Brooke slips in and I sit directly beside her. I like sitting next to her as opposed to across from her. "Here are some menus. Your waitress will be right over.

"Thank you." Brooke gives her a smile and we both begin looking over the menu.

There's so much to choose from for a small place, I'm quite impressed. The place is simple with just a few pictures scattered about the walls. The smells coming from the kitchen have my stomach rumbling. "I think I'm going to get messy and have some ribs." I put my menu down and wait for Brooke to decide.

She places her menu on top of mine and tells me she's all set too. The waitress comes over and we place our order. She's going with pulled pork. "How's the sleep been going?"

"Not too bad. I've been trying some things that the app suggests and it's seems to be helping, I guess. Brody woke me last night, but I don't remember dreaming anything, and I was able to go right back to sleep."

"He's probably learning the sounds and movements you make while you're dreaming, and so he's able to help you quicker. What are some of the things you're trying?" I chuckle as I try to figure out what to say. "What's so funny?" she asks.

I suddenly feel self-conscious over the things I've been trying, and I don't like it. That's not typically me. I think it's one of my biggest struggles lately. I feel weak, and usually I'm strong and confident. "It's just some of the things they recommend sound strange. Like there's a video about relaxing your body. I've tried it both nights. I feel foolish doing it, but if it's going to help, then I'll continue to do it as long as I'm alone. I also started drinking night time tea."

"I like night time tea. I haven't drank it in a while, but I used to get anxiety over tests and the stress would keep me up, so I would use that to help me unwind."

"It's pretty good. I don't mind the taste of it. One of the coaching tips was to change the way I think about sleep, and it makes a lot of sense, but it's easier said than done." The first time I watched the video of this woman speaking in a slow relaxed voice, I wanted to scream at the coach. See the things I see in my sleep and tell me you can change the way you think about sleep. "I'll be honest, at first I thought it was complete bullshit, but then I went through the videos and listened to them. It started to make sense." I shrug my shoulders and look down at the place mat on the table.

She puts her hand on mine and gives it a squeeze. "I'm proud of you. You've tried something outside of your comfort zone." I feel like a fucking pansy, but I bite my tongue because clearly she's happy with the effort I'm putting in.

"Thanks, I'm really trying." The waitress puts our food down in front of us. "Listen, I really want us to move forward in our relationship, I love you, but I need to take some time to pull my stuff together so I don't hurt you again." I turn to face her and she has a look of fear on her face. "Sweetie, I'm not saying I want us to break up, but I want us to sleep apart until I know I'm doing better with the nightmares. I'd never forgive myself if I attacked you again. What if I hurt you?"

"I get it, and I think it's brave of you to admit it." She digs into her pulled pork.

"You do?" I thought she was going to freak out on me. I don't want to hurt her physically or emotionally, but I need to make myself stronger for both of us.

"I do, and when you're ready for us to start spending the night together again, you let me know."

Lord, how did I end up lucky enough to have a wonderful woman like this? "Here's the thing. I haven't had an episode like I did at the beach in a while, and as a matter of fact, it only happened one other time. It's how I learned that fireworks were a trigger for me, and now I know sand at the beach can be too. I think part of the reason I had the episode at the beach was because I was tired. I'm thinking if I can get my sleep under control and continue working on the other self-coaching tips, then I'll be okay. That said, if I can keep the nightmares at bay, then come next weekend when we get together for the Bowl and Dine event on the base, maybe you'll consider staying with me at my place?"

A huge smile spreads across her face. "I'd love that." She just made my night. I know she's happy, and now I have something to aim for. I've always been a goal-based person. I'll bust my ass over the next week and a half doing my exercises to make sure I'm better for her, and then I'm going to plan a really romantic night for the two of us. "What's that grin for, Vibe?" She nudges me with her shoulder. I can't believe she used my nickname.

I laugh. She busted me in my dirty thoughts. "I'm sorry. I was just thinking about how happy you make me and how lucky I am to have such an understanding girlfriend." I wiggle my brows at her.

She bites her lip and leans in. "I find myself pretty lucky too." She kisses me gently. "And I love you."

The waitress comes back over. "Is there anything else I can get you two?"

"Shall we share some peach cobbler?" I continue staring into Brooke's beautiful blue eyes. She barely nods but it's enough to tell me what she wants.

I look up to the waitress. "We would like to share some peach cobbler please."

She laughs at our flirting. "I'll be back with your dessert and some containers for your leftovers."

"Thank you." I give her a smile and she walks off.

The waitress comes back a few minutes later with our dessert and the containers she promised. Once we pack up our leftovers, I pick up the spoon and dig into the cobbler, feeding the first bite to Brooke, who licks her lips and opens wide. When the cobbler hits her tongue, she closes her eyes and moans gently, savoring the flavor. The look of ecstasy on her face makes my cock twitch. She's slowly chewing the dessert with her eyes closed. "You keep that up and you'll be back at my house, so I can put that same look on your face."

She opens her eyes and giggles. "Sorry, but that's some pretty heavenly cobbler." She picks up her spoon and scoops some up. I thought she was going to take more for herself, but she returns the favor and feeds it to me. Damn, she's right—this cobbler is delicious. We continue feeding each other until our dessert is almost gone. That's when the waitress drops the bill. I ask her to hold on a second and I instantly hand over my credit card so she can run it. It's getting late, and we both have to work tomorrow.

As soon as the waitress returns with my slip and card, I sign it, setting it aside for her. "Are you ready, sweetie?"

"Yeah, I'm pretty tired." A yawn escapes her.

I take her hand and walk her to her car. When we get there, I feel like there's so much I need to say, but I can't come up with the right words. "Thank you for having dinner with me."

"Vaughn." She looks down for a second, and then back up at me. "I've waited a while now for you to see me as a woman and not Remy's sister. I want you to know it was worth the wait and I'm not going anywhere. Take care of yourself so we can move forward. Show me the man I know you are."

I nod. "Good night." I give her a chaste kiss and open the car door for her.

She climbs in, and just before I close the door, she tells me she loves me. I close my eyes, taking in her words. When I open them, her window is down. "I love you too, more than you know." I turn and walk away, not wanting her to see this weaker side of me.

Chapter 18

Brooke

I've had an amazing week. Vaughn and I have spoken every night, either via text or phone call, and we've had some great conversations. I'm so proud of him for trying all of these new things, and he says they seem to be working. He hasn't woken up during the night since Tuesday, and he sounds thrilled…although I'll admit he sounded slightly off last night before going to bed when we started discussing Bowl and Dine today. I think he's just nervous about me sleeping over again, but we'll see what happens, because first we need to have some fun with our friends.

Courtney is on her way over to get ready with me. I know it makes us sound like we're teenagers instead of in our late twenties, but we don't care, it's fun. I run to my closet, grabbing some things and laying them out on the bed to try and decide what I'll wear, but since I'm struggling, I grab my overnight bag and toss what I need into it, so at least that's ready. No sooner do I zip up the bag and Courtney comes bursting through the door. "I'm glad I wasn't naked or anything."

"Like it would be the first time I saw you naked." She stands with her hands on her hips.

"True. Come help me pick an outfit." She struts over to my bed to see the three outfits I have laid out. The first is shredded shorts with a floral print top that I haven't worn in ages. The second outfit has shorts that go to just above my knee, but have shred holes in them and a turquoise short sleeved shirt, and the third outfit was plain dark jean shorts and a bright pink top. She studies them like there's a right and wrong answer, and if she doesn't get it right, she'll end up in jail. "This isn't a test," I finally tease her.

"Fine, the middle outfit." She struts to my closet in search of the shirt I told her she could borrow.

I laugh and grab the other clothes to put them back. "Good, that's the one I was feeling too."

"Then why did you ask me?"

"To see if we were on the same page."

She shakes her head and rolls her eyes. "Brooke, you act like you have a single outfit in all of these clothes that wouldn't look amazing on you."

I shrug and say nothing. You always look at other people's clothes different than you look at your own. "Come on. I want to curl your hair." I grab her arm and pull her toward the bathroom across the hall. One of the upsides to this house being empty is I don't have to share the bathroom with my brothers, and soon I'll have a bathroom of my own. I finally heard back from my landlord, and of course I passed my background check, which means I get to sign the lease on my house Monday after work. I'm so excited and can't wait to tell Vaughn tonight. Courtney and I are going to go furniture shopping this week with Mama. She wants to come with us, it's going to be so much fun.

Courtney plops down on the toilet facing the wall and I get busy curling her hair. I've already done mine, but I promised her she could do my makeup. While I was in school there were so few days I would get to go out that we would make the most of them, and since I love doing hair and she likes doing makeup, it's sort of been our thing to swap off.

We both stare into the mirror, happy with our appearance, and in plenty of time for us to get over to the base. Courtney and I are riding together. I told her I would most likely be spending the night at Vaughn's house, since he hasn't mentioned a nightmare in a while. We're meeting the guys at Callen's place, where she'll leave her car, and we'll ride with them to the bowling alley on the base. "Let's roll." She flings her long hair over her shoulder and walks out the door with a sense of purpose.

"Are you two off to your bowling night?"

"Yeah, I'll see you tomorrow, Mama." I kiss her on the cheek.

"Okay, dear. You two have fun, now."

We both giggle like schoolgirls and walk out the door. I put my bag in her trunk and climb into the passenger's seat. "What's up with you and Callen?"

I question as soon as she's taken off.

She huffs. "I don't know. He seems like a nice guy and all, but come on, let's be real. You know my history."

"I do, and all your history means is you haven't found the right guy yet. Now I'm not saying Callen is him, but you won't know unless you give him a fair shot."

"I'm trying. We've talked on the phone a few times and he's taken me to dinner, but it really hasn't gone much further than that." She stops at a red light and glances over at me. "When we do stuff like this he acts thrilled to see me, but then I don't hear from him for a while."

"Have you told him about your ex?"

The light turns green so she takes off again. "Yeah, he said the guy was an asshole for cheating on a great girl like me."

"Well, there you go. Maybe he's just afraid to rush you."

"I guess, or he's really not interested in a relationship and is just trying to get into my pants like the others." She sounds defeated.

I need to change the subject, otherwise our night is going to be ruined. "I don't think that's the case at all, but I don't want to depress you. We're supposed to be having fun." I turn up the music and we both start dancing in the car. It's one of the things I love about Courtney, we both love to dance.

We finally pull up to the base and she rolls down the window. "Callen Johnson is expecting me."

"License," the guy mutters, sounding miserable with his job.

She slips it from her wallet and hands it to him. He looks it over and tells her to have a good day. She puts it back and pulls through to the gate toward Callen's house. When we get there, Callen and Vaughn are sitting on the porch waiting for us. I jump out of the car, really excited to see him. "Are we late?"

He wraps me in a hug. "Nah, we were just chillin', waiting for you." His tone is somber. He sounds off, and it makes me nervous. I hope something didn't happen, setting him back. Not because I wouldn't be able to stay with him, because although that would suck, I'd be more concerned over how he was handling the setback.

"Are you ladies ready?" Callen hits the alarm button on his car, unlocking it.

Courtney gives him a shy smile. "Sure, let's get going."

She slips into the front passenger's seat and Vaughn and I sit in the back. I'm trying to get him to look at me, but he's practically ignoring me, even though he's holding my hand. He and Callen are talking about work and the guys that are coming today. They're arguing over who will be on whose team. There are eight of us, so we can divide up evenly. Apparently this guy Tommy is coming. He never seems to go out with the guys because he's married and has a kid, but they convinced him to come today. Vaughn told him he could bring the family, but he told him it would be just him.

We pull up to the bowling alley at the same time Nolin, Max, and Liam arrive in Nolin's car. We all get out and say hi, and then head in to see if Tommy is here as well but we discover he's not. Callen gives his name, and tells the guy he's registered eight of us for the event. The guy tells us we're on the last two lanes. The event fee covers three games, and we'll be served our food in between the second and third game. He lets us know the waitress will bring us the options we can choose from and begins getting us shoes. Tommy walks in as the guy behind the counter brings Liam his. He quickly gives the guy his size and we head to the end lanes.

When we get there, Callen sits in front of one screen and Vaughn in front of the other. Vaughn programs the names. Our lane consists of Vaughn and I, Liam, and Nolin. Callen's lane is he and Courtney, with Max, and Tommy. The guys quickly introduce us to Tommy, and then we all start looking for balls to throw. I find a pretty purple ball that is a size 8 and Courtney grabs a pink one that also has an eight on it. All the guys are grabbing blue and black ones that are much heavier balls. The guys listed us first in the list. I think it's because they want to see what we've got before they have to throw, but they try to say it's a ladies before gentleman type of thing.

I'm glad to see Vaughn is loosening up a bit. I was starting to think it was going to be a crap night, but he's laughing and seems to be having fun. I step up to the lane, slowly walk to the line, and throw my ball. It slowly curves down the lane and I only manage to hit two pins. I turn around with a pout and the guys laugh, but Courtney made me look good, because she threw a gutter ball. Callen tries to encourage her, but I'm not sure it's working. Liam and Max go next. Liam gets a spare and Max gets a strike. The guys are really having a great time. They're egging each other on, and joking around, and before we know it, the first game is done and we've lost by ten pins. Vaughn is never going to hear the end of it if we don't win a game. "We'll take the next one," I taunt Callen.

"Yeah, we'll see about that." He hits the button to start the next game. The waitress brings us another round of drinks. They sell alcohol but because people have to drive, we've all agreed to stick to soda or water. I kick off the second game with a spare, while Courtney only gets a six.

I stick out my tongue at Callen and take a seat next to Vaughn. "Hey, are you all right? You're awfully quiet."

"I'm fine. I'm having a great time. Are you?"

"Yes, this is a blast." I'm full of excitement.

He gives me a tight smile. "Good." He gets up to take his turn and he gets a strike. It's puts a bit of a pep into his step.

It's my turn again and I really want to get a strike. I'm really focused when Callen decides to be a dick and shouts, "Look out."

I flinch, nearly dropping my ball. I turn around and give him a look that screams *fuck off.* "Dude, my girl is going to fuck your shit up if you keep that up." Vaughn punches Callen in the arm.

"Shit, dude. My bad. I thought it was funny." Callen rubs his arm.

"Go ahead, sweetie, take your time." I line myself up and focus on my shot. This time Callen is smart enough to keep his mouth shut. I throw my ball and it hits perfectly, knocking all ten pins down. I jump up and down, full of excitement. I step down from the lane and Vaughn gives me a high five. "Nice job, sweetie." I wiggle my brows at him and take my seat.

Our food arrives just as we're finishing the second game and things are getting competitive. I'm almost afraid to see what the third game will be like. My arm is getting tired, as is Courtney's. Neither of us are used to repeatedly throwing an eight pound ball around, and who would have thought it could be so exhausting.

Everyone gathers at the table where the waitress has set our food and we dig in. Everyone is starving at this point from the activity, so we eat pretty quickly. Vaughn sits next to me, and again he's really quiet and distant. His leg is bouncing a mile a minute under the table, and he's no longer interacting with his buddies. I'm starting to wonder if it was a bad idea for Courtney and I to come today. "Let's play," Vaughn announces, and storms off to start the next game. What the hell has crawled up his ass? Courtney looks at me with fear in her eyes, and I simply shrug my shoulders, because honestly I have no idea what that was about, but I'm getting frustrated because he's gotten more and more distant as the day has gone on. Even after winning the last game he was cranky. I wonder if he's really not sleeping well and he told me he was because he doesn't want me on his ass. I shake off my thoughts. There's no way he'd lie to me like that. "Let's go, Brooke." Wow, I went from sweetie to Brooke. Well, all right. I walk up the lane and toss my ball haphazardly, not really caring at this point. I knock down three pins with the first ball and manage a spare with the second, and then I take a seat behind him. I'm watching the others bowl while Callen is giving him shit for his attitude. Tension is getting high, and I'm not sure what to do. I'm about ready to storm off, only I can't, because I promised I would be there for him.

The game is going by quickly, and in between throws, Callen tries to get Vaughn to pull his head out of his ass, but it just seems to be making things worse. I take my next two throws, and with only one more turn left for me, I kneel next to Vaughn, trying to be discreet. "Hey, is this attitude because I'm supposed to be spending the night?"

His head whips to mine and he narrows his eyes. "What are you talking about? I never told you we were going there." Tears well in my eyes at his nasty tone.

"When we had dinner…you said that if you were doing well, and you told me you've been sleeping, so I assumed…"

He runs his hand through his wavy hair. "Well, that's the problem. You shouldn't have assumed. Now if you'll excuse me, it's my turn."

I stand up, floored he's talking to me this way. I'm fighting my tears because we're with his friends in a public place and I have nowhere to go. I came with Courtney, and her car is at Callen's still. "Dude, you're being a dick. What the fuck is your problem, man?" Callen stands off with Vaughn, but Vaughn steps around him and throws his ball down the lane, getting a gutter ball. Now he's even angrier.

"I think it's time to call it quits." Tommy starts taking off his bowling shoes and the other guys follow suit.

Vaughn collapses into the chair. With his head in his hands, he looks to the floor and whispers an apology. Callen takes care of everything at the counter while Courtney and I change. By the time we're done, the other guys have all run off. Callen puts his hand on Vaughn's shoulder. "Let's go, man. We need to get the girls back to their car."

"You take them. I'm going to walk, I need to clear my head."

He stands up and his eyes meet mine. "I don't know what has come over you, but when you've gotten your shit figured out, call me. I've tried to be supportive, and to be there for you, and I even understand how I hurt you running out on you after the beach, but that gives you no right to treat me the way you have today. I love you, Vaughn Anderson, but you will treat me the way I deserve to be treated, or you'll lose me forever." I hold my head high and walk toward Courtney, who puts her arm around me comfortingly.

Callen spends the entire car ride apologizing for his friend's behavior. He tells me that he's never seen Vaughn look as good has he has the past week and a half, and now all of a sudden he was on edge today. Maybe we were rushing things when we spoke about spending the night, but if so, that's fine. He should have just said so. I was so on edge the entire time we were together I didn't even get to tell him the good news, and now, I don't care to.

Chapter 19

Brooke

I climb out of bed and stroll over to my window seat. Getting comfortable, I sit and stare into the bright, blue sky. It's a beautiful Saturday morning, and I want nothing more than to spend the day with Vaughn, but I can't. He pushed me away last week and I pushed back. Now I haven't spoken to him other than some text messages back and forth that only led to him telling me he was fucked up and not sure when he'd be able to see me again. A tear runs down my cheek as I think about the sweet man I love running around his backyard with Brody, so calm and carefree. I smile remembering the day I met him. He was leaner than he is now, but just as handsome. We spent the entire week sneaking little touches and flirting with each other behind Rem's back. He was so sweet as we leaned on that tree, and he fed me cotton candy. That night he came so close to kissing me for the first time. I chuckle, but as usual Rem got in the way. I wipe the tears running down my face. Last Fourth of July he was at the house and I was so tempted to talk to him.

That wasn't the man I saw last week, and I want to know where he's gone. His smile plays in my mind repeatedly, as well as the look of relief on his face when I told him I love him, and I do. Now when I'm finally done with school and ready to have a life with the man I love, he's pushing me away. It's time I fight for him, and I think I know the man to help. Remy and Kenzie are coming over for dinner tonight, and I think it's time I fill him in on what his friend is going through. Vaughn won't open up to me, but he will to my brother.

I run off to the shower to get ready for my day. Mama, Courtney, and I are going to my new place to do some cleaning, and then we're going to pick some furniture before we have to be back here for dinner. As soon as I'm done, I hurry downstairs to find Courtney in the kitchen with Mama. "Hey, girl. How you holding up?"

"I'm okay. I know it's only been a week, but I miss him." She rubs my arm. "Actually, I feel like it's been longer because the man we hung with last week, that wasn't my Vaughn. I don't know who that was, but—" I close my eyes. "That wasn't my man."

She nods. "What are you going to do?"

I chuckle. "Well, my big brother always wants to come to my rescue, now he can. I know Vaughn won't open up to me about the things he's experienced, and I understand. He doesn't want to fill my head with that stuff. I get it, but he has no reason not to open up to Rem, and if there's anyone that can help get him on the straight and narrow, it's Remy."

"You really love that man, don't you?" Mama hands me a bottle of water.

I look up at her, proud. "From the moment his lips first touched mine."

Mama puts her arm around me. "I think you loved him even before that. You know you remind me so much of me, sweetie. Your father and I had a similar situation. He never deployed or served, but we fell instantly in love, and I knew from the moment he first touched me I would be spending my life with him."

I rest my head on her shoulder. "Thanks, Mama. I just hope he can see it too."

"He will. Men are difficult, girls," Mama says to both of us. "But when you have someone you love with all your heart, you have to hold on tight and enjoy the ride no matter where it takes you. Love is not meant to be all peaches and cream. There are ups and downs and so many bumps along the journey. It's how you handle the bumps that make your relationship stronger. You have to learn to rely on one another, and right now that's the part Vaughn is having a hard time with." I nod and wipe away a tear that escaped me. "Don't you fret, your brother had the same problem with Kenzie. He came around and now look at them. They'll be here later to regale us with stories of their honeymoon. Now no more depressing talk. We need to have some girl time shopping." I chuckle and the three of us get up from our stools. Mama grabs a basket full of cleaning supplies, and we head out to my house.

When we get to the house, it's dark because all of the blinds are closed. The first thing we do after we've unloaded the vacuum and mops that I've bought is go around letting light in. "Brooke, you start here in the kitchen." Mama drops a few things for me to use. She hands Courtney a duster. "Courtney, you get to dust everything, and I'm going to clean the two bathrooms."

I pull my phone from my back pocket and open up a playlist of music for us to listen to while we clean. I start with wiping down the very top of the cabinets and then move to the inside of the cabinets, down to the countertops and sink, before I clean the lower cabinets. Now there's dust all over the floor. I grab my vacuum and clean it all up until I'm happy with the way it looks. It's taken me a while to clean it, but I'm happy it's ready for some dishes and everything else I'll need to keep in here. I continue vacuuming into the living room, helping Courtney take care of the dust from having the house closed up. By the time we're done with these two rooms, Mama is done with my master bathroom. I take the vacuum into the two guest rooms, and then into the master.

When I'm done, I store the vacuum in the hall closet and get busy mopping the kitchen while Courtney dust mops the hardwood floors in my living room. It's taken us a good few hours, but the house smells fresh and clean. It's now ready for furniture to be delivered.

Mama comes out of the guest bathroom. "This place looks great. You picked a beautiful home, Brooke. I'm proud of you."

"Thanks, Mama. I love this house, but I was just thinking about how much stuff I'm going to need." I shake my head.

"One day at a time, sweetie." She puts all the supplies back into the bucket and places it under the sink.

"Mama, why are you leaving your bucket under there?"

She smiles. "That's your bucket. I bought it for you to have here. There was no sense in taking my supplies to bring them back home when you would need them, anyway."

I chuckle. "Thanks, Mama."

"You're welcome. Now, let's hit the store."

We pull up to the furniture store a short time later. We picked one not too far from my house, hoping to make delivery simple and cheap. We walk in and we're all shocked by how big the place is, you would never know it from the outside. There's a woman sitting at a counter as we look around in amazement. "How can we help you ladies today?" the woman greets us.

"My daughter is renting a home and needs to furnish it. We're looking for a bedroom set, living room set, and a table with chairs."

The woman smiles at the prospect of a huge sale. "Let me get you some help." She speaks into a walkie talkie and a woman approaches us.

"Hello, ladies. I'm Marcie, how can I help?"

I tell her again what we're looking for and she walks us over to the bedroom sets first. Eventually I would like to furnish the other two rooms as well, but like Mama says, one day at a time. I need to start with necessities. She leads us to an elevator and takes us up a level. When we step off the elevator, we are surrounded by bedroom sets. After about thirty minutes of wandering around, I finally spot my set. It's a solid oak queen size bed. It has a bureau with mirror, nightstand, and dresser. "Mama, do you think it'll fit?"

"For sure. It's beautiful," she agrees.

"I'll take it." The woman makes some notes on her clipboard and we move on to the living room next. After another hour and a half of shopping, I finally find everything I need, but I'm exhausted. Who knew furniture shopping could be so tiring? We follow the woman back to the front of the store, where she finalizes my order and sets up the delivery. Unfortunately, in order for everything to be delivered on the same day, it will take almost two weeks for them to get it to me. I mark the delivery date into my phone, along with a reminder to ask that I not be on-call that weekend. We have a new assistant starting this week, so hopefully that won't be an issue. When we're finally done and I have all my paperwork in hand, we start toward the car.

"One more stop," Mama says.

"Where?" I question.

"Don't you fret." She gets into the driver's seat and pulls out of the lot.

We pull up to this huge store that carries everything I could possibly need for the house. We grab two carts and Mama and Courtney help me pick plates, knives, utensils, and cups. We then move on to bedding. I pick a set for my room that's a turquoise blue paisley print. It has shams and curtains to match. We also pick some nice decorative pillows and a small lamp for when I want to read at night. I'm exhausted and I want to go home but Mama insists we still have to pick towels and curtains for the two bathrooms. Of course I can't disagree, I couldn't shower at my place if I wanted to because there are no curtains hung in either shower.

When we get to the bathroom section, I find a seashell set for the guest bathroom that is really pretty. We collect everything including hooks, matching towels, a trash can, and floor mats. I look at my cart and shake my head at the dent that I'm about to make in my savings account. Then we move on, looking for my bathroom. I find a set that is the same colors of turquoise and blue, again grabbing everything we need. We pile it all into my cart. I look at my mom with my brows raised. "Anything else you can think of?"

She checks her watch. "No. I think we've covered it. Plus we have to go. Your brother will be at the house any minute." I close my eyes and try to take a deep breath, because I've been trying to get her out of here for a while now, so she wouldn't be late for my brother getting home, and now all of a sudden she's worried about it. This woman can be infuriating sometimes. We walk up to the checkout counter, and on the way mama sees a stack of welcome mats. She stops. "Wait. You can't have home without a welcome mat. It's like a curse." She exaggerates, but makes me pick a mat and throws the one of my choice into her cart.

224

I begin unloading the cart onto the belt and Mama approaches the cashier, asking if they can bring another cart over. The bagger runs off to get one and I continue to unload. By the time I'm done with the first cart, they've already filled the empty one. Mama hands mine off to the girl and I continue to unload. I finally finish emptying the second cart and the girl asks for it, because they were small and overflowing with stuff. I push it down to her as Courtney pushes one out of the way. I go back to the register, and when the gentleman says my total, I nearly vomit, but I dig into my bag for my credit card. Before I can take it out, he hands my mother a receipt and tells her to have a nice day. "Wait, what just happened?" I look at my mother in total confusion. "You did not just pay for all that stuff?"

"I did, and it was your father's orders. Consider it a housewarming and a graduation gift. We're proud of you."

"Mama, buying me dishes and maybe some utensils is a house warming gift. Not setting up my home." My eyes are wide with concern.

"You listen here. You're our baby girl and we're proud of you. We have done similar things for each of your brothers, and we will do this for you. Now I will not hear another word about it."

"Yes, ma'am." We make it out to the car and we load as much as we can into the trunk, squeezing the rest into the back with Courtney. As soon as the door is shut, I wrap my mama into the biggest hug. "Thank you so much, Mama. I love you, and really appreciate all you and Dad have already done. You didn't need to do this too."

225

She rubs my back. "We did it because we wanted to, not because we needed to. We love you too, dear. Now let's go, your brother is going to be waiting."

Chapter 20

Brooke

We pull up to the house and there are far more people here than expected. Keaton's truck is in the driveway along with Remy's Audi, and Dawson's SUV is in the street, which means Mama is having the entire family over. "I thought it was just Remy and Kenzie tonight?" I look at her with my brows raised.

She shrugs. "I guess your brothers wanted to come over too."

"Mmhmmm." Why do I feel like this woman is up to no good? I shake my head and climb out of the car, grabbing my bags with the help of Courtney and Mama.

When we get inside, everyone is in the living room and there are gifts on the floor.

"Congratulations," everyone shouts.

"Y'all act like I bought the house. I'm only renting it."

"Yes, but you're still moving out on your own,

227

and we're proud of you." My dad wraps his arm around me and hugs me.

I look up at him. "Thanks, Dad."

"Courtney, will you join us?" Mama asks.

"I'd love to, but I'm sorry, I have to get going." I give my friend a big hug and thank her for all of her help today. She tells me she'll see me at work.

Keaton comes over and hands me a plate of my favorite BBQ chicken pizza. "Thanks, Bro." We all sit around enjoying some pizza. As I look around at my amazing family, I realize the only one missing is my man. It makes me sad. I can't help but wonder what he's doing tonight. Is he even okay? I hated the look on Remy's face when he came back here to get his head on straight. He looked sad and defeated. Now, my man is going through the same thing.

"Hey, are you all right?" Remy takes a seat next to me. I was so lost in thought I had no idea everyone was watching me.

I turn to my brother. "Can we talk later? Alone."

He gives me a small smile. "Of course, but only if you promise to have some fun with your gifts for now."

I chuckle. "Okay, I'll try."

"That's my girl." He takes my plate and puts a gift on my lap.

I give my brother a big smile, because who can resist being excited about gifts? I rip through the paper to reveal a gorgeous pot and pan set, and that's when I realize my mom never pressed me to buy pans. She was on me about everything else but stuff to cook with. "You told Mom what you were getting me, didn't you?"

"She made me," he whispers and winks at me.

I can't help but laugh. He puts another gift on my lap. This one is from Keaton. I rip through a big box and inside is a ton of spatulas, spoons, and every other cooking utensil I could possibly need. "Thank you, Keaton, but how did you know what to get? No offense, but you're not much of a cook."

He laughs. "None taken. I asked Mama and she gave me a list of what you would need." I thank them both.

I grab another gift off the floor. It's a pair of really nice wine glasses, a bottle of Moscato, along with a bottle opener set. "That one is from Dawson and I." Kayla smiles. "The one on the floor is from the kids."

"Thank you." I put down their gift and quickly pick up the other one, because I can't wait to see what the kids gave me. I rip through yet another package to reveal framed pictures. There's four in the box. One of the entire family, one of each child separately, and the last one is of the two kids together. They're gorgeous, and I'm thrilled I'll have a piece of my family to keep in my house with me. "Thank you guys so much. I love them and can't wait to put them up in the house."

Becky comes running over. "Auntie Brooke, do you like my picture?"

"Oh, I love it, sweet girl." I pick her up and squeeze her.

"Remy and I are having some pictures printed for you as well. We'll show them to you once we've cleaned up. Unfortunately they're from the wedding, so we couldn't have them ready in time for tonight."

I jump up and hug her. "Thank you."

I turn to my family. "Thank you all. You've all helped make my home special. I can't wait for it to be set up."

"And we'll all be there on moving day to make sure you're squared away." Dawson puts his arm around me and kisses the top of my head. I'm so lucky to have such an amazing family. It makes me feel for Vaughn all that much more. He's thousands of miles away from his family. He has none of them to hug him and tell him it will be okay. This makes me that much more determined to help him understand that we're there for him and that we'll support him.

"Let's get cleaned up so we can look at some pictures." The guys all get busy getting rid of empty pizza boxes while Mama and I put the leftover pizza in the fridge.

Once we're done, Kenzie sets up her laptop. Mama, Kenzie, Kayla, and I all huddle around the kitchen island to look over the pictures from the wedding while the guys are in the other room. She opens a disc that reveals the pictures in order, starting with the guys getting ready at the house. There are some great pictures of Remy and Vaughn together, and although I would like one, I decide to wait until she tells me which ones she's ordered for me before I say anything. After the guys, it's us getting ready and getting into the limo. There are pictures of us climbing out of the limo and waiting to walk into the yard, and then pictures of us making our way down the aisle. Of course there are tons of pictures of the ceremony, pictures of them with the honor guard, and pictures of us on the front lawn. The photographer easily took a thousand shots when all is said and done. "Kenzie, the pictures came out beautiful."

"Thanks, we're quite pleased. I pulled the ones I wanted to make for you and put them in a folder." She opens a folder on her laptop to reveal a few shots.

She clicks on the first one to open it up bigger, and the first picture is a really fun one. It's of all of us girls wearing our t-shirts and shorts with our sneakers. "I love that one." I clap my hands, excited. She clicks the arrow to open the next picture, and it's of her and my brother. She's still in her wedding dress and Rem's in his uniform.

She turns to Mama. "We've ordered you an eleven by fourteen of this one, Mama."

"Thank you, sweetie. Dad and I will be ordering some others. I really would like one of the entire family. The one in the living room is a bit outdated." I'll say it is. Remy wasn't even in the service yet when we took that photo. We took one picture at the wedding that included everyone, even Rebecca and Beau are in it, and it came out beautiful. Kayla put Beau in an adorable little suit with a bowtie.

She clicks the next arrow, and I can't help but smile even as a lone tear runs down my cheek. It's the picture of Rem and Vaughn. "Thank you," I manage, though barely a whisper.

Kenzie rubs my back. "He'll be okay. It's clear

as day he loves you, and if nothing else, that's enough to make him fight this." I nod my head, silently praying she's right.

She clicks the arrow one more time, and the final picture she has for me is my favorite. It's a picture of me and my three brothers. "You guys are awesome. I can't thank you enough. I'm so excited that I have such nice pictures of my family to put up in my home."

"Sometimes when you live alone, you need a reminder that there are people who love and support you. Even if you're not living under the same roof as them." Kayla hugs me.

"Now," Kenzie announces. "When is moving day?"

I wipe the tears from my eyes. "In two weeks. That's when my furniture will be in. I scheduled it for a Saturday. That way I wouldn't need to request a day off. I'll just have to ask Dr. Kramer to swap on-call times with me if that's my weekend."

Kenzie pulls her phone out. "Nice. I'll add it to our calendar right now." She's typing into her phone when she looks up. "I can't believe the annual block party is almost here."

"Mama, I'm so sorry. I've been so wrapped up in my new job and Vaughn that I've done nothing to help you plan." I feel horrible. That's been something Mama and I always do together.

"It's fine, sweetie. Actually, some of the neighbors are doing a lot of the planning for us this year because we were so busy planning the wedding. We've done this for so many years now, it's not like there's a lot to actually plan anymore.

We're doing everything as we have every other year." She shrugs. "The planning meetings are more of a way for us neighbors to get together once in a while."

"I can't wait. I love the block party."

"It was a lot of fun last year, even if I did leave early." Kenzie giggles. She and Remy were having their own issues last year. She came with Lilly, basically ate, hung out for a few, and then left. Mama was so upset with Remy over it until Kenzie told Mama it was her choice to leave, that she was avoiding him because of her own fears.

"Well, this is fun, but I need to get my children to bed." Kayla hugs us each goodbye and then goes to get Beau from Remy, who is always hogging him. He thinks because he's his godfather he can constantly hold him and be in control of him. He's always playing with him and throwing him in the air. It's quite cute, actually.

Keaton is the next to go, leaving Kenzie and Remy left. I take a seat next to my brother, and as if my father can read my mind, he walks into the kitchen, knowing I want to talk with my brother. "Spill."

"You know I went to Vaughn's house after the wedding?"

"Yeah, everyone does."

"Well, the next morning we had this great conversation about him getting help with his nightmares and flashbacks. After finding houses for me to look at, we did some research and found him some self-help coaching. He was thrilled. There was an app and everything."

"Are you sure he was thrilled?"

"Rem, he got up and ran to grab his phone to download the app. I didn't pressure him or force him. As a matter of fact, when we started the research, I told him he didn't have to commit to anything, I just wanted to see what opportunities were out there for him to consider, and he agreed."

He shrugs. "Okay, so what went wrong?"

"I don't know. He asked me to sleep here for a while. Said he needed time to try these things out and see if they'd work before we could continue sleeping in the same bed." I run my hands through my hair. "I agreed, I supported him. We were talking through text over the course of two weeks. He was thrilled with the progress he had made, and told me if he kept doing well, he wanted me to spend the night after the bowl and dine we planned with his boys." I look down, trying to maintain my composure. "He was off at bowling. He wasn't his fun, flirty self—he was cruel, and no matter what I did, nothing made him happy. Then when I mentioned staying the night, he lost it. Even Callen freaked out on him. We didn't even finish the final game. Tommy called it quits and everyone followed suit. Now he won't talk to me and I'm scared." I finally look up to see Remy's jaw tight. I can tell he's pissed—he's cracking his knuckles. I place my hand over his. "Rem, he needs your help. He won't talk to me about his problem, but I know you can get him to open up."

Remy closes his eyes and takes a deep breath. "I'm angry because I told that fucker if things got worse to come to me, but does he listen? No. Now

I'm going to hunt his ass down tomorrow and make him wake the fuck up before he loses the best girl he could ever have."

"What are you going to do?"

"I'm going to go to Callen's, pick him up, and the two of us are going to his house for an intervention. Hopefully he's not in too bad of shape."

"Do you know where Callen lives?"

"No, but you do. Listen, I know the guy from the base, but give me his address. Trust me, he'll be cool with this."

I nod. He kisses me on the cheek and walks into the kitchen. The last thing I hear before I run up the stairs is Remy tell Kenzie that he has to go to the base tomorrow.

Chapter 21

Vaughn

I stare into the mirror with four days' worth of scruff on my face. I'm a fucking mess and I'm contemplating calling out again tomorrow. I haven't done my exercises in days, and my lack of sleep goes to show they work, but it doesn't matter now. Nothing does. I grab two aspirin from the cabinet, pop them into my mouth, and swallow them down with my beer. It's after five somewhere, right?

Plopping down on my couch, I glance around my living room. It's a mess again, and I hate living in a mess, but I have no desire to clean, either. The only thing I've done outside of eat, drink, and sleep, is take Brody out to use the bathroom. There's dog hair all over the place, and he's sitting at my feet with a sad look on his face. "Welcome to my world, buddy. Welcome to my world." I pat the top of his head. He jumps up onto the couch and rests on my lap. I chug my beer, lay my head back on the couch, and close my eyes while I rest my legs on my coffee table. Fuck, I'm so tired.

Change the way you think about sleep, I tell myself. Sleep is okay, nothing bad will happen in your sleep, it's just a way to rest your body. The fuck—that's so far from the truth. Horrible things happen in my sleep. Trucks blow up in my sleep, I lose men in my sleep, and I lose the only woman I've ever loved in my sleep. If I can't have her, then I want no one. I open my eyes one more time, but they're heavy. I don't want to sleep. I don't want to see the look of devastation that was on Brooke's beautiful face the day I blew it, but I can't fight anymore. My lids close, and there's her gorgeous blue eyes, her silky blonde hair, and her brilliant smile. She whispers to me *I loved you, Vaughn.* Loved, as in past tense.

I jump up, panting. Brody's at the door barking, and there's pounding on my door. Brody barks louder. "Brody, stop." He comes running back over to me.

"Open the fuck up." I hear a voice from the other side of the door. I can't quite make out the voice between the fog in my head and the solid door—it's muffled. Whoever it is, they're determined, pounding again. "We know you're in there. Open this fucking door or I'll bust it down." Fuck. Now I know who it is.

"Go the fuck away, man," I shout through the door.

"No. Open up."

"No."

"Callen, you have your key?" Remy asks him. Fuck, he has Callen with him. I hear him putting the key into the lock. I gave Callen a key when I first moved off base in case I ever locked myself out or he needed to get in for anything. It's come in handy because he's taken Brody out for me when I've needed him too. The door opens, and when they get their first glimpse of me, their eyes go wide. Yeah, yeah, I'm a mess. If you're here to judge, you can go fuck yourself. Brody barks, jumping up and down…he's full of excitement.

"Hey, boy." Callen pets him trying to calm him down.

"I think my dog is happy to see you." I take a pull from my beer and walk back to my couch, plopping myself down in the center of it, spilling beer on my naked chest. It causes me to laugh.

"I don't think this funny." Remy walks over and takes a seat. "This place is a mess, you're fucking drunk at ten a.m., and you smell like dirty ass."

"I may be drunk, but I don't remember inviting you over." I finish my beer and put it with the others on the coffee table. I watch Callen put a leash on Brody and take him to the backyard. He thinks he's so smart, I took him out a little while ago. Remy glares at me with an angry look on his face. "What's your problem?"

His brows shoot up. "My problem is you promised me if shit got out of control you'd come to me. I don't fucking call this coming to me."

I laugh. "Let me guess. Your sister ran to you and told you she's worried and you needed to come check on me." I use a baby voice.

"Listen, you fuck. My sister is worried about your sorry ass. She wants to help you and support you, and you fucking pushed her away."

I get up and start pacing the room. I run my hands through my hair, I'm losing control. "I'm not one of her animals that she can fucking heal. I told her I was broken." I'm seething.

"So did you lie to her when you told her the self-coaching was helping?"

"No!" I shout at him. "It was helping."

Callen comes back in with the dog. "Brody, go lay down, boy." He runs off to the other side of the room and collapses on the floor. My loyal dog won't go too far from my side. "Dude, your dog just pissed like he's been holding it for days."

"Bullshit. I think...I just walked him what, a few hours ago." Callen raises his brows, questioning me. "I don't know what time it was." I shake my head. "My days are all running together."

"That's the lack of sleep," Remy barks at me.

My head whips around to meet his glare. "Thanks, Captain Fucking Obvious."

He jumps up from the seat. "First, if you're going to be a dick, I'll remind you I'm a fucking major. Second, we're not leaving until you pull your head out of your ass, so the way I see it, you have two options. You can talk to us and tell us what went wrong and we'll figure it out together, or you can have us up your ass all fucking day long, because I know how you feel about my sister, and losing her permanently isn't an option."

"I need a beer."

"Oh no, you're done drinking for now." Remy steps in front of me. My fists clench at my sides. "Before you even think about swinging, remember

I'm an officer, and it doesn't matter if I'm in your home, the charges are the same." I scream out, not knowing how else to exert my frustration. Brody jumps up and starts barking like crazy. Callen has to run to him and calm him down. I bend over with my hands on my knees, panting. "You can scream and shout all you want, man, but we're not leaving. We're your boys, and you're going to get through this. You've hid this and carried the weight of whatever is bothering you for long enough. It's time to get help. I'm personally bringing you to meet my doctor tomorrow morning. Your commander already knows."

"You spoke to my commander?" My eyes go wide, I've never even mentioned a sleeping problem to my commander. I've always hid it and hid it well. I don't know whether I should be angry or thankful that he finally knows.

"Yes, first thing this morning. I have to say he's quite surprised. You've hid this well up until now. He said only recently he started becoming concerned, and when you called out on Friday he was planning to talk to you tomorrow. He's glad we're stepping in."

I look to the floor. "What if I don't want to go to this doctor?"

"Then you'll have to deal with your commanding officer, but I'm pretty sure you won't like what he has to say." He's softened his voice.

I sigh. "I fucked up, bad."

"Maybe so, but it's not too late to fix it." Callen comes over and touches my shoulder.

When I look up, my eyes are welling with tears.

He pulls me in and I lose it. "I don't want to lose her, but I panicked. I couldn't let her see how weak I was, and that's how these fucking exercises make me feel, embarrassed and fucking weak." I pull away, taking a seat back on the couch with my elbows on my knees. I rub my forehead, silently begging my headache to go away.

"Dude, there's nothing weak about you, and you should be proud of yourself. You took steps to better yourself without any professional help, and it was working. I don't get why you stopped."

I puff out my cheeks, exhaling a huge, cleansing breath. "I freaked out. I knew I had been telling Brooke that the exercises were working, and that meant she was going to want to spend the night. At first I was thrilled. I was even going to plan a romantic night for us. I was planning to make her a nice dinner and everything."

"Okay?" Callen has a look of confusion on his face.

"How romantic is it to say 'Excuse me, Angel, I have to do my sleep exercises before we can make love,' or 'thanks for making love to me, but now I have to go meditate'? I was going to sound like a fool and ruin our first night together. Of course I had the option of skipping the exercises and scaring the shit out of her with a nightmare because I didn't do them. That's always a great welcome back to my bed moment."

"Sorry, man. I didn't think about any of that, but you realize this woman loves you and would do anything to help you." Callen's voice is full of sincerity.

"I don't know. Once I screwed up I didn't know what to do. The hurt on her face has haunted my sleep ever since. I'm not sure I can ever fix this, and I'm not sure I blame her." Another tear runs down my cheek.

"Listen, Vibe. She wouldn't have come to me for help if she didn't love you or want to fix things with you. It was a tough thing for her to do. She gave you time and you weren't getting better on your own. She did what she thought was right for you, not her. Trust me, I was livid when she told me, and she knew I would be. She was just wrong about the reason why I was angry. I'm not mad because you hurt her feelings…well, I am…but that's not what made my blood boil. You promised me you would come to me, and you broke that promise."

I look down again, no longer able to look one of my best friends in the eye. "I'm sorry, man. I was afraid to tell you how badly I had behaved, and I was embarrassed by it. I acted like a fool to my girlfriend in front of my crew, and I've been a dick ever since." I sniffle and wipe away more tears.

"You have, but you know what? Your crew, they're all worried too. We've talked about it. I didn't tell them everything, but I've told them enough. You owe them an apology, but get your shit together and they'll be there for you just like they were before." I nod my head at Callen, not sure what else to say.

"Here's how this is going to go down." Remy gets up from his seat. "The two of us are going to help you clean this pit up, and then I'm going to spend the night right here on this couch. Tomorrow morning, I'll follow you to the doctor's office and get you settled. From there, everything will be left up to the doctor."

My eyes shoot up to his. "I'll start my exercises again tonight. That guy cannot hospitalize me. I'll go crazy in there."

"I don't think he's going to do that, but it's up to you. You have to be honest with him and tell him everything. You can't hide it like you did after your last deployment."

"I got it." My voice is rough.

"Good, let's clean up this mess." I stand up from the couch. Remy grabs my hand and pulls me in for a hug. "You're going to be all right, man."

"Thanks. I'm sorry," I say past the lump in my throat fighting back my tears.

He pulls away. "It's all good. I've been there."

I nod. "Hey, do you mind if I shower first? I think it'll help me feel better."

"Sure, just let me take a piss first."

"I have two bathrooms."

"You do, and I was trying to be discreet, but since that didn't work I'll tell you upfront. I don't trust you, so I'm going to remove all razors and pills from your bathroom."

I roll my eyes and shake my head. "Go for it." Remy walks off to the bathroom. Brody sits by the back door. "Callen, will you hook my dog up?"

"You got it, man." He walks over to the drawer with his leash and takes him out again for me. I've really fucked this up even with my dog. He's tries to wake me up from these nasty nightmares, no matter how much I've ignored him and now I need to make it up to him too.

"You're good to go, man." Remy comes back into the living room and starts cleaning up.

I thank him again and walk off to my bathroom. Turning on the water as hot as I can take it, I climb in and let out a good sob. I haven't cried this hard ever, but I lean with my arm on the shower wall and really let it all out. I cry for the guys I've lost or have gone home with missing limbs, I cry for my girl because of the pain I've caused her, and I cry for myself because I was too stupid to get help sooner. I feel like I've been here forever, but when I finally have no tears left, I wash my body and jump out to get dressed. If I don't get my ass in gear, Remy's going to come bursting through this door, and I don't need to worry them more than I already have. I slip on a pair of running shorts and a t-shirt. When I get back to the living room, the guys have already collected a bag of trash and put it by the back door. I grab the vacuum from the hall closet to clean up all of Brody's dog hair. As soon as that's done, I load my dishwasher, run it, and then wipe down my sink.

"Are you good?" Callen asks.

"Yeah, I'm good, and it's not like the Major is going to let me out of his sight." I chuckle.

"You fucking got that right," he busts my balls.

Callen slaps me on the back. "I'm going to update our commander and I'll see you tomorrow after your appointment." I silently nod and then thank him again. He leaves me with Remy.

"I'm going to take Brody out back for a bit. I owe him some time." My voice is low and my eyes are welling with tears that I'm trying to hold back.

"Go. I'll be here."

He stands in the door watching me throw a ball around with my dog. Brody is thrilled to chase after it and quickly brings it back to me. I laugh, watching as his face is full of joy. He comes running at me and jumps, but I'm not expecting it. He knocks me to the ground and starts licking my face. "Down, boy." He doesn't listen, he's so excited he continues licking me and I can't help but laugh. "Oh, I'm sorry, boy." I pet his head, and as if he understands my apology, he climbs off me and I throw the ball again. I look over to see Remy smiling at me from the door. He walks off and I can't help but wonder if he's going to call Brooke. I'm still sitting on the ground when Brody comes back over with the ball. "I miss her, boy." Brody drops the ball and barks. I toss it again and he runs off. I need to figure out how to fix things with her but I want to make sure I'm solid first. I become so deep in thought thinking about her, I don't notice Brody come back with the ball. I throw it again, and then place my head in my hands. "Do I call her and let her know I'm working on it and I'm always thinking about her?" I whisper to myself.

"Probably a good place to start." I jump.

"Holy shit. I didn't hear you come out."

"I know. I saw you on the ground and thought you might need me."

I get up. "Come, Brody." He comes running over and my stomach growls. I haven't eaten much of anything over the last few days.

"It's a good thing I've ordered some pizza. Come

on. It should be here any minute." I thank him and then thank god for giving me amazing friends.

Chapter 22

Brooke

It's finally here. Moving day. I spent most of last night packing up the last bits of my room and talking with Vaughn. We've been sending each other text messages since he went to the doctor over a week ago. I begged Remy to tell me how things went when he got to Vaughn's on that Sunday morning, but he wouldn't spill. He said it's Vaughn's story to tell, and he'll tell it when he's ready. I got the first text from him around lunchtime the next day. It was short and simple.

Vaughn: I'm sorry. I hope you can someday forgive me. I'm trying to get better.

I cried so hard after reading that text. Part of me wanted to stay silent, but I couldn't, not after I ran from him the first time.

Brooke: I love you and I'll be here when you're

ready.

He thanked me and then went quiet for a few days. I could tell he was doing better each day because his text messages started to change, but now I haven't heard from in him in almost two days and I'm trying not to panic.

I shake my thoughts of him and take one last glance around my room. It's completely empty except for my furniture and the bedding. I throw my bag over my shoulder and run down to my waiting parents.

"Ready?"

I nod and run out to put my bag in the car.

When we pull up to my new place. Remy and Keaton are sitting on the front step and Kenzie is in between them. "Hey guys, sorry I'm late."

"Everything all right? You're never late."

"Yeah, I just took an extra moment to look around before I left." They all gave me a knowing smile and followed me into my home. This is the first time Remy and Kenzie are seeing it, and I can tell from their reaction they like it. "Feel free to walk around and check the place out. The furniture will be here any minute." I drop my bag in my walk-in closet. I need to wash all the towels my mom bought me. I run to the laundry closet and get a load going. I'm glad I ran to the store yesterday and did some shopping. There's a huge supercenter up the street from my house with everything I'll ever need. After I brought the food home and got it all put away, I washed all the dishes and cups. I was definitely smart enough to run some through my dishwasher, otherwise it would have taken me forever.

"Mama, what do you think of how I set up the cabinets?"

She starts opening them up. "I was wondering where everything was." She has pride in her voice. "You did a good job, but you'll probably move things fifty times. It takes a while before you figure out what works for you."

The doorbell rings and I clap with excitement, thinking my furniture is here, but when I open the door there's a delivery man holding two boxes. "Can I help you?"

"Brooke Bennett?" he questions.

"Yes, sir."

"I have a delivery for you." I open the door, sign for the packages, and thank him. Excited, I rip open the package to find a dozen long stem roses with a card.

Brooke,

I'm really sorry I'm not there with you on this important day, but I want you to know I've never once stopped thinking about you or loving you. I'm working hard and getting stronger and stronger each day, and I promise you I will explain everything to you soon. Please, I beg you, do not give up on me. I need you in my life, like I need air to breathe.

Love,

Vaughn

Tears well in my eyes. "He's so sweet. Even with all he's going through he thinks of me." I wipe away my tears and open the other box. When I see the contents, I crack up laughing.

"What is it?"

"Peach cobbler." I laugh through my tears.

My brothers are looking at me like I have ten heads. "Why is that funny?"

"Because we shared a peach cobbler together after we came to look at this house." I put it in the fridge to save for later. I can only imagine what he had to do to get a florist to deliver peach cobbler. I shake my head and grab my phone to thank him.

Brooke: I got my flowers and peach cobbler, thank you so much. I love you and have not given up on you. I can't wait for you to be better so we can share cobbler again.

Vaughn: I promise you I'm working on it. I can't wait to have you back in my arms.

I send him an emoji blowing him a kiss and put my phone away to get ready for the delivery guys to get here. Mama keeps busy grabbing my duster and dusts all around the living room and bedrooms once again. We did it not too long ago, but since the house is all closed up and empty, it needs it again. When she's done, she grabs the vacuum and starts vacuuming while I switch the load of towels to the dryer and put in another load.

The doorbell rings again and this time it's the furniture. I jump up and down, clapping with excitement. "Ms. Bennett?" the delivery man questions.

"That's me."

"We're bringing in the bedroom set first. Can you show me where it's going?"

"Sure, right this way." I lead him to my room and point out how I want the set put together. He agrees and they get busy unloading the bedroom set. That's when I realize I messed up. I never washed my bedding. It's all still sitting in the bag. I'll have to wash it next. When I get back to the living room, Kenzie is cleaning all of the windows around the living room and opening blinds to let sunlight in.

"You have a great yard," She says, excited.

"I know I can't wait to see Brody running free back there." I know he'll be here soon.

She wraps an arm around me in silent support. "The landlord good with the dog?"

"Yup. He figured since I'm a vet, I know how to handle them."

"Brooke," Mama calls from the kitchen. We both turn. "Do you know how you're setting up the living room? They're almost done in the bedroom."

"No, but I figured that's why I have these muscle men here." I wiggle my brows at my brothers, who both roll their eyes.

Courtney comes running through the door. "Hey,

251

sorry I'm late."

"It's all good. There's not much to do. We're all sitting around waiting for furniture to come in, and since I forgot to wash my sheets, I can't make my bed until the load in the washer finishes."

"Okay." She gives Mama and my dad each a hug, and then comes to give me one. "The place looks great!"

"Thanks. All I have left to do is open and wash the pots, pans, and utensils."

"Well, I guess I have something to do."

"The boxes are in the spare room." She runs off to grab the boxes and begins opening them while the movers bring in my couch. It's bigger than I thought, but I like it. They place it down against the wall where the TV is going to go and then head off to grab the two chairs I ordered, as well as a coffee table and two end tables. After this, all they'll have left to do is the kitchen set and they're done.

I exhale a deep breath. It's coming together, but there's still so much I need. I haven't gotten a coffee pot, I need a toaster or toaster oven, oven mitts, kitchen towels, and some sort of Tupperware containers for leftovers. I shake my head. Moving out on your own is exhausting, but I'm excited and nervous at the same time. This place is going to get really quiet later. I really wish Vaughn was here to spend the night with me. I shake off my thoughts and grab my phone to make note of the things I need to get tomorrow from the super center. I want to try and be as settled as possible before I go back to work on Monday. "Are you okay, sweetie? You look deep in thought."

"Yeah, Dad. I just realized I need to get some things from the store tomorrow. I was starting a list, that way I won't forget anything."

"I thought you got everything? What did you forget?"

I go over my list with him and he laughs. "It's funny how you forget something like a coffee pot until you go to make coffee and you don't have it."

"Yeah, it'd be hard to make the English muffins I bought without a toaster."

The movers have now finished moving my living room set in, and as soon as they leave I'm going to move it around. I don't like how it's set up, and apparently neither do my brothers, because they're already discussing it. My father stands beside me. We both watch my brothers animatedly discuss how the living room should be set up, and as with most things in life, they disagree. Their conversation turns into an argument. Keaton tries to punch Remy in the arm, but misses because Remy steps out of the way. Now Remy's laughing his ass off at Keaton, pissing him off more. I find this all quite funny, but my father doesn't. "Cut the crap, you two. Your sister doesn't need you guys breaking her stuff before she even gets to use it."

The tables and chairs for the dining room don't take them long to unload. They had to put the table together, but the six chairs they simply carried in. "Okay, ma'am. You're all set. I just need you to sign here." I scribble my name on the line. "Here is your warranty information." He hands me an envelope with papers in it. "Have a great night." They leave, and instantly Remy and Keaton start rearranging the living room furniture.

"Hey, sis. What are you doing about a TV?"

They delivered the stand for a TV but I haven't bought one for the living room yet. I have a TV in my bedroom and it was hooked up earlier this week, along with the Wi-Fi. "I don't have one yet."

Remy and Keaton each look at one another and then back at me, and at the same exact time they say. "We'll be back." They both run out the door.

"Where you going?" I shout to them, but they don't answer, they just continue on their way. I turn back to everyone else. "Shall I order pizza?"

Everyone nods, agreeing they are hungry. I grab my phone to order, Mama changes my laundry, and Kenzie grabs my sheets from the spare room to put into the washer. Once I'm done, I take a seat on my new couch, put my head back, and close my eyes. It's been a tiring few days, and I want nothing more than to sit and relax. I exhale and jump up to keep going. I realize I still haven't set up the bathrooms.

"Courtney, want to help me with the bathrooms?"

"Of course." We go into the spare room to find the bags with the bathroom stuff. The bags are all mixed, so we sort through them. She takes the main bathroom and I take the stuff for mine. I'm glad it doesn't take much to put down some bathmats and hang a shower curtain because I'm seriously spent. Mama peeks her head in to see if I need any help but I'm almost done. When I walk out, I admire my furniture for the first time. It fits nicely in my room and I love it.

A short time later, the pizza has arrived. I grab

plates, cups, and napkins. As we're digging in, Keaton and Remy come walking through the door carrying a huge TV. "Are you two crazy?"

They both shrug their shoulders and continue carrying the TV into the living room. "Consider it an early birthday/Christmas present, if that makes you feel better."

I laugh. "I can't believe you guys bought me a forty-six inch TV."

"Listen, if we're going to have movie nights, we need a TV. Without one, you can't force me to watch this." Remy pulls my favorite movie from his coat pocket and I can't help but burst into laughter.

"I can't believe you bought me *Twister*. I thought you would be thrilled I didn't have access to it anymore."

He kisses me on the head. "A girl has to have her favorite movie on hand."

"You're the best, Rem." The guys lean the TV against the stand and then grab some pizza. "Now I have to work on getting a DVD player and a surround sound system."

"Let me know when you're ready and I can help you pick one, but for now at least you can get cable."

Mama smiles at my brothers with a look of pure pride. As soon as they've scarfed down two slices, they get busy opening the box and carefully putting the huge TV on its stand. Remy grabs the remote, turns the TV on, and scrolls through the smart TV options. "Sis, I need your Wi-Fi password." I run to the drawer I have it written down in and hand him the slip of paper. Once he has it plugged into the

TV, he shows me how to watch Netflix and then shows me how I can play music.

"You guys are the best. I'll have to call the company and get another cable box, but this will be great for now." In true Keaton and Remy fashion, they both wrap me in a hug, squeezing me between them. It's something they used to do to me all the time. "You guys are going to break me," I whine.

"Never." Keaton kisses my head and then gives me a noogie.

"Really. You done messed up my hair." I smack him playfully.

"On that note, I'm out of here. See ya, sis." Keaton kisses my mother goodbye and shakes hands with my father on his way out the door.

Next thing I know, it's just Courtney and I. She helps me set my bed up and then hangs with me for a bit. We chill on my new living room furniture, making plans for a movie night and dinner later this week. "Do you need help with anything else before I go?"

"No, I think I'm good. I'm going to take a shower and read for a bit. Thank you so much for all of your help."

I walk her to the door, she gives me a quick hug, and then runs down the walkway to her car. I lock the house and shut the lights on my way to my room. I grab my phone to check for messages before I hit the shower. It's so quiet in the house. I put on the TV to a music channel and lower the volume. I have no messages, but I'm hoping Vaughn will answer a text from me.

Brooke: Thank you again for the flowers. I love them and they look gorgeous on my kitchen island. I miss you and wish you were here with me.

Vaughn: I'm sorry, Angel. Why don't we get together for dinner this week and we can talk?

Brooke: That would be awesome. Why don't you come to my place and I'll cook. How's Tuesday?

Vaughn: Tuesday works. See you soon, Angel. I love you!

Brooke: Love you too!

I put my phone down feeling so much better that I at least know I'm going to be seeing him soon. I gather what I need for the shower so I can get some sleep, I'm exhausted from the busy day.

Chapter 23

Brooke

I arrive at work full of energy and excitement. I've spent the last two nights in my new place. I've shopped for my home, prepared clothes for the week, and even prepared some meals for myself, hoping I wouldn't forget to eat or eat poorly, but nothing could have prepared me for the vision in front of me. I park my car, taking in the police, ambulance, and fire department all sitting with lights flashing blocking the entrance to the clinic. I leap from my car and run to the front door to find Dr. Kramer on a stretcher with an oxygen mask over his face. "What's going on?"

"Who are you?" the officer asks.

"I'm the other veterinarian that works here." I can't take my eyes off of my dear friend and mentor. My body begins to tremble and tears are welling in my eyes. "Please, what's going on?"

"He's had a severe heart attack. We need to get

him to the hospital. Who is his next of kin?"

I shake my head and close my eyes. "He has no one." I burst into tears and instantly Courtney is at my side. She knows how much Dr. Kramer means to me. He's like a second father to me. He's been a mentor and taught me all I know. I can't lose this dear man. "I'm the closest he has to family."

"Ma'am, I know this is difficult, but we may need you. How can we reach you?" I reach over and hand him one of the brand new business cards that Dr. Kramer just had printed for me. I can hear sirens screaming as the ambulance rushes from the parking lot.

"How could this be happening? He's a fit man. He works out, eats healthy for the most part. I don't understand."

He shakes his head. "I'm sorry, ma'am. I wish I had answers for you, but I don't. Sometimes no matter what we do, it's not enough." He rubs my arm. "Will you be okay here?"

I swallow through the lump in my throat and nod my head. "Yes, I have a clinic to run." I hold my head high, knowing that Dr. Kramer would want me to run the clinic today, and I plan to make him proud. The nice officer nods and heads toward the door. "Officer?"

He turns back to me. "Will you please make sure I get an update?"

He gives me a tight smile and nods. "On my way there now."

"Thank you." My voice is barely a whisper as I fight the tears prickling my eyes.

I turn to my friend. "Will you give me a minute

and then meet me in the back?" She nods and I walk away.

I grab my cell phone and call my dad.

"Hey, sweetie," he answers cheerfully.

"Daddy, Dr. Kramer is on his way to the hospital. He's had a heart attack."

"Oh dear. I'm so sorry, sweetie."

I'm now sobbing into the phone. "Can you make some calls and find out what's happening? I'm at the clinic and I can't just leave. I have animals I need to tend to."

"Of course. I'll be in touch shortly. Hang in there, sweetie." He cuts the call. I grab a tissue and dab my eyes, trying to not totally destroy my makeup even though I know it's a mess. Courtney comes walking into the back. She says nothing, but sits next to me and quietly waits. I exhale a deep breath. "We need to get through this day as quickly as possible. I'm waiting on an update from either the police or my father. Please call and cancel any appointments that aren't urgent, and ask others to come in early. I'm going to start checking on the animals we have here and see who can be sent home and who needs to stay." I exhale another deep breath. "I'll need to catch Raeanne up on everything. Is she here yet?"

Her eyes go wide. "Poor girl is probably standing at the door. She doesn't have a key yet." She jumps up and runs to the door. I follow behind her to see not only is Raeanne standing there, but so are the first patients of the morning.

I let out a sigh. "Let's open and get things rolling." I turn to Raeanne. "Can I see you in the back?"

She nods, looking nervous, but follows me to the back. As soon as we're out of earshot of our clients, she finally asks with a shaken voice, "Did I do something wrong?"

I shake my head. "No, Dr. Kramer was rushed to the emergency room this morning. He had a heart attack. I really need your help to get through today. We're canceling clients that are not urgent, and trying to bump others up so I can get out of here and get to the hospital."

"I'm so sorry." Her voice laced with concern. "Why don't I start checking the patients we already have here for you and you can do the checkups that are walking in now?"

"That's a good plan. Let me know if you have any concerns or need my help." She rubs my arm and walks off. With one more deep breath, I pick up the carrier of my first patient, a Siamese cat.

***

Vaughn

I'm walking out of my morning appointment with the good doctor when my phone vibrates in the clip. I pull it out to see it's Remy. "Hey, man. Yes, I went to my appointment and things are going great." I roll my eyes because he's been checking on me for over two weeks now. I'm finally seeing Brooke tomorrow, and he of all people should know that means I'm feeling good. The doctor and I just met about it.

"I'm glad to hear it, but that's not why I'm calling." There's panic in his voice, and now I'm freaking out. Lord, please tell me that my angel is all right. I stop in the middle of the parking lot, silently praying while I wait for his next words. "Brooke is at the clinic, but she's going to need you. Dr. Kramer was rushed to the hospital today."

"How do you know?" I start walking toward my car again. I need to get a hold of Brooke and make sure she's okay.

"My father called me. He wants me to go by and check on her, but not sure I can get out of here early today to do that. Keaton is going to stop by and see if she needs anything, but you should too. She'll want to see you."

I exhale a deep, cleansing breathe. I'm just getting strong enough for myself, am I strong enough for her too? I have to be. I love her and I need to be there for her. "I'll get there as soon as I can." I jump in my car and head straight to work. The guys are all busy working on vehicles when I walk through the doors. The bays are full, and there's more that need work in the lot.

I go straight to my commander's office and knock on the door. "Enter," he barks from the other side of the door.

"Good morning, sir."

"Staff Sergeant Anderson, how are you today?"

I close the door behind me and step closer to his desk. "I'm doing well, sir. I want to thank you for your understanding while I work through my issues. I'm getting better and better every day. I've actually slept through the night for almost two weeks now."

"That's good to hear. I don't like seeing my men not at their best. If you need help, son, you need to come to me. That's what I'm here for." I look down at the floor, trying to figure out how to bring this up without sounding like an asshole. He's already been so flexible. "What is it, son?"

"Sir. You know Major Bennett, right?"

"Yes, of course. He called me before heading to your house that morning." His southern accent is getting stronger as he gets more concerned. I need to spit this out.

"I've been dating his sister for quite some time now. As a matter of fact, I love her, and I hurt her deeply with the way I handled the situation I was in. Now, she needs me, and I'd like to be there for her. I know you've been understanding with my time, but can I please take leave for the afternoon?"

"Is she all right? Does the Major know?"

"She's fine, and he called me, sir, he knows. It's her boss and mentor. He was just rushed to the hospital. We're waiting for an update, but from the way the Major was sounding, it doesn't look good. I'd like to take her to the hospital to see him. She's very close to the man, and I don't want her to have to go alone." I looked down. "I didn't allow her to be there for me the way I should have, now I need to be there for her."

"Listen, son. When you retire from this man's Army in another couple years, there's going to be a few select people at your side. A few men here and there that you manage to stay in touch with because you've caught up at multiple duty stations and became close friends. Other than that, all you have is your family. What I'm telling you is, especially at this stage in the game, family comes first. I didn't always believe that, but after some recent events, I came to realize I was wrong. You get done what you can while you wait for an update, and then you do what you have to do, but make sure your men are squared away here, also."

"Yes, sir. Thank you, sir." I start to walk back toward the door but before I leave I turn back to him. "Sir." He looks back up at me. "I hope your family is well."

He gives me a tight smile. "Thank you, son." I nod and walk out the door, straight to the bay where my men are.

Leaning on the counter, I take a minute to watch my men at work. I've been on this base for a year now, and my time in is almost up. At one point I dreaded the thought of my career coming to an end. Always wondered what I would do with my life when it was time for me to retire, now I'm counting down the days. I'll be retiring ahead of Callen, and I hope he's serious about staying down here and opening a shop with me, because that's exactly what I plan on doing right after I marry the love of my life.

"Listen up, guys." I hear tools drop and see heads pop out from under vehicles. "Everyone gather around, please." The guys all come over to the counter I'm leaning on. "First, I need to apologize to you guys. I know I've been a surly dick lately, and I'm sorry. I had some things going on that I should have admitted to, and instead, like the thick headed numbskull I am, I tried to fix

264

things myself, and it cost me dearly. I hope you guys can forgive me." The guys are all quiet for what feels like an eternity. I'm about to speak up and say more but I'm stopped.

Max punches me in the arm. "We're just glad to see you back to yourself, Sarge." I'm one lucky fuck. My guys forgive me, and now I need to pray my girl does too.

"Thanks, guys. Now that I'm getting better, I have one more thing I need to take care of. I know I haven't been here as often as I should because I've been busy getting my shit together, but I may have to leave early today. Brooke's boss and mentor is in the hospital because of a heart attack, and it's not looking good. I'm waiting for a call, but will probably have to run out as soon as it comes through so I can get her over there to spend some time with him." The guys pat my back in support and if feels good. I wish I had realized I had all of this sooner. "As usual you'll have to deal with Callen being in charge."

"What the fuck?" Tommy bellows angrily. I can tell from the look on his face that he's joking, but it's still funny.

"You're such an asshole. You know I'm so much easier to work for than this dickhead." He slaps me on the back.

The guys all burst into laughter. "Okay, comedy hour is over. Get back to work. I have shit to do." I walk to my office and the guys go back to the vehicles they're working on. I take a seat at my desk and boot up my laptop. While I wait I send a quick text to Remy.

Vaughn: Spoke to CO, I'm good to go. Let me know.

I put my phone down and begin going through emails. There's a shit ton of them because I haven't been checking it as often as I should. As I go through I realize that my boy really covered my ass while I was doing my thing. I'm trying really hard to concentrate. I'm about a quarter of the way through before I check my phone and notice I have nothing from Remy yet. It's really hard to think about work when I'm waiting on something so important.

I put my phone down and continue working. I take time to check on parts, see what we have up that needs to be worked on, and be sure to set a priority for the guys. Callen is pretty good at all of that, but it will be good to have it done for him while he's out there working on vehicles too. I'm finishing up processing some paperwork. It's been a busy morning, I've worked straight through lunch because I know I'm going to have to leave soon. Placing my clipboards back on their appropriate hooks, I shove the last of my granola bar into my mouth when my phone chirps.

Remy: Get her there ASAP. It's not good.

Shit, I mutter to myself. Grabbing my phone and keys, I run out the door. "Got to go, Callen." I run to my CO's office his door is open. I knock and peek my head in. He looks up from his computer. "I got the call, sir."

266

"Go." I thank him and run back down the hall. Going straight to my car, I send Remy a text as I start it up.

Vaughn: On my way.

I have to be careful driving on base, the MPs are everywhere, and despite the fact I fix their fucking vehicles, they'd give me a ticket in a fucking heartbeat. The second I'm through the gate and on the main road, I fly to get the clinic as quickly as I can. I'm happy it's only a few minutes away, and thanks to my speeding, I shaved a few minutes off the commute. As soon as I walk through the door, I spot Courtney. "Where's Brooke?"

Her eyes fill with panic. "In the back, why?"

"Get her, please. I need to get her to the hospital." Her eyes well with tears as she jumps from her seat and runs to the back. While I stand in the entry waiting for her, I take deep breaths, trying to maintain control, but internally I'm a bit freaked out. I haven't seen her in a few weeks, and now I'm whisking her away to the hospital to see a man she cares deeply for.

"Vaughn?" Her eyes are pleading.

"Angel, we have to go."

Her eyes well. "But how do you know?" Her voice is laced with concern.

I place each of my hands on her arms. "Angel, look at me." I wait for her to look into my eyes. "Remy called. I need to get you to the hospital. Grab your purse." I shake her gently. She nods and runs off.

When she gets back, she turns to Courtney. "I'll call you in a bit. Have Raeanne take care of whatever she can. If there are any emergencies, they'll have to take them to the larger hospital outside of town until I know what's going on. Call or text me if you need me, but I'll be in touch soon." Courtney nods. I take her hand and run her out the door to my waiting car.

Chapter 24

Brooke

We arrive at the hospital and Vaughn drops me off at the door with a promise I would text him the room number as soon as I have it. He pulls away to find a parking spot and I run inside. There's an older woman sitting by the door with a headset on, chewing gum. She's dressed like she's from the eighties, but is really much older. It almost makes me laugh. "Excuse me." My voice is rushed. "I'm looking for Dr. Joel Kramer, please. He's a patient here. He was rushed in this morning." I'm rambling now but she types away on the computer, still chomping on her gum as if she's a teen who doesn't know better.

She looks up at me. "And you are?

"Dr. Brooke Bennett." She looks back down at the computer and back up at me. She notices my name on the lab coat I forgot to take off.

"Room three fourteen." She nods with her head toward a hall. "Take the elevators over there up to the third floor, hang a right when you get off, and his room is down the hall."

I nod and run for the elevators, sending Vaughn the text he's waiting for. Once I'm in the elevator, I send him a second one with the instructions Chompy gave me. Yes, I really just nicknamed her Chompy, there's no other name for her. When I get to the third floor, I follow the directions, finding his room and my father. "Daddy." I run over to him. He wraps me into a hug and rubs my back, consoling me. "How is he?"

"I'm sorry, sweetie, but it's not good. He's holding on by a thread. They really need to operate but can't. He's not strong enough." I close my eyes, taking in his words. I want to scream at the doctor, force him to do something, but I know darn well they're doing all they can. I have the same hurt my clients have when they want me to heal their pet when there's nothing else we can do. He hugs me one more time. "We just have to wait." Doctors are doctors. I just gave that same line to a client not too long ago. It will do me no good to be angry. "Why don't you go sit with him?"

"Vaughn is on his way up." My dad nods and I stroll into the room. It's dark with the curtain drawn and the lights off. His eyes are closed, and the only sign to tell me he's still with me is the ventilator breathing for him and the beeping of the heart monitor. I pull a chair up to his side, lower myself into it, and take his hand, hoping he knows I'm here for him. "You can't leave me yet. I'm not ready." I squeeze his hand. I exhale a deep breath. "After you left today, I lost it. I was scared. I've always had you by my side, you've been there to help me make the right decisions, to ensure I do a procedure correctly, to support me, and train me to be the best I can be." I wipe the tears from my face. "I'm not there yet. I have so much more to learn from you. I'm not sure I can go in every day and not see your smiling face. You taught me about paying it forward and supporting others. Well, now I'm here to support you in return, so you have to fight. You have to get better."

I can feel his eyes on me as I talk with my friend. He walks up behind me and wraps his arms around me and I lose it. I drop Dr. Kramer's hand and hug Vaughn at his waist, sobbing with my face pressed to his stomach. He rubs my back and tries to console me as I fear losing my dear friend.

A doctor walks in a few minutes later with my father. He checks his vitals and makes some notes on a chart. "We discovered that Dr. Kramer had two people listed as next of kin, you and his attorney. His attorney was by earlier to see how he was doing, and we told him the same thing I'm going to tell you. I'm not sure he's going to make the night. His heartbeat is erratic and his blood pressure is extremely low. We're doing what we can to make him stronger, but there's not much more we can do until things level out. His lawyer did ask that I give you this note." He hands me an envelope. I rip it open to find two slips of paper inside.

Dear Ms. Bennett,
I was asked to hold onto this note until this day came. The day when we were losing our

beloved Dr. Kramer.
Warmest regards,
Jacob Fox

I flip to the second sheet of paper and it's a letter from Dr. Kramer.

My dearest Brooke,

If you're reading this, it is either because I've passed on, or am seriously ill and things aren't looking good. As you know, I'm not good at expressing my feelings or dealing with emotion, but I wanted to have a chance to tell you how proud I am of the grown woman you've become, and this here letter is the only way for me to do it. You have done amazing things while working with me at the clinic. You managed to not only work hard in school, but maintain quite a schedule so you could take on as much hands-on training as possible. Your dedication to your academics as well as the clinic and your family has not gone

272

unnoticed.

When you started working the front desk of my clinic all those years ago, I thought you were just some young kid looking to make money, but I was wrong. I had no idea the friendship we would build in working side by side. When I lost Carly and Bobby, well, it broke my heart, but you were there for me. You helped me pick myself back up and get through the hurdle. You became my family.

Even now as I write this, I'm struggling to express how much you've come to mean to me. I know I could never replace your father and I'd never want to, he's a fine man, and has done an amazing job raising you and your brothers, but you're like a daughter to me.

I imagine if you're reading this, you will be meeting my attorney in the *coming days. I've never told you this, and part of me wishes I had better prepared you, but I simply couldn't bring myself to discuss it. My attorney has my will, and in it you will learn that I've left you the clinic. There is no one on this earth better equipped to run it than you. I know you will be an amazing doctor. The care I see in your eyes when you handle the animals is like nothing I've ever seen before. Do good things with it and continue to make me proud.*

Your dear friend

Joel Kramer

I sob, holding the paper pressed to my chest. I can't believe he's leaving me the clinic. He needs to fight, not give up. "Why? Why are you giving up already?"

I drop the paper on the chair and sit on the bed next to him. "I've been so lucky to train by your side, and I'm honored to do as you ask, but please don't give up yet." The steady beeping of the monitor suddenly changes to one long, constant beep. It's like he knows I've read it, and so he can let go, but I'm not ready. I'm not ready. The doctor—I hadn't even realized he'd left—comes running back in with some nurses. Vaughn wraps me in his arms and pulls me away to allow them some space to work. He runs his fingers through my hair and consoles me in my time of need.

I look up into his eyes. "Please don't leave me tonight?" My lip trembles.

"Angel, I'm not going anywhere. I'll always be here for you. As I should have allowed you to be for me." He kisses me on the head and wraps me in his arms yet again.

From where I stand in the corner of the room, I hear the dreaded words no one wants to hear. "Time of death. Three-thirty-five."

I take a deep breath. "I need to call my staff."

He places his hands on my cheeks. "Why don't we go home? You can call from there." I nod my agreement, and hold up my finger, asking him to give me a minute.

I walk back over to the doctor. "Thank you for doing all you could for him. May I have a moment?"

"Of course."

"You dear man. Thank you so much for taking me under your wing and teaching me so many amazing things. You are loved dearly and will never be forgotten. I promise to work hard in your clinic, honoring your memory." I kiss him on the forehead and walk out of his room where I find my brother Remy, my father, and Vaughn. Remy thanks Vaughn for being here for me. They shake hands, we all hug, and the four of us leave the hospital together.

When we get back to my place, I take a seat at my brand new kitchen table and rest my head in my hands for a second. Vaughn is with me, but he's silently moving around in the kitchen, probably trying to learn the place since he hasn't been here since we first looked at it together. My head is pounding and I need to call the office. Part of me wants to go there, but I can't, not now.

"Angel, what can I get you?" His voice is soft and caring.

"Tea and some aspirin would be great." I grab my phone, noticing that I have texts of condolences and some laced with concern.

I let out a breath and dial the clinic. Courtney answers and I can tell she's been shaken up, waiting to hear from me. "Dr. Kramer's office, how may I help you?" I lose it at her greeting. "Hello. Brooke, is that you?"

"Yes. I'm sorry. I just left the hospital. He's gone." I cry so hard into the phone.

Now I can hear Courtney crying into the phone. "Who is left in the clinic?"

"We have one client left, and then it will be Raeanne and I."

"Close as soon as you're done. Call our patients for this week and tell them the clinic will be closed due to the loss of Dr. Kramer. Be sure to let them know that the clinic is not closing permanently, and that we will re-open in a week or so. I'll stop in to check on the animals that weren't ready to go home."

She sniffles. "There are only three still here." She gasps. "Wait—did you say it's not closing?"

"No. I discovered today that the clinic is being left to me. I need to work things out with his lawyer, but it will remain open."

"That's great, Brooke. Get some rest, and let us know about arrangements." She sniffles once again.

"I will. I'm sorry I couldn't come back in. I just need the night before I go in again."

"I understand." She cuts the call. I'm so drained, and it's only a little after four.

Vaughn hands me a cup of warm tea and the aspirin I asked for. "Angel, why don't you lay down for a while? I'll make you something to eat."

"What about Brody?"

He pulls me toward the couch. He puts a coaster down on the table and places the hot cup on top of it. "I'm going to call Callen and ask him to walk him and bring me some clothes."

"Will you ask him to bring Brody here?"

A small smile appears on his gorgeous face. "You want him here?"

I nod. "I miss him and I think he'll cheer me up."

"Rest, I'll make the call."

I lay on the couch and close my eyes while he calls Callen. I can hear him asking if he would mind bringing Brody to the house with a change of uniform and clothes for him. My eyes are heavy, and despite my fighting it, I doze off.

I wake to my buddy Brody licking my face. It makes me laugh. "Okay, Brody, okay." I laugh some more as he barks, excited to see me. I sit up on the couch to stretch, and that's when I take in the wonderful smells coming from the kitchen. "What are you making? It smells heavenly." My stomach

277

rumbles, reminding me I skipped lunch.

"Chicken stir fry." I wrap my arms around his waist, pressing my cheek to his muscular back while he stirs our dinner.

I close my eyes and inhale his manly woodsy scent. "You smell just as yummy."

He chuckles. "Are you hungry?" He looks over his shoulder to try and see me.

"I'm starved. I never ate lunch."

"Me neither. I had a granola bar, but that was it. When Remy called, I knew I needed to work straight through so I could leave when you needed me."

"Thank you so much."

He shuts off the pan and turns to me. "Thank you for allowing me to be there for you. We have a lot to talk about, and I promise you we will talk soon, but I want to help you past this first." He looks up at the sky for a brief second and then back down into my eyes. "I just want to say I'm sorry I pushed you away, and I swear to you I'll never do it again."

I push up on my toes, pressing my lips to his. "You're forgiven. I love you so much and I'm so glad to have you by my side."

"I love you too, Angel." He kisses my forehead. "Now let me finish dinner so I can feed you."

I grab a few plates and cups while he finishes up. I grab us each a glass of water and set it on the table. He brings the plates over and we both sit to eat. "Vaughn, this is really good." I devour my food. I'm really hungry and I hadn't realized how much until just now.

"Thanks, I'm glad you're enjoying it. I was

afraid you were going to fight me on eating."

I shake my head. "I'm a stress eater. I'll eat like crazy until this is all over, so I hope you'll still love me when I'm fat."

He bursts into laughter. "First, I'll love you no matter what. Second, there's no way you're getting fat. I've known you for what, ten years now, and never have I seen you put on a pound."

I shrug and continue eating. He's right. I have a crazy metabolism and can eat just about anything and hardly gain a pound. I love it, but my friends hate me for it. When we're done eating, he offers to clean up, and while he does, I take Brody to the yard. There's a spot in the far corner where I want to train him to go. I call him over to follow me, and when he does what I want him to, I reward him with a treat. By the time I get him back into the house, Vaughn has everything cleaned up.

"Why don't we lay down and watch some TV? That way you can rest. Once you're asleep, if it's okay with you, I'll go into the spare room to do my exercises for the night."

"That's fine." I change into shorts and a t-shirt while he strips into lounge shorts. We climb into bed together with me lying on his chest, breathing in his scent as he draws small circles on my back. It's calming, and in no time I'm sleeping once again.

Chapter 25

Brooke

I've spent a long day going over things with Dr. Kramer's attorney. The man is incredibly sweet, and I learned some things from him. He is a friend of the families, and so Dr. Kramer found it easy to trust him with his final wishes. Dr. Kramer has everything laid out and paid for. He has some distant family that do not live close to him. The attorney contacted them to let them know of his passing, and they said they would not be able to fly out for a service. This made me sad. This man literally died with only friends for family.

His wishes were that he be cremated, and he has an urn he has chosen for his ashes to be stored in. I have requested that we receive a small portion of his ashes to keep at the clinic, along with a photo of him. The urn with the rest of his remains will go to a beautiful Columbarium niche. That way if his family ever wants to visit him, they can.

The clinic is going to be named The Kramer

Clinic for Pets, and his attorney is going to take care of changing the name for me. I want his legacy to live on. The man has served this community for well over thirty years, he deserves this.

"Thank you so much for taking care of all of this for me." I give Mr. Fox a tight smile.

"You're a sweet girl. I can see why Dr. Kramer cared so deeply for you. I'll make all the arrangements. He's also asked that I continue to represent you in any matters related to the clinic. If you have any concerns, please feel free to come to me."

"I will. Now the small service will take place next week. We've finalized the obituary for you to get into the paper. Is there anything else we need to do?"

"No, I've already taken care of making sure the cremation is all set. Now we just wait for that to be completed and I'll take care of everything as far as the clinic goes."

I nod silently. "Can I ask you a question?" I bite my lip, wondering if I should get personal with him.

"Of course." He steepled his fingers in front of his mouth and waits for me to ask.

"Is it crazy that I feel weird running this clinic without him? I mean, I've been working side by side with him for the last eight years and now it's mine, and it feels…" Words fail me. "I don't know. It doesn't feel right." A tear escapes me, but I quickly dash it away.

"I think what you're feeling is completely normal, but I think you're also struggling with fear, maybe fear of making a mistake, or feeling like you failed him in some way." Another tear streaks my face because he's right, and all I can manage is a nod.

I close my eyes, wipe away my tears, and stand from my seat. "Thank you so much for your time. I look forward to hearing from you."

"You're most welcome. Please contact me if you need help with anything at all."

"Will do." I turn and leave, walking straight out to my car. I start it up and crank up the AC to cool off the car before I leave. I need to clear my head. I'm about to take on a thriving clinic by myself and I'm not sure I can do it. "Damn. Why did you have to leave me so soon?" A tear runs down my cheek. I need to get my crap together. I'm driving, and the last thing I need is an accident. I drive aimlessly for what feels like forever when I find myself on the same street as the clinic.

I pull in with the excuse I need to check on the animals. Unlocking the door, I step inside and lock it again behind me. I go straight to the back where I have three pets still here, a dog and two cats. I take the dog out of his kennel first and bring him to the back for a quick walk. He was quite ill, but looks much better today. When we're done, I put him up on the table to give him a quick look over. "You, my friend, are ready to go home." He barks and licks me, thanking me for the good news, I'm sure. "Okay, back in your kennel while I call your mama to come get you." After I've made the call, I check on the two cats. One of them is recovering from emergency surgery but is no longer a threat, and the other could have gone home yesterday, but according to the chart, the owner couldn't get here to pick him up before we closed.

It dawns on me that I'm going to need to send out a newsletter to our email list, letting them know what's happening and when we'll be open again. I head to the back office, the office that will now be mine, and I take a seat behind his desk, where I let out a sob. It feels strange being behind his desk. I feel like I'm betraying him in some way, taking what's his. I pick up the phone to call the owners of the three pets. I reach one, and he's on his way. The other two I've left messages for, giving them my personal cell number and ask them to call me to make arrangements for their animals.

I glance over at the clock and note that Vaughn will be getting out of work soon and he's coming to my place again tonight. I gave him a key and told him to make himself at home if he beats me there. I want to get out this brief e-newsletter and then I'll leave to meet up with him. I open the email service and begin typing a quick notice to everyone. It informs them that the service details will be in the paper and the clinic will open again in two weeks under the name of The Kramer Clinic for Pets to honor Dr. Kramer. I apologize for any inconvenience closing the clinic has caused, and I send the email out. I shut down the computer and walk to the front to wait for Mr. Patterson to pick up his dog, taking a seat at Courtney's desk. I notice she's cleared the calendar and left me the notes she told me about. The place is quiet now that it's empty. I'm really going to miss this man.

I jump at the knock on the door. I run over to

open it, letting Mr. Patterson in. "I'm so sorry, Dr. Bennett. I didn't mean to scare you."

I shake my head. "No need to apologize. I'm jumpy with everything that's happening."

"It's understandable. I'm sorry for your loss."

"Thank you. Sparky is all set. If you'll follow me." I walk him to the back where Sparky is sitting in a kennel. When he sees his owner, he perks up with excitement.

I open the kennel and Sparky goes right to Mr. Patterson, who's waiting with a leash. "Thank you again. I know you're closed. Do you need me to write a check, or pay for the services with a credit card?"

"You know what, is it okay if we bill you? The computers are all shut down and I'm not good with the billing side of things. That's Courtney's department."

"Not a problem. I'll be in touch for his check up in a few months."

"We'll be here." He shakes my hand and takes Sparky home. I check my cell one more time, and since I've heard nothing, I make a quick call to Courtney, asking her if she can come back if I need her to meet up with the other two owners and inform her that she needs to bill Mr. Patterson. Being the sweet girl that she is, she's agreed to deal with it for me so I can go home and rest. She's also aware of all of the arrangements and has offered to call Raeanne to fill her in. I know she hasn't worked here long, but I'm sure she'd like to know.

I shut the lights, lock the doors, and head straight home. When I get there, Vaughn is already there and in the yard, letting Brody run around. My yard is fenced in, so it's easy to let him run free. I lean on the frame of the slider watching them, they are amazing together. He whistles to him from the corner I want to train him to go and he runs over. He leans over to talk to him, and if I know Vaughn, he's encouraging him to be a good boy and do his business. Brody is too excited, though. He runs off after the ball and brings it back to Vaughn. I can't help but laugh. Vaughn picks up the ball and holds it. He tells him to sit and then tries again. Brody obeys and does his business in the corner, and once he's done, Vaughn rewards him by throwing the ball. Brody sees me in the door, ditches the ball, and comes running at me, barking, from the other side of the door. "Hey, boy." I squat down on the back patio. "I saw you make your potty like a good boy. Who's my good boy?"

"Did you see him run from me at first?" Vaughn's voice is full of laughter.

"Yeah, it made me laugh. He never disobeys you."

"Maybe he knew you needed to laugh today. He seems to know things."

"Maybe." I pet him on the head. "Dinner smells good. What are you making?"

"Baked ziti." He pins me to the door, slips his hand into my hair at the nape of my neck and presses a kiss to my lips. "Are you ready for a quiet night for two?"

"More than ready."

He licks across my lips. I open to him and our tongues collide. I love the taste of this man. He pulls away, leaving me with my panties wet and wanting more. I whimper. "Later, Angel. Dinner is ready." I've never wanted to eat dinner so quickly in my life.

I've missed my man, and I want to show him how much. He even has plates and cups ready to go. He feeds Brody, washes his hands, and pulls dinner from the oven. He serves up dinner and we each take a seat at the table. "Thank you. This smells delicious. I'm starving."

"You're welcome." He looks down for a second and then back at me. "I enjoy cooking you meals. I've really missed you." He takes a bite of his meal.

"Vaughn, I like you being here with me. I want us to move forward, now that you're getting help." I take a bite. "Mmmm, this is so good." I wipe my mouth. "Especially if you're going to continue to cook for me like this."

He laughs. "Listen, I've made some great progress with my doctor, and in a short period of time. He's told me he's proud of me but he also says one of the things I need to do is communicate with my friends and family better. He says I need to stop hiding things I'm feeling and that are happening to me because it's making it worse." I nod in silent understanding. I don't want to stop the flow he has going. "I've spoken to my mom and told her some of the things I was going through. I also told her about you and how much I love you." My brows shoot up in shock. "She's thrilled." A huge grin spreads across his face.

"I'm glad you spoke to her. I hope it helped."

"It did, but I haven't spoken to the most

important person about it yet. You. I know I've said it before, but I need to say it again. I'm so sorry I kept all of this from you. The nightmares are brutal, and after the incident at the bowling alley, they got worse. It went from bombs and killings to me losing you forever, and that really messed me up." He looks down again, taking a deep breath. "Listen, this is a heavy topic that I was planning to have tonight, and then I was going to wait because I know you're grieving a loss." He exhales a deep breath.

"Hey, it's fine. I want to be here for you, and to be honest, it helps take my mind off of it for a while. I went to the clinic before coming home, and it was incredibly hard to be there, but we need to move forward."

He nods. "I love you and I wanted to spend a romantic evening with you, but I didn't feel I could do that until we talked." He pauses. "And I have a lot I need to say." I encourage him to keep going and so he does. He tells me about his treatment with the doctor and he even shares some of the things he's witnessed while overseas that have contributed to his PTSD. I'm so proud of him. I can see this isn't easy for him, but with a little support, he manages to get through it. We talk about the nightly exercises he's been doing, and he's excited when I offer to do them with him.

After about an hour of talking, we both feel so much better about our relationship. We've even talked about living together once his lease is up at the end of fall. We've discovered we're both goal-oriented people, and with some goals in place, we're likely to do well. I've even shared some of my fears over managing the clinic myself, which is what led to me agreeing to do the exercises with him. It sounds like it will be just as good for me to do them and it will help us grow as a couple.

He stands from the table and pulls me into his arms. "I'll never be able to thank you enough for not giving up on me. You truly are my angel." He kisses me on the forehead.

"You've thanked me plenty. Now let's clean up so I can show you how much I've missed you." I wink at him and he throws his head back in laughter. It takes us all of ten minutes to get things straightened out in the kitchen. As soon as we're done, he takes my hand and leads me to the bedroom, closing the dog out.

He whimpers, begging to join us, but Vaughn shouts to him, "Go lay down, Brody." We hear him plop down outside the door. It makes me laugh.

"He's going to hear us," I joke.

"Tonight, Angel, the whole fucking town will hear us." His lips crash into mine. It's a heated passionate kiss, he's showing me how much he loves me. He tugs at my shirt, peeling it over my head. The second it's off, his lips are back on mine. The kiss is needy, his hands glide up my back and go straight to my bra. He fumbles with the clasp and pushes the straps off my shoulders, causing it to drop. Pulling my hair to the side so it's just shy of painful he nips and kisses his way up my jaw to my ear a his free hand massages my hardened nipple. I grind my hips against the bulge in his pants, but he pins me to the door, stopping me. He licks up the vein in my neck, sending shivers rampant through my body. "I haven't come since we last made love. You need to stop that," he whispers into my ear. I bite my lip at the thought of him saving all his pleasure for me.

Tugging at his t-shirt, I remove it and toss it across my room. I want to feel his bare chest on mine. He presses me to the door, grabs me by my ass, and lifts me. I wrap my legs around his waist and he carries me off to bed. He gently places me down with my ass hanging off the edge. He makes quick work of the button on my pants and peels them down along with my thong. He drops them to the floor. "Lie in the middle of the bed, Angel." I do as he asks while he strips. Just looking at my man makes my panties wet. I'm one lucky woman. He climbs on top of me but goes straight for my breast, sucking my nipple into his mouth while his fingers slip through my folds. I arch my back, pleasure shooting through my body. He buries two fingers inside me, fucking me with them while he licks across my chest to pay equal attention to my other breast.

"Babe," I pant. "I'm going to—" My words fail me. I'm about to explode, because just like him, I haven't come since the last time we made love. He pulls his fingers from deep inside of me and rubs my juices across each of my nipples before sucking them into his mouth. He moans at the taste of me and then sucks on his fingers next. He finally kisses down my body to my pussy, wasting no time, he goes right for my clit, licking it hard and fast. He has his arms over my legs, holding me still while he

289

parts my folds. He's switching between fucking me with his tongue and sucking on my clit, and the feeling is amazing. He sucks my clit into his mouth one more time, scraping his teeth gently over it, and sending me into the most intense orgasm of my life. My entire body is a quivering mess as he laps at my juices, ensuring he doesn't miss one drop. When he's finally satisfied his hunger, he jumps off of me and goes for his jeans, pulling out his wallet and fishing for a condom. "I'm glad you're thinking, because I don't have any brain function. Although I'm on the pill and probably would have said fuck it."

He laughs rolling a condom over his shaft. I never drop the 'F' word, so to say he knows I mean business. "That's good to know, because I only have one. That means either forego round two until we go to the store, or we say fuck it." I giggle as he climbs up my body like he's a predator and I'm his prey.

He kisses me, letting me taste myself on his lips. When he pulls away I pull him back down, wanting more. He moans into my mouth as he buries his cock balls deep inside me, rolling his hips to make sure he hits my sweet spot. I roll mine, meeting him thrust for thrust. Staring into my eyes, he lifts my legs over his shoulders as we move, never breaking eye contact. It's so deep this way. He picks up the pace, my body already climbing, working back up to another orgasm. "Vaughn…baby…" I close my eyes and pant.

"Open them for me, Angel." He slams into me. "Come for me." I feel like he's staring deep into my soul as he continues the rhythm he's set. My muscles tighten around him, my legs shake, and I have to fight to keep my eyes open while I ride out another intense orgasm. "Fuck," he growls out, planting himself inside me and finding his release. He never breaks eye contact as he's panting, his skin glistens with sweat. He's gorgeous and he's all mine.

"I love you so much, Angel."

"I love you too. Shall we shower and then start those exercises? I'm exhausted."

"That'd be perfect, but first I want to hold you for a minute." He slips out of me. Lying beside me, he runs his fingers through my hair. "You're so beautiful." He stares down at me.

"You're not too shabby yourself." My voice is full of laughter.

He chuckles and presses his lips to mine. "Let's get cleaned up."

I watch his naked body climb off the bed and strut into my bathroom. I could definitely get used to this.

Chapter 26

Brooke

Despite the fact I lost one of my best friends, we've had a great week. Vaughn and I have made great strides in our relationship. We've been practically living together even though we said he wasn't going to move in until the fall. It's nice having dinner together each evening, and before bed we meditate and do his exercises on the floor in the spare room. It's something that has brought us even closer as a couple

The clinic is back open, and my clients are amazing. Supporting both me and the clinic. Referrals have been coming in, and they've praised us on the new name. They all love the picture I put up in the clinic of Dr. Kramer. I also have a small pet urn there on a shelf with his ashes but I couldn't bring myself to tell them that. I wanted to keep that for us. We all agreed it's only fitting we put him to rest in a place he loved so dearly.

Today we finally get a day for fun. We're

heading to my parents' house for the annual block party and we're both excited. We're even bringing Brody. Vaughn is in the kitchen packing up his things while I pull my hair back into a ponytail. It's an extremely warm day, and we'll be outside for most of it.

"Babe, are you almost ready?" I find Vaughn sitting with Brody, petting him.

"Yeah. I just got done taking him out. He should be set for the ride."

"Great. Let's get going. I promised Mama I would be there early to help her collect the food and set it up on the tables."

We pack everything up in the trunk and get Brody into the backseat. He gets comfy on the new seat cover I installed. I found it online. One end connects to the headrest of the front seat and the other side connects to the backseat, so it almost cradles him. It certainly contains his hair and it can be washed should he have an accident.

Vaughn holds open the passenger's side door for me. I love that even though we've been dating for a while now he's still such a gentleman. Once he closes my door, he climbs in behind the wheel and we're on our way. I turn to check on Brody and he's fast asleep. This dog is so like a child, he's always sleeping within five minutes of being in the car. Vaughn parks the car on the next street over, knowing we don't want cars on our road because of the event. I climb out and grab Brody's leash while he gets our stuff from the trunk and we walk the short distance to my parents' house. When we arrive, Keaton, Remy, and Kenzie are already here.

Dawson and his family will be here a little later. The DJ is just beginning his set up and my brothers are setting up tables.

"Awww, look who's here," Kenzie shouts, running over to meet Brody for the first time.

She leans in to kiss me, but Brody starts to bark. "Sorry, he's protective. Let me introduce you first." I pull Brody's leash. "Brody sit." He listens, but never takes his eyes off of Kenzie. "This is Kenzie, be a good boy." Kenzie puts her hand out for him to sniff, and then she starts petting him. He licks her hand and just like that, they're friends.

She leans in again and kisses me on the cheek. "Um, is he your dog or Vaughn's?" She giggles.

"Oh, he's protective of both of us. Ask Remy."

At that very moment, Remy comes walking up behind her. "He's way protective of Vaughn. When I went to his house that morning, this guy was freaking out." Vaughn starts laughing. "Dude, it wasn't even funny. I thought Cujo here was going to bite my balls off."

Now Kenzie and I are laughing too. Brody is the sweetest dog ever. His bark is bigger than his bite. We all get out of the street and head into the yard to get Brody settled. We're tying his leash to a tree in the back where he can run around a bit in the shade, but we can still do stuff and keep an eye on him. Dad has promised to install a line for him between two trees. We'll hook him to it and he'll have free rein of the back part of the yard while we're over, but it's not installed yet, and today's not a good day for that anyway.

We're getting Brody settled when Mama calls

from the back door. "Brooke, can you and Vaughn come here for a moment?"

"Be right there, Mama." We finish hooking the leash and Vaughn pours water into his bowl. "There. You be a good boy now, ya hear?"

Vaughn links his fingers with mine and we start toward the house. We're approaching the patio when he tugs my hand. "I have a surprise for you."

I smile. "You do?"

"I do." He pulls me into the house, and when he does, my jaw drops. There are two strangers standing in my parents' kitchen, and if Vaughn wasn't a spitting image of his parents, I wouldn't have clue as to who they are. I look from Vaughn to his parents, and back.

"How? When?"

"Mom, Dad, this is Brooke." He has such pride in his voice. "Brooke, this is my mom, Adriana, and my dad, Tucker."

I put my hand out. "Mr. and Mrs. Anderson. It's a pleasure to meet you."

His mom takes my hand and pulls me into a hug. "Please call me Adriana." When we pull apart, Mr. Anderson shakes my hand and asks me to call him by his first name as well.

"When did you get in?"

Mama smiles. "Vaughn called me and told me he wanted to surprise you with a visit from his parents. He arranged their flight and picked them up yesterday, and then brought them here to meet us. They're staying upstairs in the spare room."

"Mama, you're the best." I wrap my mama in the biggest hug.

"She's very sweet, and has made us feel very welcome."

"Thank you, Mama Bennett." Vaughn kisses Mama on the cheek.

"How long are y'all down for?"

"Y'all bring us to the airport on Monday." She says 'y'all,' trying to mimic our accent.

It makes me laugh. "Please tell me you'll join us for dinner at my house tomorrow night."

She rubs my arm. "We'd love to." I look up at Vaughn, thrilled that he's surprised me with this. He knows I've been concerned with having the opportunity of meeting them at some point. I only wish they were staying longer.

Remy comes walking into the house. "Hey, y'all gonna help us or what?" Remy puts his arm around Vaughn's shoulder.

Vaughn turns to him. "You got it, man. What do you need?"

The guys head outside and us women stay in the kitchen making punch, adult tea, lemonade, and some desserts for the dessert table. Adriana has regaled me with stories of Vaughn's childhood, and told me how he was once quite the wild child. When we get outside an hour later, I find my man hanging with my brother. I can't help but tease him. "Hey, wild child."

He rolls his eyes. "Clearly you've been talking with my mother."

I giggle. "Isn't that what you wanted? Me to get to know your mother?"

He shakes his head. "Of course, Angel." He turns to my brother. "Hey, you and Kenzie up for some

Cornhole?"

"Yeah, we're going to kick your asses."

I give him a look of shock. "Are you serious right now? You know damn well I'm the queen of Cornhole."

We all run over to the game, grab the beanbags, and get a game going. Kenzie's at one end with Vaughn, and I'm at the other end with Remy, and we're playing couples. I make the first throw, sinking my shot. I'm so excited, I wiggle my brows at Remy. Remy and I each land one more bag on the board. "That puts us up by three." I shove my brother. He grabs me in a headlock and ruffles my hair. "Rem, stop. You're messing up my hair."

"Then stop talking trash." I manage to jab him in the ribs, forcing him to let go of me.

"Are we going to play or are you two going to wrestle?" Kenzie shouts, collecting the beanbags so her and Vaughn can take their turn.

Lilly and Keaton come walking over with beers for everyone. "Can Lilly and I play the winners?" Keaton asks.

"If you're okay with playing against Vaughn and I." I give Remy a cocky look. Vaughn takes his shot and he almost sinks it. Kenzie throws hers next, it slides off the board but knocks Vaughn's in. Vaughn's next bag lands on the board and I'm jumping up and down, full of excitement until Kenzie sinks her next one, leaving us with only one point. It takes us a little while, but Vaughn and I finally win the round. Remy's pissed, but walks off to get us another round of beers while we play a round against Keaton and Lilly.

"Angel, we need to check on Brody," Vaughn reminds me.

I gasp. "Oh my, I forgot about him, poor thing."

"Don't stress it. I'll go check on him," Kenzie offers.

"Are you sure?" Vaughn asks.

She shrugs. "Yeah, I don't mind." She heads in the dog's direction.

"Hey, Kenzie. If he starts barking at you, just come get me." She nods and runs off to the back while we start our game.

What a great day this is turning out to be. The street is filling up with people who have come to celebrate the end of summer, and the smell of food is in the air. The DJ is playing music and there's a girl set up with a table for face painting. At the end of the street I spot Dawson walking Becky to the bounce house, which is set up in its usual spot two houses down from Mama's. I take my shot, and go back to admiring everyone wandering the street, having a great time. Vaughn's parents are sitting on the front lawn in chairs with Mama, relaxing. They look like they're having a blast.

Kenzie comes back to tell us that Brody is fine. He's relaxing in the shade. He let her pet him for a while and she told him she'd be back to check on him soon. Remy comes back and hands off the beers. We start drinking another round, and Remy tells us we need to stop to eat after this game. We're having a blast playing, but thirty minutes later the round is over, and Keaton and Lilly won, and we're all out of beer.

As promised, we let someone else enjoy

Cornhole for a while, and we go grab some food. There's tons to choose from as always. There's pulled pork, ribs, burgers, hot dogs, fried chicken, and more sides than you can imagine. We all make a plate and head to the backyard to chill with Brody for a bit. Remy runs to the house to grab a huge blanket so we can enjoy dinner on the lawn. While we set up, Vaughn puts food in a bowl for Brody, who starts chomping down instantly. Vaughn takes a seat next to me and we all dig in. "Brooke, we should have the pictures soon. I'll bring them by as soon as they come in."

"Thanks, Kenzie. I can't wait to have more pictures up in the house."

"Speaking of pictures, lean in, Angel." I press my back to Vaughn's chest. He pulls out his phone and snaps a selfie of the two of us. He tells me it's for him to send to his mom, that she wants a picture of us, but he's instantly made it the wallpaper on his phone as well.

"I'm so glad you don't mind taking photos, because I love pictures, and it would kill me if I had to fight you for one." I giggle. While we finish eating, I convince him that we need a picture of him and I with Brody for my house. He thinks I'm taking the picture thing a bit far, but he's happy to take it to please me. The two of us sit with Brody between us. Kenzie takes the picture for us with my phone. It comes out great, and I do as Vaughn did, I save it as the wallpaper to my phone. Once we've cleaned our mess from eating, Remy and Keaton take off with Lilly and Kenzie to play some more Cornhole, but Vaughn and I want to walk Brody.

He needs to get used to being around people. I untie him from the tree and we bring him to the front of the house to meet his parents. Brody is being a bit shy. I sit on the lawn next to his parents and he takes a seat next to me. Brody lays down with his head on my lap. "It's okay, boy. They're Vaughn's parents." He whimpers and continues lying on my lap.

"What's wrong with him?" his mama asks nervously.

"He's just shy. He's not used to being around all of these people. His last owner was an elderly man who passed away, and then Vaughn adopted him, and it's usually just the three of us. The only other people he's met before tonight was Callen and Remy." I pet him, trying to calm him down. "Plus he's still young."

She smiles at me. "You really do love animals, don't you?" I nod. "I can see it in your eyes. You light up talking about him, and you can see how much he loves you."

"He's very protective of Vaughn and I. He takes good care of us, doesn't he, babe?"

He kisses me. "He sure does."

"Yeah, well. You remember, fur babies are nice, but you, my son, are an only child, and my only chance at grandbabies. Now I'm not trying to rush you, but don't go thinking this will replace them for me." Vaughn's eyes go wide with panic. We haven't even talked about marriage yet, and she's bringing babies into the picture. I, on the other hand, think it's hilarious. I burst into laughter.

When I finally calm back down, I look her dead

in the eye. "Ma'am, I can promise you I'm a fan of having babies someday, and yes, that was plural, because I'd like more than one." Vaughn's shaking his head as Remy and Kenzie come walking over.

"Hey, man, help me out here. These women are talking babies."

Remy's brows shoot up. "Dude, I love you like a brother, but you get my sister pregnant before you say I do, I'm gonna kick your ass." Everyone bursts into a fit of laughter.

"Dude, I'm not rushin' it. My mom's the one started all the kid talk."

Remy looks to Vaughn's mom. "No offense, ma'am." He tips his head to her.

"None taken. I agree. They need to marry first. I'm simply letting them know they will hear from me if they think a fur baby is going to be enough to keep me from having grandchildren." Keaton and Lilly come over and take a seat with us. Mama introduces them, and they start discussing what they do for a living. Mama fills her in on the order of her children, and as she's finishing, Dawson and his family join us. Now we're all sprawled out on the lawn. Mama takes some pictures of us all sitting and hanging out. Our little family has grown and I can see how happy mama is.

It's starting to get late and Brody is panting. I think he's having a hard time dealing with all the people. "Babe, I think it's time to go. We need to get him settled down."

"Okay, Angel. I'll gather his stuff from the back."

"Leave it. You're coming here tomorrow. You

can get it then," Mama tells him. "Before you two go, though. I would like to take a picture of you two with Mr. And Mrs. Anderson." We all get up from our seats. Vaughn and I stand together, Mrs. Anderson is by me, and Mr. Anderson is by Vaughn. Mama snaps quite a few picture and we call it a night.

As we walk back to the car, I thank him for the wonderful surprise. I can't wait for dinner with them tomorrow night.

Chapter 27

Brooke

Tonight we're having dinner with Vaughn's parents, and I'm so excited. We contemplated having everyone over, but we decided that we really want to spend time with them alone before we have to bring them to the airport in the morning. Now, I wish I had bought a spare bedroom set, because we would offer for them to stay here with us instead of at my parents' house, but for now, on such short notice, it's our only option.

As I'm preparing greens, my mind wanders back to yesterday. His mama is really sweet. She's a short woman with black curly hair that hangs to her shoulders. Her chocolate brown eyes lit up when she saw us walk through the door yesterday. I can see the pride written all over her face when she looks at her son. She clearly adores him. His father is tall and lean. Vaughn gets his hazel eyes from his father, but his curly hair from his mother. His father's hair is a bit lighter and straight. He's a gorgeous combination of his parents. I can't help the smile that spreads across my face when I picture him hugging his parents. He hasn't seen them in a few years, but in that moment there was nothing but love between them. I'm glad he's getting at least a little time with them.

His parents will be here shortly. We're going to spend part of the afternoon with them, and then after dinner we'll take them back to my parents' for the evening. Mama is going to the airport with us in the morning to see them off. It appears my parents have really hit it off with them. For dinner I'm making them homemade southern fried chicken, mashed sweet potatoes, collard greens, green bean casserole, and salad. Vaughn and I tend to eat quite healthy, and since I'm not sure his parents will eat collard greens, I want to have some other options available.

"Angel, I'm going to go pick my parents up. Do you need anything while I'm out?"

I shake my head no. "I'm good. I'm almost done with this and will be free to sit with y'all when you get back."

He presses his lips to mine. "I love you."

Hearing those words coming from his lips never fails to make me smile. "I love you too."

Now that he's gone, the house is silent. I grab the remote for the TV and tune to my favorite country music channel. I'm a fan of almost all music, but country is my favorite. I go back to finishing up what I need for dinner later, and then clean up. Brody is now whimpering at the back door, his sign that he needs to be let out. I run over, open the door for him, and he runs free. He truly enjoys my backyard. I stand out on the back porch watching him and soaking up the sun's rays. The warm sun makes me wish I had some furniture for the yard.

Slipping my phone from my back pocket, I dial Vaughn. I'm lucky he answers right away. "Yes, Angel."

"Have you left Mama's yet?"

"No. I'm getting ready to leave now. Do you need something?"

"Yeah, it's a gorgeous day, and I have no furniture for the yard. Can you ask Mama if we can borrow some folding chairs? Then we can sit out and enjoy the sun for a little while."

"Good plan. I'll ask." He pulls his mouth away from the phone but I can hear what's going on, so I know her answer before he tells me. "She said yes. I'll collect four chairs and be home soon."

"Thanks, babe."

"Love you, Angel."

"Love you too." I cut the call, thrilled we'll have something to sit out and play with Brody on. I'll eventually get my own furniture, but with all the money I just spent furnishing the inside, it's nice to borrow some for a little while. Grabbing some of Brody's toys, I start playing around with him. He loves to fetch a ball or a Frisbee, but I think he's getting bored with it. I got him this long chew toy that he loves to attack while I pull on it. When I call his name and hold up the toy, he drops the tennis ball and comes running. "Sit, Brody." He listens, but as I lower the toy he jumps for it. "No. Sit, Brody." He does as I ask. I hold the hand with the toy in the air and the other in front of him telling him to stay. "Stay." I lower the toy. "Stay." I lower it more. "Stay." I'm practically touching it to his nose, and like a good boy, he still hasn't moved. I start to move my hand, but still warn him to stay. "Get it, boy." He grabs the toy with his teeth, growling as he attacks it. I pull slightly, and he fights harder, growling louder.

"Angel. Are you okay?" Vaughn comes sprinting into the yard, his voice full of panic.

"Brody, sit." He doesn't listen the first time. I'm about to say it again when Vaughn whistles to him through his two fingers. Brody goes running over to him and sits at his feet.

"Good boy. Next time listen when Brooke tells you to sit." Vaughn pets his head and comes walking over to me. "I heard Brody growling and I panicked."

"I'm sorry, I was training him." I pat my leg. "Come, boy." Brody runs over. "Sit." Brody drops down on his rear and stares up at me. I turn to Vaughn, and now his parents are with us. "Watch this. You know how he reacts to this toy, right?"

"Yeah, he gets all hyped up over it."

I do the trick all over again telling him to stay until I'm ready for him to attack. When I give the command, he responds, grabbing the toy and shaking his head, pulling me along with the toy. "Brody, sit." Again he doesn't listen. Vaughn is about to whistle when I stop him. "Brody, sit." He's too wrapped up in his toy, he's not paying attention to me, but I know what will get his attention. I pull the toy snug, forcing him to pull back, and as soon

306

as he does, I let go. He rolls to the ground and I walk away, ignoring him. When he realizes my back is to him and I'm no longer playing, he comes over and drops the toy at my feet, because he wants my attention and wants me to play with him more. I keep my head up and my arms crossed until he whimpers. "Do you want to play?" I pick up the toy. "You need to listen. Let's try again." This time when we're about to start, I ask Vaughn to grab me a treat. "Listen." I give him a stern look. He was trained well, I know he gets it. I say the commands again, allowing him to attack the toy. When Vaughn comes back out with a treat, he sneaks it into my free hand. Brody is growling at the toy and pulling on it as he does. "Brody, sit." My voice is stern. His ears perk up, he drops the toy, and sits with his tail wagging a million miles an hour. "Good boy. Here you go." I give him the treat and tell him to go lay down.

As soon as he runs off, Adriana comes over. "You're amazing with him." She hugs me.

"Thank you. I'm sorry about that, but I needed to teach him the lesson in the moment or it would be gone, and he wouldn't learn that what he was doing was wrong." I hug her back.

"No need to apologize, it was great to witness you teaching him like that. We've never had any pets, so we've never witnessed animals being trained." Tucker steps forward and gives me a hug.

"Now that I know you're fine. I'm going to go grab the chairs from my trunk." He runs back out of the yard, leaving his parents with me. "I figured we'd hang out here for a while and then we can go in. I'm going to make some fried chicken for dinner."

"Sounds good to us," Tucker says.

Vaughn comes back into the yard carrying two chairs in each arm. He sets them up and we all take a seat. Brody comes over with a ball and he drops it at Tucker's feet. He's all too happy to throw the ball. He tosses it across the yard and Brody chases after it. "How's the clinic coming?" Adriana asks me leaning back in her chair and enjoys the sun.

"It was tough at first. It still feels weird sometimes being there without him. I try to remind myself that this is what he wanted and carry on."

She gives me a gentle smile. "Vaughn told us the story. I'm so sorry for your loss."

"Thank you. I think the toughest part for me right now is hiring someone. I need to bring in another vet, but I'm struggling to even run the ad. I need the person to be a perfect fit. Someone who's going to understand that we're more than a clinic, we're a family, and this is more than just a job to us."

"I can see why Vaughn loves you so much. You care about so much more than yourself and your individual family. You care for and love all those around you." I blush at her kind words. I've always loved caring for any breathing soul, human or animal. It's in my blood, it's who I am, and what I do. I think that's why when Vaughn wouldn't let me in it hurt so bad, and it's also why I felt I had to go to Remy. It was my way of helping him without being there for him directly.

"Even as a child Vaughn was stubborn," Adriana

carries on, pulling me from my thoughts. "He insisted on learning to do things on his own. It didn't matter if he was learning the hard way as long as he could take the time to do it for himself, he was happy."

I turn to him. "He's a stubborn man."

"Most of them are. He's just like his father, and they are both very lucky to have found women who love them enough to stand by them when they put us through all kinds of shit." She raises her brows.

I giggle. "I love your son very much. I'm not sure if he told you, but he's planning on moving in come the fall when his lease is up."

"That's great. I think it's smart that you two live together before you move onto marriage. A lot of kids these days rush to get married having no idea what true love is, and then they're divorced before you know it." I nod, agreeing with her because it's true. I've seen kids I went to high school with get married right after high school and now they're divorced and single parents because they rushed off and married their high school sweetheart without any true understanding of what being in love really involves. I feel like you have to experience loss and hurt to know when you've found love.

"If you'll excuse me, I'm going to get the fried chicken started." I stroll into the house, leaving Vaughn outside with his parents.

***

Vaughn

"Thank you guys so much for coming down. Not only am I excited to see you, but Brooke kept asking when she'd get to meet you."

"We've missed you, Vaughn, but I'm glad to see you're doing well for yourself. She seems like a fine young lady." My mom's voice is laced with pride. I wish she'd have more time to see just how amazing my woman is. Although she was not there directly, she helped me through all of this, and it's thanks to her I'm doing better and have managed to keep my career intact. She went to Remy and got me help when I needed it most, and kept reminding me that she was here waiting for me. She showed me how much she loves me and that was what helped push me to go to the good doctor, who's been helping me get through this. She was right that night outside her bedroom when she hugged me and told me that love can heal many things. If she hadn't been there loving me, lord only knows where I'd be today, but I guarantee you it wouldn't be sitting in a backyard enjoying an afternoon with my parents.

"We should go help Brooke inside." Mama stands from her chair. Dad and I follow her in. We put some football playing on the TV and sit quietly watching the way we used to when I was younger.

I can hear them giggling in the kitchen while we watch the replay of the Giants pre-season game from the other night. They lose to the Patriots, which sucks, because my father and I are both Giants fans. "They aren't looking too good this year." My father sighs.

"No, they're not. If they keep this up, they won't even make the playoffs."

I don't get to watch games too much anymore. I'm always busy doing stuff, and to be honest, it's not the same not having my dad to watch the games with. He was always a bit more into it than me, but I enjoy the sport and the time with him.

"Dinner is ready," Brooke calls from the kitchen. She has a bunch of serving bowls on the table and there are settings for four already out. I grab everyone water to have with dinner while Brooke lets my parents help themselves to food. Once I'm back and I've made my plate, Brooke makes hers. I chuckle to myself, because no matter how much I try to get her to eat first, she never listens. She always waits for me to have my plate made. We all sit and dig in, continuing the conversation from outside in regards to my childhood. Mom even brought some pictures to show her, but I'm lucky, because she left the really embarrassing ones at home.

After about an hour or so of laughter and fun, we realize we need to clean up from dinner. Everything is sitting on the table cold, but we don't really care because it's been a great night. "Brooke, thank you so much for having us over. It was really nice to spend some quality time with our son and getting to know you."

"Oh, trust me, it's been a pleasure." Brooke stands from the table and begins the process of cleaning up.

Mom stands as well. "What can I help with?"

"I've got this, why don't you enjoy the time with

Vaughn? I know you have to get going soon."

She sighs. "Unfortunately, you're right. It's already after seven and we have an early flight."

"Mom, do you want me to bring you back so you can get ready for the morning?" She looks to my father, who gives her a gentle nod.

"Give me five minutes to help Brooke a bit." Mom grabs some food off the table and helps Brooke pack the leftovers away.

I look to my dad. "Is she okay?"

He nods. "I think now that it's time to leave, it's sinking in just how much she misses you."

"I miss you guys too. I'll talk to Brooke and see if maybe we can take some time to come north for a visit."

My dad stands from his chair. I put out my hand to shake his, but he pulls me in for a hug. "That would be great, son. We love you."

"Love you too, Dad."

When we pull away, Mom tells us she's ready to go. There are some tears shed, but they say goodbye to Brooke and I drive them back to her mom's house while she takes care of Brody. When we pull up to the house, I walk them to the door. "Thank you again for the flight, son. Although the visit was short, we've had a great time."

"Thanks for coming, Mom."

"You take care of that girl. She's a good one."

I look my mom dead in the eye. "I plan on marrying that girl."

She nods. "I know you do, son. I know you do." We hug one more time and they step inside.

"I'll see you tomorrow morning," I reply

watching them close the door behind them. I exhale a deep breath before climbing back into my car and heading home to the love of my life. My parents are the first people I have told I want to marry Brooke. Now I just have to get the courage to ask her father and her brother for permission, but I'll figure that out soon enough.

When I pull back up at the house, Brooke is relaxing in bed, waiting for me. "Shall we do our exercises?" she asks the second I'm through the door.

"No, not tonight. Tonight I want to make sweet love to my angel, and then hold her in my arms and never let her go." I strip as I make my way over to the bed, and when I slip in next to her, she lowers herself onto her back. I look down into her eyes. "I love you, Brooke Leah Bennett. You're my angel, and you've helped heal me. Thank you." Before she can say a word, my lips are on hers, showing her just how much she means to me.

The End

Epilogue

Brooke

I can't believe we're about to land in New York. I'm so excited I hardly slept a wink last night. I've never traveled outside of Georgia, and I've certainly never flown before. Vaughn's parents are picking us up at the airport, and we're going to stay at a hotel. Callen has Brody while we spend four days up here, and he's promised us he will take good care of him while we're gone.

We've just landed, and the captain has announced that we're free to get up to claim our carry-on luggage. "How was your first flight, Angel?"

"It was amazing. I was a little nervous at first but once we were in the air I was fine. Although the landing was a little scary too."

He laughs. "Well, you have to do it at least one more time so we can get home." I shrug, not really caring. It wasn't that bad, and now that I've experienced it once, it probably won't bother me again. I'm probably more nervous over the fact that I closed the clinic for four days. I still haven't brought myself to hire another veterinarian, and of course Vaughn used this as another chance to remind me why I need to. Had I done it already, we'd still be open right now. Of course he's right, so I've promised him I would start looking as soon as the holidays were over. It's two weeks before Christmas, certainly not the ideal time to try and hire someone.

We walk off the plane and Vaughn instantly takes my hand. "This place is a zoo," he warns, holding me close. There are holiday travelers everywhere, and no one is paying attention to anything other than themselves. I shake my head, shocked. We hurry through, trying to make our way to baggage claim. We only have one bag, but there's no way I was flying to New York without luggage. I told Vaughn for starters I'm going to freeze my ass off, and second, I want to have room for souvenirs. He laughed, but caved, and let me pack a light suitcase. Taking my brother's advice, I flagged our suitcase with some ribbon so it would stand out from the rest of the bags on the conveyor belt. The light starts flashing and the belt starts to move, carrying bags into the room. We're both watching for our basic black rolling suitcase. It takes a few minutes, but it appears, as do his parents.

They come running over to greet us with a hug and a kiss. "Welcome to New York, dear."

"Thanks, Mama Anderson." I've recently started calling her that because I have a hard time calling her by her first name. We were speaking over the phone one day when I explained that it's simply my upbringing. In the south we rarely refer to someone older than us by their first name. When I offered this as a compromise, well, let's just say she was thrilled.

We're heading out to the parking lot when Vaughn gives his father the name of the hotel we're staying at near Rockefeller Center. I clap my hands, excited. "I can't believe I'm going to get to see it. The lights are going to be just beautiful." Everyone around me looks at the southern girl with the thick accent. I blush and take Vaughn's hand as we approach the car.

"I'm sorry we don't have a room for you to stay with us." Mama Anderson blushes.

"Mom, I've told you. I want to stay in a hotel with Brooke. As excited as we are to visit, this is our vacation too, and it's the first time Brooke has left Georgia. I want to show her around." His mama nods.

Traffic is a mess as usual, but we finally make it to the hotel. "We'll see you two for dinner in a little while." They wave goodbye and pull away.

"If they're leaving, how are we getting to their house for dinner?"

Vaughn chuckles. "Angel, we'll take the subway and then walk." My face lights up yet again. My first flight and now my first train ride. I feel like a little kid again. I'm getting to experience all these firsts with my love. We walk into the hotel and straight up to the counter. Vaughn gives the woman standing there his name. She pulls up our reservation. He signs a paper and she gives us two keys with directions on how to get to our room. When we get up there, I'm thrilled. The room is small, but has a gorgeous view of Rockefeller Center. It's breathtaking.

I can see people skating around on the ice and there are lights all over the place. Vaughn comes up behind me, wrapping his arms around my waist. He whispers in my ear, "Have you ever ice skated before?"

"No, where am I going to find a frozen lake in Georgia?" I give him a look that screams *really*.

"They have indoor rinks," he says like it's common knowledge.

"I guess, but no, I've never ice skated, and I don't know of any indoor rinks."

He laughs. "Okay, do you want to change before we go out?" I shake my head no, and continue to look out the window. It's already after five and I'm starved. We probably should have gone straight to his parents for dinner, but he wanted to get us settled first. He takes my hand and pulls me toward the door. "Let vacation begin."

***

Brooke

I just experienced my first night in New York and I'm in awe. I got to ride the subway to Vaughn's parents' place. They rent a small apartment that only has one bedroom. They moved after Vaughn left, knowing he wasn't going to move back home. It's a cozy place with a doorman and a nice view of the city, but it's small. After dinner we walked a little, and then took a cab back to the hotel where we made love, and then did our relaxing exercises together. He hasn't been doing them much lately, but being that we are out of our comfort zone, and we don't have Brody, we thought it was a good idea to help us relax after a busy night.

Today we're going down to Rockefeller Center to walk around. We'll go do a little shopping, stopping to check out the window displays as we go, and have dinner.

"Ready, Angel?" Vaughn is bundled up in a coat, beanie, and gloves, waiting by the door. I quickly slip into my stuff and he takes my hand, leading me down to the lobby of our hotel and out to the streets of New York. It amazes me that his parents don't live far from this beautiful attraction. There is so much to see in this area alone, and I'm so glad we came at this time of year, because it's absolutely stunning. He pulls me close, holding my two hands, and says, "What would you like to do first?"

I shrug. "I just want to walk around and check everything out. Maybe pop into some stores."

We walk down the street hand in hand, pointing out lights and all the Christmas decor. Now don't get me wrong, we decorate for Christmas in the south, but nothing like this. I mean, this is an entirely new level of decor. I'm simply in awe, pointing places out that make me smile.

We loop around and make our way back to the Center, and I notice Vaughn has started walking a bit faster. "What's the rush?"

"I wanted to surprise you, but it took us longer to walk around than I thought. We have tickets to go to the Top of the Rock." He tugs me, hurrying along. "I don't want to miss our slot." We finally arrive and Vaughn pulls two tickets from his pocket and shows them to a gentleman who leads us to where we need to go. We wait in line with the rest of our group, and it takes a little while but when we finally get up there, the view is breathtaking. Vaughn and I take a ton of pictures together with my phone from different angles with different views in the background.

"Babe, this is amazing. Thank you so much."

"Thank you for being here with me. This view may be stunning, but it'd be nowhere near as beautiful without you." He leans in and presses a kiss to my lips.

When he pulls away, I have a huge grin on my face. "Aren't you becoming quite the romantic?"

"Oh Angel, you haven't seen anything yet." We make our way back down, and when we do, we stop to get a pretzel from a street cart. I'm too excited about walking around to stop and eat. The sun is setting, and more and more lights are starting to illuminate the night. It's getting cold, but I really don't care, because it's such a romantic night being out here with Vaughn, hand and hand. I spot a small shop and we decide to duck in. I want to buy something for my niece and nephew. The place is amazing. There are toys of all kinds around me, things for all ages. I find a bear for Beau and a doll for Becky. Thrilled with my purchase, we head back out, and now Vaughn pulls me back toward the ice skating rink.

"What are you doing?"

"I want to take you ice skating."

"But I've told you I've never been ice skating."

"You've never flown either, but you did it, and you're here. You can't come to Rockefeller Center and not ice skate, or at least attempt to." He gives me his full on *you're not going to win this one* sexy smile.

"Fine. Let's do it."

"I'm glad you agree, because we have a scheduled time to be on the ice, and we need to get our skates." I laugh and shake my head. This guy has all kinds of things planned for us today. He walks me toward the skate house, where he gives them his name for his reservation. They ask for our shoe sizes and they hand us skates. We take a seat to lace them up, only Vaughn takes my leg and rests it on top of his. "It's important that your skates be laced up tight." He quickly ties my lace so the skate is snug around my ankle, and then does the other one. I stand, trying to balance on my skates as I walk to the railing at the edge of the rink, while Vaughn takes the ice like it's no big deal. He steps on and takes my hands, pulling me with him, and suddenly I feel like a newborn deer learning to stand. I'm wobbly and feel like I'm going to fall, but lucky for me, Vaughn knows what he's doing and holds on to me. He starts teaching me how to push off, and slowly I'm getting a little better. At least now I can move a bit. The view is amazing. Everything is beautifully lit up, making for a romantic evening. That's when I notice the ice is starting to clear, and I'm in a panic, thinking we have to get off, and I'm in the middle of the rink. I'm slow, and there's no way I can move as quickly as the people around us. The music fades out and suddenly *One Call Away* by Charlie Puth starts playing as Vaughn pulls me around the rink. He's facing me, holding my hands and skating backward, singing to me. It's the most romantic thing ever. I can't believe he's managed to get the entire rink just for us. My eyes well with tears, Vaughn is singing the song I once sang to him, letting him know I would be there for him. Now that he's strong enough to be my superman, he's letting me know it. He spins us around, nearly causing me to fall, but of course he catches me with laughter in his voice. When I'm finally steady on my feet once again, he drops to one knee in the middle of the rink, reaches into the inner pocket of his coat, and reveals a tiny black box.

My eyes go wide and my hands go to my mouth. "Angel, I've been going over this entire proposal in my head for the longest time now, but nothing I came up with seemed like the right words to tell you how much I love you and need you in my life. You were my superwoman when I needed you, and now I want to return the favor. Please let me spend the rest of my life being there for you the way you were for me. Please, will you marry me?"

I instantly nod my head yes as my hand trembles. He slips this beautiful round cut diamond onto my finger and then stands, spinning me around, he screams out, "She said yes" with laughter in his voice. The crowd around us claps and cheers as he pulls me around the rink for one last loop before others join us. When we get to the exit, his parents are there waiting for us. His mom is crying tears of joy, and now I'm crying too, because I think it's beautiful with all they've missed from his life with him away, they got to witness this special moment. Then she shows me the phone she's holding with my entire family on the screen watching, and it causes me to let out a sob. Hundreds of miles away and my entire family was still a part of my engagement.

They're all waving and laughing at the look of shock on my face seeing them in the phone. They congratulate us and wish us a safe flight home before we hang up. People are now walking off the ice and congratulating us on our engagement. "Thank you so much. I've had the time of my life, and you certainly pulled off an engagement I'll never forget."

"You're welcome. I love you, Brooke, and I meant it when I said I want to spend my life supporting you and being there for you. Together we can get through anything."

His parents each hug us one more time. "Now let's go, our dinner is waiting," his dad says.

We all laugh and walk off toward the restaurant to enjoy dinner with my future in-laws.

To our troops who need help!

Do you have a family member or know someone that is suffering from PTSD? There are a number of organizations available to help soldiers through this trying time. Here are a few that may be able to help.

VETSports
www.vetsports.org
Veteran's Phone Line
(813) 284-0587
the_toc@vetsports.org
Public Inquiries
301-323-8063
the_toc@vetsports.org

Veterans Crisis Line
www.veteranscrisisline.net
1-800-273-8255 Press 1
You can learn to recognize signs of suicide at
www.veteranscrisisline.net/SignsOfCrisis/Identif
ying.aspx

Honoring The Sacrifice
http://honoringthesacrifice.com/
info@honorhingthesacrifice.org

Gary Sinise Foundation
https://www.garysinisefoundation.org/
gsf@polarispr.com

Acknowledgments

First and foremost, I always give a shout out to my husband, who constantly puts up with my book-writing obsession. I love what I do, but I work hard, and sometimes that means he suffers a bit without much complaint. Thanks, babe, for always supporting me and being there for me. I love you and thank you for all you do so that I can be home writing.

To my girl Deena! Thank you so much for backing me with my military writing. I love that I can go to you and bounce all my crazy military ideas off of you.

To my betas team! Thank you ladies so much for all of your input. Your dedication to helping me make my work the best it can be is greatly appreciated! I love you all for your individual thoughts and strengths.

To Mello's Militia, you are one amazing group of women. You are a team for sure, and I need you to know how much I appreciate all you do for me. You are constantly out there, posting, sharing, entering me in contests, and, best of all, making me laugh when I need it the most. You ladies are the driving force behind my writing. When the going gets tough, you help me through whether realize it or not.

Clayr and Stracey! I truly love you two and have no idea what I would do without you. You're two amazing leaders, and my Army wouldn't be the same without you.

Thank you to my editor, Toni, for taking me on

last minute and providing me with awesome feedback, and thank you to Team Limitless for not only taking me on, but for working with me on all my crazy ideas.

Thank you to all of my author friends and followers who have supported me throughout my writing journey. The list of friends and supporters is endless, and there's no way I can thank you all individually, so if you have supported me or helped me in any way, no matter how big or small, I thank you and hope at some point I get to return the favor.

About the Author

Alison Mello is a wife and stay at home mom to a wonderful little boy. She lives with her amazing family in Massachusetts. She loves playing soccer, basketball and football with her son.

After having her son, Alison started reading again and fell in love with Contemporary Romance. Reading made her happy and gave her something to do when she had downtime. As she started to read more, she started to notice things she really enjoyed in a book and things she didn't. She began to have ideas for writing one of her own. One day she literally woke up and started writing. She realized that if there was ever a time for her to write, it was now. She had a part time job to give her something to do. The hours at work were slow and she was bored with what she was doing, so while her son was off enjoying his friends over summer vacation she got started.

Alison finished the first book in two weeks and decided that she really enjoyed writing, so she kept going. She already had ideas in mind for books two and three, so she kept writing. That is how the Learning to Love Series was born. Somewhere along the line, one of my Beta readers convinced me that Michael, a character from Finding Love, needed his own story. That is when Alison added the fourth and final book. Alison hopes you enjoy her books as much as she enjoyed writing them.

She's so glad she started this writing journey and hopes you will stay with her for the ride. Chasing Dreams is scheduled to release in April and the first two books of the Love Conquers Life series will be out this summer!

Facebook:
http://www.facebook.com/alisonmelloauthor

Twitter:
http://www.twitter.com/alisonmelloauth

Newsletter:
http://www.alisonmelloauthor.com/

Goodreads:
http://www.goodreads.com/alisonmelloauthor

Instagram:
http://www.instagram.com/alisonmelloauthor

Printed in Great Britain
by Amazon